Comings & Goings
in
Charlford

Comings & Goings
in
Charlford

W. Henry Barnes

Copyright © 2023 W. Henry Barnes

All rights reserved

Paperback **ISBN**: 9798398598452
Hardback **ISBN**: 9798398802221
Imprint: Independently published

DEDICATION

Everything I have ever done has been for all my family who always supported me in my plans, career paths and hobbies. For my venture into writing fiction, my thanks go mainly to my lovely wife Margaret who encouraged me and gave me the freedom and the time that the books demanded. But I doubt if the books would have gone beyond manuscripts if son Ian hadn't helped me with his knowledge of literature and experience of publishing over the Internet. Son David, with Susi's support, nursed me back to health after Margaret was snatched from us by a massive stroke. The growing musical career of granddaughter Laura (Lo Barnes) fills me with admiration and hope. My love goes to them all and to Margaret's family.

Chapter 1

Charlford is a pleasant village at the eastern edge of England's West Country and takes its name from a shallow ford by which vehicles can cross the young river Charl. The stream marks the end of the road from the nearby city of Salchester, so the ford is little used except by farm vehicles going to and from fields, sheds, and occasional livestock shelters that lie beyond the stream. However, the narrow footbridge that accompanies the ford makes an ideal place to pass the time of day, leaning on the handrail and watching the gentle flow of the stream below. And that rate of flow is matched by the pace of life of most of the six hundred or so residents of the village.

The village centre is considered to be the green, overlooked at one end by the parish church that supports the souls of the residents, and at the other by the village inn, the Red Lion, that feeds and waters their bodies. A detailed map of the village shows many homes are reached via lanes and paths that meander off among fields and small woods. The newest houses are the council-owned row that runs along the outer edge of The Crescent that surrounds a small copse.

Most houses lie along Salchester Road, and the front rooms of one or two have been given over as part-time premises for one-man businesses. These tend to change according to their profitability, but the photographer and the dry-cleaning agency have stood the test of time and are seen as permanent fixtures, saving their clients the time and cost of travelling into the city. But there are two established businesses that are well-supported; a general store, with an often-busy Post Office counter; and its next-door neighbour, a small garage. Owned and run by the Post Mistress's brother-in-law, the garage offers a minor repair service, has a couple of fuel pumps, sells bottled camping gas to tourists, and boasts a free compressed air line!

Overall, Charlford is home to a community where most people know their neighbours, but it does accept incomers, as happened a few years ago with the licensee of the Red Lion, Jim Parker. The fact that Jim rescued the village inn from probable closure could well have influenced people's attitudes towards him. After some timely refurbishments he returned the inn to its rightful place in local society as the distribution hub, and sometimes the origin, of village news and views.

Returning to the map of the village, it also shows a short road starting roughly at the side of the Red Lion and curling away from the village, through a small wood. It ends at Charlford Manor, a large country house having outbuildings in a decent-sized stable yard.

The manor's owner, Tony Philips, had bought the place on the rebound from a divorce, using funds created from a large part of his share in a business partnership in Salchester and from the sale of his former marital home. These funds had been resting in a local bank account because his ex-wife's new husband, the self-important owner of a local butcher's shop, 'Wouldn't lower himself to take money from a rag-and-bone man' – Tony's business had dealt in scrap metal and road haulage.

Folk generally agreed it was a good thing that Tony had bought the manor as, before it was put up for sale, it had been uninhabited for over ten years while the scattered family of the previous owner squabbled about what to do with it. While Tony had saved it from what had looked like an inevitable fall into a total ruin, many knew of his perhaps questionable beginnings and wondered about his real intentions. No-one could deny the effort and the money that he'd put into restoring the place, along with his plans to bring in new businesses to work there. But there were still some doubters – country folk don't take lightly to change – and when any of this group aired their views, it was usually after consuming a pint or three in the bar of the Red Lion.

One regular contributor to such discussions was Harriet (known as Hattie) Scattergood, complaining from her chosen seat at the end of the bar furthest from the door.

'How can they call that renovating', she would ask, 'when everything's different from what it was before? Renovating means renewing, but when it was new there was a proper family living at the manor, looked after by a team of real servants, and a carriage for the master to drive round the estate…' Once she was in full flow, nobody interrupted – it went on exactly the same each time.

'Yes,' she'd say, 'the house is being lived in again, but the only family is that jumped-up scrap-metal dealer and his daughter! The only servants, if you can call them that, are them well-past-it old codgers trying to teach old tricks to young fools who should know better!' She'd pause at some point for a lubricating sip from her half pint of shandy, then go on, 'And what about the carriage? I heard it was found and then given away to somebody – it belonged in our community!!'

'All right, Hattie,' Jim would interrupt, 'we've heard it all before, but you're right, things haven't gone back to how your mother tells you they used to be –'

'You leave my mother out of this! She knew how it used to be at the manor and it was better than it is now!'

'How is your mum these days?' would intercede Tom Grover, in an attempt to calm things down. He'd once been sweet on Hattie's mum when they were at school together and he sometimes wondered if things might have worked out differently for him if he'd spoken up about how he felt about her – but he'd been afraid of rejection and probable humiliation. Tom had never married but often thought that, even now, there might be a spark between him and Hattie's mum.

'She's staying with me,' Hattie always replied. 'And she doesn't want to see you – she's not up to leaving the house and doesn't want visitors to see her as she is now, so you can keep your nose out and your hands to yourself, Tom Grover – in fact you all can – I've had enough of you all and I'm going home! But it's been lovely to have a nice chat.' Then, with a broad smile she would stride out amid a flurry of laughs and derisory comments about her attitude, her dress sense and her general appearance, all of which she seemed to totally ignore. Hattie also carried an unusual, often not very pleasant, aroma, and this ensured that no-one got close enough to know if the comments affected her.

A frequent witness to these exchanges was long-term resident and local bus driver, Graham Bartlett, who would often call in for a quick drink on his way home after an early shift. He would sometimes be pumped for more information about Hattie simply because his wife, Eileen, had had some dealings with the Scattergood family in her days as a District Nurse. Graham always stated quite firmly that she never brought her work home with her, but the questing for inside information on the Scattergoods, and Hattie in particular, never went away. When Graham mentioned this to Eileen, she always defended Hattie, knowing that Mrs Scattergood had been in need of real care when her daughter had come back to the village to stay with her – but that was as far as Eileen would go in discussing the matter.

Getting back to the effects of the changes at Charlford Manor, two other residents to be affected were Monica Tillotson and Jenny Cole. Monica ran the Post Office and shop, while Jenny was the wife of DC Cole – her husband was known as Loada and, as he lived in the village, was regarded by many as the village bobby.

Like in any rural community, the Post Office was the place to be for gaining fuel for the gossip engine, and Monica regularly found herself being pumped for information that, sadly, she was unable to provide. 'Yes,' she'd agree, 'there's been a lot of extra mail to and from the manor, but it's all been typically boring-looking legal, financial and other business stuff.' Sadly, for all concerned, she had been unable to deduce any whiff of intrigue or scandal.

In the Coles' case, at the time when the manor was being renovated, Jenny's husband had taken his turn in monitoring the site on the lookout for criminal damage and to prevent thefts of materials etc. Then, a bit later, they had both been more closely involved when one of a group of lads visiting from Bracknell had been attacked by a local thug.

But, unlike Monica at the Post Office, the Coles' lips were sealed, as they always were around police matters.

After a while, interest in the regime at Charlford Manor dwindled as new topics, such as Mrs Little's latest litter of pups and Alf Webster's new car, came on the scene.

Chapter 2

Tony Philips was born and raised in the West Country city of Salchester, and on his very first day at school he became inseparable best pals with Reg Harris. The pair were always either competing with, or supporting, each other in playground games, school sports, and so on.

In their teens, they went together to find Saturday jobs with the local scrap-metal dealer, Mr Hady, tidying and sweeping the yard, washing his trucks, and so on. They proved to be reliable and interested, were liked by the other staff and by most of the customers, and really enjoyed the work. So it was no surprise to anyone when they eventually approached the owner with ideas for expanding the transport side of the business, if he would take them on full time.

By that stage, having driven trucks and old cars around the site, they had easily obtained their driving licences, so Mr Hady took them, and some of their ideas, on board – business improved, and they never looked back. Then, when the owner was ready to retire, Tony and Reg knew the business well enough, had promising ideas for expansion, and had saved enough money, to get a bank loan to fully take it over. The business then grew to the point where, when Tony's marriage was breaking up, Reg was able to do a part buyout of Tony's interest so as to help cover his friend's expected costs.

As the divorce settlement eventually demanded no cash from him, this money, together with the proceeds of selling the family home, had helped Tony to buy the long-empty manor house in the nearby village of Charlford. But Tony's divorce had affected him more than he had realised or expected. Getting the manor house into a habitable state had been therapeutic but, as the task neared completion, he had been at a loss to know what to do next.

During the manor house's restoration, Tony and his teenaged daughter, Anna, had lived in what had been the servants' cottage in the manor's stable yard. On weekdays, when Anna was boarding at her school in Salchester, Tony often had his main meal at the Red Lion, and this became the obvious place for Reg to come and find him every so often. Away from business in Salchester, and keeping out of the way of the building works at the manor, they would sit and idly chat. Topics drifted between their pipe dreams, their ambitions, and their plans, but usually began with reminiscences of the good old days of their Saturday jobs with old Mr Hady.

Then Ted Bailey had come on the scene. He suggested that the outbuildings in the manor's stable yard could be used as craft workshops and had even gone so far as to say that he would love to have the chance to move his home, as well as his cabinetmaking business, from Bracknell to the manor. This fact, and Ted's positive attitude, had rekindled Tony's business interests. So, on a meeting with Reg soon after that momentous visit, Tony got straight down to talking turkey.

First off, he explained that he didn't simply want to be a landlord, letting out premises and collecting the rent; he wanted to be a bit more involved – not in the activities themselves, but in providing, or at least offering, some of the support services they might need.

'What sort of support, and how do you plan to do it?' asked Reg.

'That's the problem – I just can't think what people would need! In the yard business we just collected or moved stuff – we provided trucks and blokes, or did it ourselves, but the rest of it's all a bit hazy now.'

'I reckon we had it easy when we inherited Julie,' replied Reg. 'We didn't have to think about it; she kept the books, paid the bills, dished out pay packets, kept the council and the tax man off our backs, and all the rest of it. But you've really been in a world of your own, Tony, if you've forgotten Julie! Remember how she scared the pants off us if we dared enter her office without knocking and getting permission! And she's still the same, of course!'

'That's it, Reg, I've got to offer that sort of service.'

'OK, but you'd better get a name for it – you can't just say "I can offer a service like..." See what I mean?'

'OK, so what do you call Julie's job, then? And would she do the same for Ted Bailey's business, do you think?'

'Well, officially she's the Office Manager, and mainly she does the books, but not for much longer – she told me last week that she'll be leaving as soon as I can find a replacement.'

'Oh, so much for that idea, then.' A pause for thought. 'Has she said why she's leaving? If she hasn't got another job to go to, maybe she'd work for me?'

'It's definitely worth a try, so come in to the yard in the morning and you can ask her – rather you than me, though! Remember how we used to call her the dragon – and she can still be pretty stern.'

'OK, but I've got a few things to clear up here first – that'll give me time to gather my thoughts. And, thanks, Reg.'

Two days later, on meeting Julie again for the first time in a couple of years, Tony found her to be all sweetness and light, and quite happy to chat about the work she did and, rather surprisingly, why she was looking to leave the firm. 'I've been doing the same things for so long I'm getting bored, plus the fact that I'm not fully occupied. But why do you ask?'

'Well,' he started, rather hesitantly, 'you may not have heard, but I'm planning to rent out some of the outbuildings at Charlford Manor to a few craft workers and such, but I don't want to be just the landlord. I was looking for a way to get them to feel somehow connected to each other and to me. I was thinking perhaps I could offer them some sort of support services.'

When Julie didn't immediately respond, Tony blundered on, 'But I don't know exactly what to offer, or what to call it, and Reg said I should ask you – not to do it, because you work here and you're leaving – but to tell me what I should offer and what I should call it and that sort of thing...' and he ran out of steam!

To his complete surprise, the dragon, Julie, burst out laughing. 'You men,' she said at last. 'Reg has told me a bit about your plans and I thought you'd never ask! Now, do you want me to just tell you what services you need, and what to call it, or would you like me to take it on? If you want me to take it on, when should I make a start?'

'But I thought you were leaving the yard, and I've not got anything that needs doing at the moment,' he replied, looking as confused as he felt.

'No, I'm not leaving, though I've thought about it a few times. Don't forget, I've been with the firm just a bit longer than you and Reg. I've had lots of pleasure from seeing and helping you two build it up from Mr Hady's day, but it's so repetitive these days I could do with a bit of a change. So, if you'd like me to help with your project…'

Tony just had to interrupt her there. 'I've not kept anything secret about the manor, but I can't believe you'd be interested in helping me after I sort of walked out of here.'

'You don't know, do you?' she asked.

'Don't know what?' looking completely baffled.

'When you were in the middle of that divorce – and I could still scratch her eyes out for how she treated you and Anna – you asked Reg to buy you out. But he couldn't quite manage as much as you needed, so he asked me, and I raided my savings pot. So, I've got quite a strong interest in it all working out – you could perhaps call me a shareholder.'

'Well, blow me! OK then, if you're not leaving but would like to help with Charlford, how do you see it working – and what should I call it when I'm talking to them?'

'Unless you want a posh name, I'd just refer to it all as Admin Support. As for how it could work, anything I did would have to be separate from the yard and transport here. Perhaps I could go over there for a few hours a week, probably on a Wednesday when it's generally quiet here, if that suits their needs.'

Tony nodded for her to go on – it still sounded too good to be true.

'Of course, it all depends on what support a person might need. If they already have their own books and so on, I could offer just to check they're set up in a way that makes life easy when it comes to dealing with audits and tax returns and such. And I could perhaps help with order forms, and invoices, and stock records and that sort of thing – if somebody comes to you just as they're starting to turn a hobby into a business, that's the sort of thing that easily gets in a muddle and lets them down.'

'Wow, Julie, you've obviously given it some thought, but I wonder if new people just turning their hobbies into a business might find it a bit off-putting if you go in suggesting that all that lot needs doing? I know I had little idea of what it was you did to keep the yard running properly.'

'Oh no, I'd not go barging in like that. The best idea would be for me to only go to see somebody who wanted admin services. I'd just ask what it was they needed, and take it from there.'

'That sounds fine,' said Tony, 'but what about costings? If somebody's a new trader, we can't face them with a hefty charge on top of the rent etc.'

'As I said, it will have to be costed separate from my yard and transport work, so it's something the three of us would have to sort out. Obviously if I'm working at Charlford, the yard shouldn't pay for that work. But, on the other hand, as I helped Reg to finance your leaving here and buying the manor, we can probably call ourselves Charlford Manor shareholders and justify the yard in subsidising my efforts!'

'Julie, will you ever cease to amaze me? That sounds great but, as me and my people – hopefully there'll be more than Ted Bailey – would get all the benefit, I'll have to leave it to you to sort out the money side with Reg. Is that OK?'

'That's fine, Tony, but before you go, I must mention a couple of things that I couldn't do for your people.'

'Ah, I thought there'd be a catch – what are they?'

'For a start, when their books needed auditing, I couldn't do that – but I reckon our auditors would probably give a good price, and the same goes for advertising and printing.'

'Perhaps you could check that out with them and agree the whole package with Reg, then I'll know what to offer Ted Bailey and anybody else that's interested. Thanks for all this, Julie, you've really taken a worry off my mind.'

Next day, Tony got a call from Reg to say that he'd agreed all the points that Julie had mentioned and they'd start to set out details for Tony to consider. They had also decided that it should all be named in a way that separated it from the yard and transport business.

Tony had often tried to come up with a name for the expected collection of small businesses – to give it an identity to separate it from Charlford Manor, as that would be his home. Julie suggested the name Charlford Enterprises and it seemed to fit the bill.

However, the name would later be changed when Ted Bailey objected to it on the grounds that it seemed to imply that each trader was an enterprise belonging to a Charlford parent company, rather than individual businesses that just happened to be based at the manor and took some support from it. After much confused discussion, Tony, Reg, and Julie – with Ted's agreement – decided to change the name to 'Charlford Enterprise'. In their final opinion, this name better described an umbrella company that was simply Tony and Reg's enterprise. (*Subtle? It's beyond me!*)

Charlford Enterprise went public by means of an advertisement they placed in the local paper, the Salchester Chronicle. This was then beefed up by an article after Reg got hold of the reporter who had covered the explosion at the manor during its refurbishment; this also meant that it reached the front page and many more readers!

Unfortunately, the initial surge of interest was mainly from sensation seekers and only a couple of serious enquiries. But these were from totally unsuitable businesses – a vehicle paint sprayer and a boarding kennels. Word of the situation did eventually reach Kelly Summers, whose sandwich delivery service – Kelly's Kitchen – became the first business to fully move into premises in the stable yard.

Next to respond to the advert was Joan Fletcher. 'I'm looking for a room that's clean, dry and warm, to house a studio or workshop,' she explained when she rang and spoke to Tony.

'Depends how many people you want space for – we've got converted stables and coach houses.'

'It's only me, but I'd hope to have a visitor or two sometimes – customers or for lessons – so perhaps I'd better have a look – if that's OK?' she asked.

Arrangements were made, Tony put the phone down, and it rang again before he'd finished noting details of the call. This time he was greeted by a man's voice, identifying the caller as Doug Beacher, a saddler.

'I imagine you like the idea of our stables then, Mr Beacher.'

'Yes, that's what attracted me.' And arrangements were made for a meeting to include an inspection of the premises on offer.

Both visits resulted in stables being booked, and the occupants moved in just two weeks later. Although Joan arrived the day before Doug, he was settled in and working before her.

'Have you got problems, Joan?' he asked while stretching his legs during a coffee break.

'No, but I was wondering how you got settled so quick – I know these rooms are clean and nicely decorated, but I'm having to check everywhere to make sure my fabrics and yarns don't snag on any hidden splintery bits. Was your place better prepared than this?'

'I don't think so but, of course, my materials are sturdier than yours. I can even use some of the original hooks, shelves, and so on, to hang or store things – that was one of the attractions.'

For two people working in quite different crafts, they could have been seen as incompatible neighbours, but quite the reverse evolved – each enjoyed a calm atmosphere with the occasional chat, and respected the other's need for quiet when tackling a tricky bit of work.

In their early natters, they naturally exchanged something of their craft experiences, particularly the things that had brought them to Charlford Manor.

Doug's situation was quite straightforward. Some of his clients needed to bring their mounts to him for measurement, fittings, and so on, but a new housing estate being built near his previous location had made access difficult and so had put a stop to that. Although Tony wouldn't allow animals to be kept in the stable yard, the occasional business visit was OK. But, even then, Doug preferred such visitors to come along the lane outside the yard, and he'd go to them through the gate – problem solved.

As for Joan, this was her third and, hopefully, final studio. Her venture into the world of full-time craft work began when her husband landed a good, well-paid job. This allowed her to give up her own part-time job and turn her hobbies of spinning, knitting, and crochet into a mini business. She hadn't thought of it as a business until she took a stall at a local Christmas craft fair, where she sold a lot, and took orders for more. There wasn't really room to do things properly at home, so she took a small studio in a permanent craft centre, only for her confidence to take a real knock. Some of the others in the centre seemed to be simply selling cheap imported artefacts, with the result that her higher priced, but better quality, goods just weren't selling enough to cover her costs. The move to Charlford brought her nearer to home and allowed her to choose her outlets – she was really optimistic about her future.

Whilst both of them appreciated the calm of their working environment, they agreed eventually that it could be too quiet at times, particularly during the afternoons – Kelly arrived very early in the mornings but was usually away making her deliveries by eleven-ish. So they were really ready for the background sounds that they expected Ted to bring with his workshop, his family and his home – it would help them realise that they weren't the last people on earth.

Chapter 3

The large brown van left the Salchester road at the turn beside the Red Lion and moved slowly until Charlford Manor came into view round the final bend in the approach road – it then came to an abrupt halt. The driver, Ted Bailey, couldn't believe his eyes. In the passenger seat beside him his wife, Alison, roused from a slight doze, rubbed her eyes open and felt the same shock of surprise – the whole place looked deserted.

'Oh, Ted, what on earth has happened?' she almost wailed.

Quite clearly, Ted didn't know, but he found himself giving voice to a little worm of doubt that had been quietly bothering him for a few months. 'I'm sorry, love, but it's beginning to look like I've been taken for a ride and really dropped us in it!'

'Oh, come on, Dad,' interrupted his teenage son, Whacker, squashed in on a box just behind his mum. 'Tony's a genuine bloke. And what would he get out of doing a disappearing trick? I know you've signed up to his Enterprise thing, but he's not taken any serious money, has he?'

'Course not, lad,' Ted said, 'but me signing up helped make it all look legit, and he could have cashed in on it somehow. And don't forget, we've gradually brought all my workshop tools and materials down here over the past few months, so there's the value of that lot in his hands. But the big thing that's bothering me is that we've cut our ties with Bracknell. I know we've still got the house but, if it's all gone belly-up here, I've given up the workshop and wouldn't be likely to get another one in a hurry.'

'Oh, Ted,' his wife managed to continue, 'why didn't you tell me all this that's been bothering you? We should have talked it over, and you know I'd have supported you if you'd wanted to back out of the move.'

'Well, like Whacker says,' Ted replied, trying to calm the mood, 'Tony seemed to be a genuine bloke, and you'd have thought I was having cold feet when I wasn't – not really. Just trying to be cautious before it was too late. Anyway, what do we do now?'

'I know it's late,' Alison said, 'but we can still get back home to Bracknell – I'd only have to put the hot water on and make the beds and we could have a proper night's sleep. Then you can suss out the situation regarding the work unit in the morning. So it's not all totally lost, is it, love?'

'Come on, Mum and Dad,' again interrupted Whacker, 'aren't you giving in a bit quick? We've no idea what the situation is. Tony might just have had to go out for the day and not got back yet. And don't forget that Kelly is usually closed down by this time, so there's not always signs of life in the stable yard. I vote we carry on down to the workshop, or at least to the front door of the manor, and get out and look. You can't just turn around and drive away, Dad!'

'You're right, son, and I am going in there, if only to check all our stuff's OK. But first, I've got to think about what to say or do depending on what we find – I don't want any more surprises and end up saying the wrong thing. But I still can't believe Tony's done the dirty on us.'

They'd first come into contact with Charlford Manor the previous year when Whacker and his pals had been visiting the village and a horse-drawn carriage was discovered in a coach-house at the manor. When Whacker mentioned that his dad, Ted, was interested in such things, Tony had asked for him to come and look at it. One thing led to another, and Ted's enthusiasm for moving in to work at the manor resulted in Tony deciding to develop the idea of what became Charlford Enterprise.

But Ted was not only moving his cabinetmaking business into one of the coach-house units, he was also moving home into the refurbished servants' cottage in the manor's stable yard. So, if Ted now discovered any serious problems, they could have devastating consequences for the family.

With all this background and possible problems running through his mind, Ted continued to sit unmoving in his van

– he just couldn't imagine what might have happened. Deciding, at last, that there wasn't really any point trying to work out how to deal with the unknown, he released the handbrake and eased them towards the stable yard, set back a bit from the manor house entrance.

There was no sign of life until, suddenly, a blond head appeared round the gatepost and as quickly withdrew. The van paused, they heard a cry – 'They're here!' – then all three let out the breaths they'd been holding, and Ted eased them through the gate to be confronted by the waiting group standing in front of his work unit. Its door was festooned with large sheets of paper carrying the words "Welcome to Ted Bailey, Cabinetmaker, and Family" – though they were placed a little haphazardly and could easily have been read as "Ted Cabinet and Bailey, Family Welcome Maker", but who cared?

As they climbed, grinning, from the van, Tony Philips came forward, shook Ted firmly by the hand, gave Alison's cheek a quick kiss and ruffled Whacker's already untidy mop of hair.

'Welcome to Charlford Enterprise and your new home!' he said. 'Give your legs a stretch, say hello to everybody, then you're all invited to come up to the house and have a drink and a bite to eat.'

'Thanks, Tony, but what about the van? Can't leave it here cluttering up the estate, and we've got the last of our worldly goods inside,' Ted was still feeling a bit unsettled.

'Give over, Ted,' interrupted Alison. 'If there's tea on offer without me having to make it, I'm not missing out. Thanks, Tony, it'll be most welcome.'

Turning away, she almost bumped into Kelly whose sandwich-making kitchen was next door to the new family home. 'Good to see you again, Kelly. How's business? Hope you'll be able to add us to your client list for days when I leave the lads to their own devices,' she asked with a smile.

'It's really fine, Alison, and a couple of extra sarnies for your two will be a pleasure – but I've got to run just now to make sure all is ready for your party – see you there, OK?'

And, with that, she trotted off up to the manor house, leaving Alison wondering what all the fuss was about.

Meanwhile, Ted was renewing acquaintances with the rest of the group. First of all, also wanting to hurry off to help in the manor house, were Mr and Mrs Wilkinson – they'd been part of the household staff of the previous owner some time ago and last year had called in during a pre-retirement trip round old haunts. Finding the new owner in a state of not knowing how to manage a house of that size, they had stayed to help Tony to get things in order. They then became involved in training domestic staff for a local agency, and were still at the manor over a year later.

Waiting to have a word with Ted were the other two crafts people already working in the stable yard; Molly Andrews, the wool lady; and Harry Beacher, the saddler. 'How's things with you two?' he asked.

With Molly seeming a little shy of speaking up, it was Harry who replied, 'Everything's fine, Ted, but it can be a bit too quiet at times. So, we're really pleased to see you, if only to know we're not the only people left on earth – sorry, that didn't come out very well, did it? What we mean is that it will be good to have a bit more company.'

'Yes,' joined in Molly, 'it's nice not having loads of people milling around and stopping you working, as can happen in some craft centres, but it's been a bit too quiet at times. We know you're not likely to be noisy, but you'll help us not to feel a bit isolated, if you know what I mean.'

'I know just what you mean,' Ted replied, 'and you probably know I'm pleased to be getting away from too much noise at times. So, I hope we'll strike a happy medium – but perhaps you won't mind if Whacker gets on his drums sometimes!' They all knew that the drum kit was already set up in a fairly sound-proofed loft in Ted's unit.

At this point they were joined by Tony wanting to get them moving into the manor house for the welcoming party. 'You've all got to come in and enjoy this cake that Anna's been making and fretting over. Leave the van there, Ted, it won't walk!'

'OK Tony, but, seriously, I have been wondering about where to leave it overnight. On the earlier trips, I put it in the coach house next to the workshop, but I guess that's now properly set up as a unit and somebody will be renting it. So where can I park?'

'That'll soon be sorted, Ted, but you're right. Your visits made me realise there was going to be a problem for all the tenants, so we're planning to have some garages built in part of what was the kitchen garden.'

'But what about Kelly's brother and his veg plot – that was going to be Kelly's Krops, wasn't it?'

'I'm afraid that wasn't working out. The plot wasn't big enough to make him a living, but at least his efforts helped get him a job at the nursery in Newton – and we're leaving enough garden for Kelly to grow some of her salad stuff. But that's enough about business, let's get you some refreshments – and for now you can still park in the coach-house next to your unit – OK?'

By this time everyone else was in the manor house and they gave a somewhat self-conscious mini cheer when Ted walked in with Tony. The Bailey family were quite nonplussed by all this fuss – as far as they were concerned, they were simply moving house to go with a job in a new area. But, for Tony Philips, Ted had provided the inspiration to create a group of businesses based around Charlford Manor and then, by moving in with both home and business, had actually turned the idea into a reality.

'Right,' began Tony, 'this is the last time I'll make a fuss like this, ('Thanks goodness for that!' muttered Ted) but...'

Before he could continue, he was interrupted as the door suddenly burst open and in walked Hattie Scattergood, looking for all the world as if she had every right to be there.

'Sorry to be late, Tony, but don't let me stop your welcoming speech.' Then, with a sweet smile for everyone, she looked around for a friendly face and somewhere to join in, but they all drew back from the expected sour odour that usually surrounded her.

'Hattie, this isn't a public meeting, so I'll ask you to leave.'

'But isn't this to welcome the new family into the community? I'm part of the community too, you know!'

'No, Hattie, this is to welcome them to the Charlford Enterprise community, so again I'll ask you to leave,' Tony managing to keep calm.

'But what about me joining the Enterprise—'

'NO!' he almost shouted. 'This is a private meeting in a private house and, if you won't leave when asked, I'll call that trespassing and deal—'

'OK, keep your rag-and-bone man shirt on, Tony, I know when I'm too good for a company, but don't come begging to me when you need more staff!! Enjoy your meeting!' And, with that, she smiled as if nothing had happened and waltzed off out leaving a sea of incredulous expressions.

Mr Wilkinson, who had been preparing to usher Hattie out of the door, moved over to the windows ready to open them to clear the air but, for once, Hattie had not left an odorous reminder of her presence.

Quickly recovering himself, Tony apologised for the interruption and continued his memorised speech.

'As I was saying, it wouldn't have been right for Ted and family to turn up, move in and start work as if it was any old day. So I'll ignore your comment, Ted, in the spirit it was muttered, as long as you'll take Alison and Whacker up to the Red Lion for your evening meal, on me – and don't tell me you've brought sandwiches!!'

'Thanks, Tony, and thanks everybody. No way did we expect anything like this, but you're right – it wouldn't have been fair to expect Alison to cook a meal after she's unpacked the van and made the beds!!' When that was greeted with hoots and howls of laughter, he felt it confirmed that he'd made the right decision to move here.

The party then got under way with Tony's daughter, Anna, and Mrs Wilkinson, cutting cakes and handing out slices accompanied by cups of tea, and Mr Wilkinson telling Alison and Whacker about Hattie.

The Baileys spent the next few days settling in as a family, following Alison's logic that the family home, wherever it may be, should always be the base to build a happy and successful life on. (*That should probably be "a base on which to build etc.", so as not to end a sentence on a whatsit – but who's checking?*) Ted and Whacker agreed and, without too much protest, accepted being banned for a few days from going anywhere near the workshop until all the rooms in the cottage were just as Alison wanted them. After that, they all felt in need of a little relaxation, and headed out to face their new world. They started with an exploration of Salchester, where they also planned to buy a family car to replace the old one that had finally refused to start and been carried off to a breakers yard in Bracknell.

Chapter 4

Hattie Scattergood lived in the woods on Parsons Lane, not far from the ford at the edge of the village. While Hattie always referred to her home as a bungalow – it was, after all, a single-storey building – most of the villagers who'd seen it would be likely to describe it as a shack. It had a wooden frame and once-white panelled walls, fronted by a rickety-looking veranda.

Her life had very little variety and most days started in much the same way – just before closing the front door as she went out, she would call 'Cheerio' to her mother and would sometimes add something like 'I'll try not to be too late'. But, by that time, the radio would be on in the kitchen and she'd long ago given up on expecting a reply, and neither waited for one nor felt miffed at not hearing one.

The regular high point in Hattie's week was her visit to Charlford Post Office, first thing on a Tuesday morning, to draw her mother's pension and then deposit a small portion of it into their joint savings account. This could cause eyebrows to raise if any of the villagers who observed it had not been around when the system was set up. On that day, the day that Mrs Scattergood qualified for her pension, she had opened the savings account jointly with her daughter, 'so that my dear Hattie has the means to make sure I'm well looked-after when I get older and less able to look after myself!'.

Hattie had blushed a little at her mother's rather effusive language, but she'd often come to wish that she had a recording of it to play in response to the looks and half-heard comments that sometimes accompanied her weekly transaction. On the other hand, people in the Post Office always seemed to treat her with respect by standing aside to allow her to get to the counter, transact her business, and be off in time to catch her bus to the city. 'Nowt so queer as folk!' as her grandma Scattergood would have said.

As this was the day the local paper came out, Hattie would buy a copy, mainly to give herself something to deter fellow bus passengers from trying to strike up unwelcome conversations. Although she'd grown up in the village, Hattie had lived away for so long that, by the time her mother became really ill and she returned to care for her, she no longer had anything in common with the locals and had decided she didn't want to change that. Hearing the tittle-tattle that filled the Post Office during her visits, Hattie knew she'd been right to keep people at arm's length so as not have to constantly repeat the same banal answers to the enquiries about her mother. 'No,' she often repeated to herself, 'it was the right decision to keep myself to myself and plough my own furrow.' Then she'd laugh at herself, realising she'd used a saying of the country folk she so disliked.

Hattie's thoughts about the locals often ran through her mind on the bus to Salchester after her Post Office visit. The fact that she felt herself to be above them all gave her the confidence she needed in order to face the unknowns that each day might throw at her – days of meeting, mixing with, and even having to give the appearance of being friendly towards, total strangers. Her aloof personality had been set in childhood when her poor eyesight meant she had to wear very basic spectacles that attracted bullying, including name-calling – the origins of 'Scatty Hattie'.

Once, when running to escape a bully, Hattie had fallen and hit her head against a wall, the injury keeping her in bed for a few days. When she recovered, she was found to have lost her sense of taste and smell. Whilst her taste buds eventually recovered, she still could not enjoy any of the pleasant scents that she'd encounter during any day. Nor was she aware of the less than pleasant aromas she carried with her on her daily stroll around the shops and sights of Salchester when doing the necessary household shopping.

This pattern of Hattie's life began to change after she heard in the shop one Tuesday that a well-loved villager had died. 'So that'll be a bit less business for the Post Office then,

Monica,' was the almost gleeful comment from the mean-spirited woman who'd raised the topic.

'Aye, it will, and a fair bit less for the shop,' replied Monica. 'Mary always bought some of their supplies from us – not like some folk who draw the pension and then only buy a paper!!', looking pointedly at Hattie.

'Oh, I'd buy much more from you,' Hattie replied, 'if it wasn't all so close to its throw-away date. And it would hardly be in a state to be used by the time I got back from carrying it around the city all day, would it? But I'd always encourage others to shop here, if only for the lovely company you keep. Anyway, it's too nice a day to be stood chatting, much as I'm enjoying it, so I'll wish you all good day.' And with a beaming smile she flounced off to catch the bus as usual.

But on this occasion, once settled on the bus, Hattie's smile disappeared as she started to ponder how the news she'd just heard might affect her. She was still in that thoughtful mood when she got off the bus in the centre of Salchester and, instead of heading for the shops as usual, she went straight to the teashop in the cathedral's Chapter House. The sun had brought the tourists out in droves and she was lucky to grab the last small table, where she opened the local paper for the first time that morning. She had just reached the Situations Vacant pages, when an elderly lady came up to the empty chair at her table.

'Excuse me, miss, if this seat is free, would you mind if I joined you – it seems to be the only one in the whole place.'

'That's OK,' without looking up, a frown growing deeper as she went from page to page. In the end she closed the paper with an audible sigh and at last looked up.

The woman had watched her with quiet concern, and eventually said, 'I hope you don't mind my saying so, miss, but you look very worried and perhaps tired – I don't want to pry but, is everything alright?'

Hattie had never been approached in a kindly way before and, at first, wondered if it might be the opening phase of a confidence trick, but relaxed and decided to play it at face value. 'Well,' she replied, 'things are OK at the moment, but I've just had a bit of a sort of shock and I'm having to think what I can do about it.'

'Oh, I see. I'm sorry to intrude, my dear, but is there anything I can do? Would it perhaps help just to talk about it? And don't let your coffee go cold, will you?'

This final remark made Hattie smile a little, start to relax, and decide to give it a try, but to put the story in the third person.

'Well,' she started, 'I've just heard that a friend's mother has recently died and it leaves my friend in a difficult position. She was caring for her mother at home, so she had her mother's pension and other allowances for the pair of them to live on. It isn't a lot, but we manage – sorry, my friend manages. I don't know what she'll do now, that's all – not my problem, fortunately, but I'd like to help, if only with ideas.'

'Does your friend have a job?'

'No, not at the moment, but she had worked until she came home to look after my mother – sorry, her mother.' And Hattie displayed a rare blush.

The woman looked at her with compassion then stated the obvious, 'It's you and your own mother we're talking about, isn't it, my dear? I'm so sorry. Did she pass away very recently – your mother?'

'Oh no, and I'm sorry, the situation isn't as bad as it may have sounded – my mother is still alive and I'm looking after her. We're living off her savings and allowances, but this morning I heard of a pensioner in the village dying and it suddenly came home to me that the present situation can't last for ever and I'll have to find a job when my mum's no longer here.'

After a pause to consider things and take a sip of tea, the woman tried again. 'So, if I've got it right, things aren't as dire as they first looked to me. Your problem seems to boil down to finding a source of income – a job – for when you have to manage on your own... I should just mind my own business and let you get on with yours, shouldn't I?'

'Not at all, it's rare to talk to somebody who won't go gossiping about my business around the village, and if you know of any jobs going in the area, I'd be really grateful – there doesn't seem to be much in the paper.'

'I'm sorry, my dear, but it's a long time since I had any contact with the jobs market – my son moved to Shropshire a couple of years ago, and my late husband and I retired here from Essex, so I'm not the best person to help, I'm afraid.'

'That's OK, but thank you for your interest. Now I must be off and get some food for home.' And away Hattie went, leaving a concerned woman deep in thought at the table.

Over the next couple of weeks Hattie saw the woman three or four times, sometimes near enough to exchange pleasantries, and it all allowed Hattie's suspicions to recede. Eventually, and perhaps inevitably, they bumped into each other, again at the counter of the cathedral teashop, and finally they sat together ready to chat, like old friends just catching up on family news etc. This time, understandably, it had to start off with introductions.

'You know, my dear, while I feel I might know you a little, simply from those few words we had and from seeing you around, I still don't know your name – nor you mine, I suppose. Perhaps I should start – I'm Mrs Gilbert – Vivian. And you are?'

'That's funny, Mrs Gilbert – I've been thinking of you as a Dorothy – so I was miles off, wasn't I? Well, I'm Harriet – generally called Hattie – and with a surname like Scattergood it was inevitable I'd become Scatty Hattie at school, but I don't get it much these days, thank goodness. And I can't afford to be scatty in looking after my mum – not that she's a burden or anything, just that I have to think of everything and do everything around the house. She can't get out and hates having visitors see her in the state she's in – but she's my mum.'

'And has the job situation changed since we had that chat – or should I say, is everything alright financially with you and your mother?'

'Oh yes, everything's still the same at home – and I haven't found a job, in fact I've not seriously looked except to see if I can see anything part-time.'

'Do any of your friends in the village have any ideas or any contacts?'

'I'm afraid I don't really have any friends in the village – the women I see in the Post Office are all entrenched villagers and don't really have any time for me – and I'm happy with that – they're not my types at all.'

'Is there no-one else in the village that you talk to?'

'Well, there's the chaps in the pub – the Red Lion – but again, they're much older and only want to talk amongst themselves about farming or football.'

'Have you thought of approaching any businesses that you know and like – they just might have a vacancy but haven't got round to advertising it – or there could be a little short term fill-in job – anything to get you back into the world of work?'

'Yes, that's a brilliant idea, and I know just the person to go and see! AND, it would give me the flexibility I need for dealing with my mother's needs – thank you so much, Mrs Gilbert.'

'Oh, lovely – but "Mrs Gilbert" does sound so formal, can you call me Vivian or just Viv?'

'How about, "Auntie Viv"? – I think I'd prefer that.'

'That's lovely, my dear – do you know, I've never been an aunt before – I rather like it! And perhaps I can give you my phone number so you can call me if you ever want someone to confide in, or to help sort out a worry – or, hopefully, to share your excitement when you get that job!'

'That's really very kind of you, and I must admit there are times when I feel a bit lost, but I couldn't impose on you like that.'

'Nonsense, my dear!' And with that, Mrs Gilbert tore an empty page from her diary and fished in her handbag for a pen. 'Here, my dear, this is my telephone number, and you must feel free to contact me if ever you feel I might be able to help, if only to be someone new to talk to. And here's to the start of what I think may become a new friendship.'

With which she raised her teacup and drank a toast, leaving Hattie for once speechless, having found a friend at last.

Chapter 5

Beginning in the kitchen of the family home where she lived with her parents and brother, Kelly Summers' business, Kelly's Kitchen, made and delivered lunches to businesses that were too small to have their own canteens or too far away from an eatery or food shop.

The re-furbished laundry room in Charlford Manor stable yard suited her needs admirably, particularly after Tony had installed some extra power lines and extractor fans that she'd suggested. Kelly was delighted that the old laundry's copper could still be heated and she tried it for making soups and broths. This was partially successful and she made soup for the occasion when Tony invited people to celebrate the launch of Charlford Enterprise. But the difficulties of transporting and delivering hot liquids soon became apparent and she dropped the idea, reverting to the original plan of dealing only in sandwiches, rolls, and eventually, perhaps, pies.

But, even from the moment she moved into the newly-fitted kitchen, Kelly felt that she wouldn't be there for ever – that was not because she didn't like the place, it was simply because she had ambitions that would take her beyond a small rural business. But, keeping her eye on the ball, Kelly stuck to her basic plan to produce simple, tasty, healthy sandwiches. These she would deliver to local offices and businesses in nearby small villages, before lunch time while they remained fresh.

To achieve this seemingly simple aim, she needed a system that brought in the customer orders early enough for her to collect the ingredients and then have enough time to make up, pack, and deliver, the end product.

In the very early days this was fairly easy to achieve, partly because she started with only a few customers; then, as the numbers grew, she had her brother on hand to help out as necessary in all aspects of the work. However, their main aim was for him to produce fresh ingredients from the manor's kitchen garden. Unfortunately, although he worked the land well enough and soon brought it back up to a good level of productivity, the site just wasn't suitable for providing the range and quantities of foods that she needed. Salad items were fine but they generally had short seasons, and there was no way that the site could be developed quickly enough to provide fruits and year-round produce.

As with many small start-up businesses, the popularity of her products was soon causing problems – customer satisfaction was spreading the word to more people at each location, and then on to other locations. So she had to get in to the kitchen earlier each day to fulfil the growing orders, then stay later to clear up after making the deliveries in the promised time-scale.

At the close of one of these satisfying, yet wearying, days, Kelly was met by Alison who had just been across the yard to call Ted and Whacker for their tea meal.

'Oh, Kelly, you look done in, you poor girl. You can't set off driving home looking like that, you'll be falling asleep at the wheel. Come on in to the cottage, put your feet up for a few minutes and have a cup of tea.' Being too tired to protest, Kelly was soon settled into an armchair with her feet up on a small stool and was asleep before her cup of tea had even arrived, let alone been tasted.

When Ted and Whacker walked in, they were quickly shushed and kept in the kitchen while Alison explained what had happened, and then dealt with the inevitable questions, such as, 'What about her folks?'

'I'll ring her mum.'

'Will she be here all night?'

'Doesn't matter.'

'Where will she sleep?'

'We'll sort something out if necessary.'

'Looks like she's doing too much.'

'You can say that again.'

'But you'd never know, would you? She's always so bright and quick and on the go.'

'Reminds me a bit of how you were, Ted, when you first left Barden's and started on your own – everything had to be done by tomorrow, the customer was always right, and so on. I reckon Kelly just needs a bit of a hand to get things in perspective – is that the right word? – and make a few rules for herself.'

'Couldn't agree more, love, but who does she know that she'd trust, I wonder?'

'Oh, come off it, you two,' interposed Whacker, 'surely Kelly knows you two well enough, and there's Tony, and even Lion Jim. You've all got experience of starting a small business, and you all like her and wouldn't try to force her into anything she didn't agree with, would you?'

'No, you're right, son,' replied Ted, 'just a matter of raising the subject without her feeling we think she's failing in any way – which she isn't – if anything, she's almost too successful.'

In the meantime, Kelly had woken up in a strange place, but it didn't take her long to work out what had happened and where she was, particularly when she recognised the voices in the next room. Not wanting to butt into a private conversation, she approached the kitchen door to wait for a convenient point to let them know she was awake. Hearing the last few comments, she realised the family were quite concerned about her, so tapped on the door and went through.

'Hi there, sorry to have put you to any trouble, but I really did need that nap, so thanks, Alison. And my apologies for stopping you getting on with your meal. I really must go now – I've got some new pie recipes to try out this evening.'

'Before you go, Kelly' started Alison, 'we're a bit concerned that you might be trying to do too much – you know, never saying 'no' to a customer's request. And I've seen that myself from how you've never turned down anything us three have asked for, whether it's for a sandwich filling or the time when we want to pick it up. If you're like that with any of your other customers, it's no wonder you're shattered at the end of the day. Isn't there somebody that could help you out a bit?'

'Well, nobody apart from my brother, but I'll think about it. Thanks for your help just now, but I must get on with what I need to sort out before tomorrow, so I'll get off home and leave you in peace.'

'Hold on a minute, Kelly, are you sure you're OK to drive?'

'Thanks, Ted, I'm sure I am – and I've imposed enough on your hospitality already.'

'Why not stay and have a bite to eat with us,' asked Alison, 'it'll be one thing less for you to deal with when you get home – come on, love, it's no trouble.'

Kelly wasn't really feeling as fit as she'd claimed, so accepted the offer and was quite grateful to be able to sit and relax a bit longer. Then, during the meal, she started to answer their questions about how she ran the business. Eventually she asked if they had any suggestions, and was quite surprised that they came thick and fast.

'I'm really surprised that you don't have a menu – just doing the fillings people ask for is fine to start with, but you can't go on that way, surely,' began Alison. 'Have you thought about making a list of the real favourites and then sticking to that?'

'And perhaps allowing others to be chosen, but at a slightly higher price?' added Ted.

'Oh, I think a lot of them wouldn't like that, and I do need the sort of quantities I'm supplying now to make it worth my while.'

'Yes, but you don't have to just dump the idea on them,' said Alison. 'Start by letting them know that it's something you're thinking about – and perhaps if you concentrated on fewer fillings and so on, your costs might come down enough to reduce some prices. That would surely make up for them having a reduced choice?'

Whacker had been quiet so far, thinking about the physical aspects of Kelly's business – that was what had seemed to him to be the cause of the current situation. He wanted to know about the practical aspects of taking the orders, getting the supplies, then making up and delivering the sandwiches.

'Well, starting from scratch,' explained Kelly, 'I approach a small business, usually out in a village somewhere, ask them if they'd like a daily sandwich delivery, take their order, get the ingredients, then make them up and add them to the delivery run the next morning.'

'OK, but when you visit a customer, how do you deliver the orders and collect the money?'

'That's easy, Whacker. When I turn up at the door, somebody puts the word out that I'm there, and people come and see me and pay. Then on to the next place.'

That seemed to be such a simple straight-forward process that it stopped further questions, and they continued quietly with their meal, each wondering where they could see any openings for improvements. At last, when simple curiosity prompted Alison to ask which villages Kelly served, the answer gave her an idea.

'Well, look, Kelly, I've been wanting to get out into the local area and see what's where, so if I could come out with you and help with the deliveries, I'd see more of the area and we'd be helping each other – think about it and let me know. Would you do that?'

'I'd certainly enjoy the company,' Kelly replied, and at last smiled, 'but, of course, unless you switched to a bus somewhere, you'd be with me for a few hours!'

'That'd be no problem – these two reprobates don't need me here all day every day, so they can manage for a whole day at least once in a while – and you never know if we might see a way between us to reduce your work load.'

This really seemed to raise Kelly's spirits and they all felt it had been time well spent, particularly when they agreed with her that she was restored enough to set off home under her own steam. Over the washing-up, after Kelly had left, all three aired their views and opinions, and these led to some positive suggestions that they would either put to Kelly, or

Alison would try out when she joined Kelly on a delivery run.

However, they all felt that they shouldn't intrude on Kelly straight off, but leave her to get on with things for at least the rest of that week, so it was the following Tuesday that found Alison popping in to see if she could order rolls for Ted and Whacker for the next day. She was more than pleased to find the young woman not only in good spirits, but asking if Alison would like to go on the delivery run that day and see if she could offer any suggestions for improvements in the service. 'If you can let me have rolls for my chaps for today as well as tomorrow,' was taken correctly as a yes.

Alison nipped back home to tidy up, get her bag, etc., then popped over to the workshop to tell Ted about the change of plans for the day. She'd only been out of Kelly's kitchen for about ten minutes, but returned to find her in heated argument with the woman she'd come to recognise as Hattie Scattergood who greeted her with, 'And don't you come high and mighty with me, madam! You only live in the servants' quarters, so don't think you can go interfering in other people's businesses and interrupting job interviews and business discussions!'

Kelly looked quite distraught, and Alison was absolutely flabbergasted. Without a word she turned around, left the kitchen, and went straight across to tell Ted what was happening and to get him to rescue Kelly.

'Hold on a minute, love. If Kelly doesn't ask for help, then we'd be interfering just like you feel this Scattergood woman is.'

'But Ted,' she almost cried, 'you didn't see the expression on Kelly's face. She looked terrified – that woman was bullying her – we've got to do something!'

'OK, love, I'll pop across to have a word with her about the order you've put in for tomorrow, and see how the land lies, how's that? And you'd perhaps best go up to the manor and see if Tony's there – just in case it's serious.' Without waiting for a reply, he was off out of the door.

Arriving at Kelly's Kitchen, Ted tried the door, as the family usually did, and was a little alarmed to find it firmly closed and locked. However, his firm knocking resulted in Kelly calling out, 'Half a minute, the bolt's jammed – with you in a sec!' And she was, but opening the door a mere couple of inches.

'Yes, Mr Bailey, what can I do for you? Mrs Bailey just gave me your lunch orders for today and tomorrow.' She was trying to sound normal, but was frowning so as to show that all was not well.

'That's fine, Kelly, but I've come to check on that shelf I fixed last week – you remember I wasn't too confident of the wall behind it. Even if you don't put too much weight on it, it might not be safe. It won't take a second if I can just pop in.'

With an unspoken understanding, Kelly eased the door a bit more open so that Ted had enough room to come in and see the scene that Alison had described – Kelly almost trembling under the malevolent stare of Hattie Scattergood.

'Make it quick, Mr Carpenter, me and Miss Kelly's got a job to discuss.'

'Doesn't look like a job interview to me – and I didn't know you were looking for staff, Kelly.'

'None of your business, Mr Carpenter, and I'm not having you steal a job from under my nose.'

Just as things looked as if they might escalate further, the door opened fully and Tony Philips came in with 'Hello, Kelly – Miss Scattergood. Everything all right? Or are you being a nuisance again, Hattie? You know these premises are private property and you can only come in if the owner or the tenant invites you in?'

'Of course I know that, and everything's fine, Tony. I also know how hard Kelly is working and I just came along to offer a neighbourly hand – didn't I, my dear? Now don't you forget my offer of help – any time.'

With a broad smile she walked out and away from the site. Realising that further discussion of the woman would only add to Kelly's upset, Tony asked her if any actual damage had been done, and would she be able to continue with her day's deliveries.

'Oh no, there's no physical damage – she didn't get in far enough – but that awful smell! What on earth is it? And how can I get rid of it quickly – I daren't uncover any food to finish putting up the orders until I feel the whole kitchen is clean.'

'There's a bit of a breeze out there, so open the window and door while I nip and get a couple of fans,' replied Tony. 'But what the smell is – Heaven alone knows, 'cos nobody in the village does!' With that, he went off and made sure Hattie had done the same and was out of sight.

'I don't want to bother you,' began Ted, 'but I think we need to see what we can do to keep her out, same for any other unwelcome visitor. And it seems to me the problem is that you've got no windows to let you see anybody that comes knocking at the door. They don't have that problem in the workshops in the stables,' – a pause, and then realisation struck – 'Of course – the answer is a stable door!'

'Pardon?'

'If you and Tony agree, I could cut your door in two, put a solid bolt in the bottom half so you can keep that firmly shut while you open the top to speak to callers – perhaps put a little counter or ledge inside the bottom half where you could keep a little note book if you wanted. How does that sound?'

'That sounds great, but what would it cost and would Tony let us do it to his property – and, of course I'd still be opening up without seeing who was there.'

'Here he is – let's ask him.' They did, and he agreed with the plan, going further by suggesting that Ted put a small window in the top half of the door, preferably with some sort of toughened glass. He also said that, as it was his property, he would need to approve Ted's plans, but then he would pay.

With that settled, and the fresh air having cleared all remnants of Hattie's presence, Kelly continued with her preparations for the day, assisted by Alison who then went on the delivery run with her, and life settled down to a new normal.

Chapter 6

Alison had rather surprised herself by how interested she had become in the local area, mainly because of the ease with which she could get to Salchester – a very pleasant half-hour bus journey through rolling countryside of wooded hills and fields. Once in the city, it was the imposing cathedral that had attracted her and received most of her attention. A close second came the twee and quirky shops in the narrow lanes leading from the cathedral to the ancient market square. Several of these had been recommended as being quite authentic, while others were more modern in their wares and service; but she had loved exploring them all.

It was in one of the city's pretty teashops that Alison's project was born when she found a free magazine called Aspire and flicked through it while waiting for her order to arrive. Half expecting it to be full of ideas for improving your life by creating targets etc, she was agreeably surprised to find write-ups of all sorts of events taking place in and around local villages and their churches. She hadn't noticed it on the shelves of any newsagents, and it didn't seem to have a price marked anywhere, so she asked the waitress about it.

'Sorry, madam, but I don't really know much about it except that a chap leaves us half a dozen copies every month or so. They're free and you can either just look at them here or take a copy away. I must say they're very popular and I'm fairly certain that's the last one out of the latest batch.'

'Oh, I'd better not take it, then. I'll just note one or two things in my diary.'

'I think I can let you have some note paper if that will help, madam,' and off she went. The half a dozen sheets of the café's headed paper that she brought back gave Alison all the space she needed to note contact details for the magazine itself, plus dates and times of events listed in local villages. Feeling quite pleased with her find, she treated herself to another cup of tea and a too-tempting cup cake.

Realising she didn't know where some of the villages were that she'd made notes about, her next stop was to get a local map at a nearby stationers, where she also asked about the Aspire magazine.

'Oh, it's a nice little thing,' answered the lady at the till, rather dismissively, 'and it gives a bit more advance notice of events than the local paper can do, so I imagine it might lose the papers a few sales. If it wasn't free, I suppose we could have copies on sale here, but I think the cathedral people insist on it being free.'

Wondering if she'd perhaps disturbed a wasp's nest, Alison quickly left and got the next bus home!

Over dinner that evening, Ted asked his usual question of the family: 'Done anything special today?' and got the usual rolled-eyes response from Whacker, while Alison described her outing.

'What's so special about this booklet, then?' Ted asked. 'Apart from it being free!'

'It's a good start on getting to know the area a bit better....'

'But looking at churches??' jumped in Whacker, with a typical teenager's lack of enthusiasm.

'If you have better things to do, young man, like getting your course work done for college, then you won't have to tag along!' Ted really wasn't happy with the way some subjects were taught these days, so kept his nose out, apart from trying to ensure Whacker was keeping up to speed.

'Leave him alone, Ted, you know he'd prefer to spend his weekends seeing Tina – far nicer company than you can be!' but her smile took any sting out of the rebuke.

'OK, but you've still not said what's so special about this booklet.'

'Well, they list events like bazaars, fetes and flower festivals at local churches and villages, so there'll be something to see apart from the church itself. But what really caught my interest was the name of the chap that produces it.'

'Reckon you've found yourself a toy boy or a sugar daddy then, Mum?' laughed Whacker, ducking to avoid the expected slap.

Ignoring the interruption, Alison went on, 'You remember I've told you about staying with my cousin Jane and we used to pal about with one of her friends called Beryl? Well, her surname was Mitcalfe, and the chap behind the Aspire magazine is a – wait for it – Broderick Mitcalfe! Now there can't be many with that name floating around, so I wouldn't be surprised if they're related.'

'Yes, but what are you going to do about it?' asked Ted. 'And what do you expect to come of it? It's not as if he'd be a relation of yours.'

'No, but if they are related, it would be nice to hear how Beryl is – Jane has never mentioned her in her letters – and I'd have thought she would do if Beryl got married, or moved away or something – they always seemed to be good friends.'

'Well, you could just ask Jane the next time you write – you're bound to be writing some time fairly soon to at least give her our new address. That way you'll also get to know what sort of a bloke he is – that is, if he is related.'

'OK, love, good idea – as usual!'

When that same issue of Aspire was first distributed, one of the people to see it was Hattie Scattergood while she was making her regular mid-morning cup of tea and a scone last as long as possible – this time in a teashop in Overton, just outside Salchester. Reading some of the notices about church fetes and flower festivals drew a snort of disgust.

'All them prissy women showing off their flowery frocks and Women's Institute Victoria sponge cakes and best manners – they just make me sick!'

She thought the remark had been just a thought, but obviously not, as it drew the attention of the proprietor.

'Having a bad day then, miss?' she asked.

'You could say that – just trailed all the way out here for a job at Jackson's bakery only to find it's for the middle of the night. How do they think I'm going to get here for five o'clock in the morning when the buses don't start till 7? It was a crumby job, anyway – sorry, "crumby job in a bakery"! Not funny really – not many jobs around just now, but you have to keep looking.'

'If it doesn't have to be in food or catering, I can point you towards what might be an opening – but I don't know anything about it at all really, except that the person doing it is leaving the area and giving it up.'

'Wow, that's terrific. Thanks very much. What's the job, though?'

'Funnily enough it's to do with that magazine you're looking at – Aspire. The chap who brings it every month or so is moving away, but that's all I know – you'll have to contact the people that produce it and see if he's created a vacancy. Take that copy, if you like, we've plenty more – and good luck.'

'I think that calls for another cup of tea to celebrate.'

Although that cup of tea was on the house, it was the only bit of celebration about the job she'd hoped she might get. Hattie's quick visit to the editor revealed that it wasn't a paid job, purely voluntary. That definitely wasn't Hattie's cup of tea and she told him so, in no uncertain terms.

In the meantime, Alison was really enjoying working with Kelly on her sandwich deliveries, and had soon helped to set up new systems with various customers, the main improvements being where the customer had a staffed reception area. Particularly in busy premises, they preferred to be the main, perhaps even the only, point of contact between Kelly and her customers. Alison found it easy to persuade them to collect the orders, receive and distribute the sandwiches, and handle the money. This saved Kelly so much time and effort that she was happy to reward such support with discounted or free sandwiches.

However, for Alison, a personal benefit of being on the delivery run was that she saw more of the local villages than she'd ever imagined. So, after she'd gained a fuller understanding of Kelly's priorities, they agreed for her to be dropped off once a week or so, to have a closer look at some of the local attractions. But this needed planning, so, armed with a map of the local area, Alison marked the villages she wanted to visit. Then, with a different coloured pencil, she marked those that Kelly visited and the route she followed. On top of all that, Alison drew the route of the local buses – and what a mare's nest she ended up with!

'What's all this then, love?' asked Ted as she plonked her papers down in front of him on the kitchen table where he was trying to sketch out an idea for a secret desk drawer.

'It's the villages – you know, the ones I want to have a look at – the ones that have fetes and things. I've told you about it and you agreed we could go and visit them – so I'm trying to work out which are the best ones to see first and which ones probably aren't worth the trouble and I don't know where to start and it's all getting too much!' and a tear silently started to run down her cheek.

'Oh, come here, my love, let's have a look at you.' And he drew her down to sit on the chair he'd vacated and wiped the tear away with a fairly clean hankie. 'Now then, if all this has stemmed from what that magazine says, why not start there, look at the dates when these things happen, and look at the villages in that order?'

'Yes, but the dates are all for earlier this year, and I want us to be ready for next year, and the villages aren't getting the magazine any more – the man has gone away!!' And more tears flowed at the utter despair that the situation produced in her.

Seeing that this was not to be resolved by a few calming words, Ted put the kettle on and made a pot of tea! There, that should do the trick, he thought. (*Wrong!!*)

At this point, Whacker whistled his way in, to say he was off to the Red Lion – 'Anybody coming?' – only to realise the scene before him probably didn't need his input.

'Not just yet, son, but when you get there, can you ask if anybody knows what happened to that Aspire magazine your mum likes – looks as if they stopped doing it, but it might just be temporary.'

'I don't think it's stopped, Dad. Somebody had this month's in college the other day – it'd got his mum's picture and a bit about something she's doing. Why not check up with that bloke with the old-fashioned name Mum was on about?'

'Thanks, lad, I'm glad you're the one we kept out of the litter. Now off you go and have a nice evening – we might just drop in later.'

Whacker's news and Ted's cup of tea had cheered Alison no end, particularly as Ted seemed to think it was a good idea for her to ring the Aspire magazine man. They found the phone number in their copy, and Alison felt the address could well be the editor's home – if so, he might be there. As she really wanted to know what was happening, Ted said he'd ring there and then, failing that, try again in the morning – he didn't want Alison to start anything while she was in her current frail state.

As luck would have it, not only was the editor there, but the magazine was still in production, and they made an appointment to meet him.

So, the following Saturday afternoon, Ted took Alison to meet the tantalisingly-named Broderick Mitcalfe in a teashop in Skelford where he'd said he could hand over the latest one plus copies of previous issues. They spotted him as soon as they walked through the door – the very image of a struggling author with unruly thick black hair, matching straggly black beard and long-fingered sensitive-looking hands. It was quite a disappointment to eventually be told he was a telephone engineer! And, of course, he had no relatives in the area where Alison's cousin lived, and none, as far as he knew, called Beryl. But that didn't dampen his enthusiasm for meeting someone wanting copies of the magazine that was the baby of his leisure time.

Broderick explained that it had all come about when he became friendly with the Rural Dean and his wife, after baby-sitting for them, and the whole project came about when they were visiting one or two churches together. At each stop he'd picked up leaflets about local events, and had come up with the idea of combining the information into a booklet for distribution throughout the diocese – this had been supported by the Dean, and had grown, with Cathedral funding and other support, into its present state. He was genuinely pleased to hear first-hand of someone really wanting copies; he also explained that, though he'd wanted to include in the magazine a simple map of the area, there were cost and copyright issues that put it out of the question – at least for the moment.

'You must get a lot of satisfaction from doing it,' said Alison, seeing it as something really worthwhile as a hobby.

'Of course, but it's not without its problems,' he replied, 'the main one being in getting it to the various tea rooms and other outlets in the area. I have one or two helpers, but I do it in my spare time – and the short gap between getting it from the printer and the dates of the first events means it can be quite a rush. But there you are, all worthwhile in the end, I believe.'

Whilst this was said in apparent innocence, Alison immediately took the bait, and her offer to help with the distribution was taken up with enthusiasm. It was something she had been wondering about, and had explained to Ted and Whacker that it would get her meeting people apart from those she met when out with Kelly and it would have a worthwhile purpose. It would also help the family in getting to know the area.

'Where would I normally find it in Charlford?' she asked. 'And would I be treading on anybody's toes if I did the village?'

'Ah!' said Broderick looking a little thoughtful. 'I normally take them to the Post Office, but I was about to warn you that you might come across a problem there, so it might be best to leave that one with me.'

At this, Ted spoke up for the first time since introductions had been made. 'I can't have my wife getting involved in any sort of controversy, and certainly not anything that's likely to put her in harm's way.'

'Oh no, I agree with you, Mr Bailey, which is why I'd suggest your wife should keep any activities for the magazine away from Charlford.'

Seeing the concerned looks that Ted and Alison were exchanging, he realised he had to be totally honest with them. 'Look, it may not be a problem, but I was approached by a young lady from your village wanting to distribute the magazine for me, but I just couldn't use her.'

A further pause while he seemed to struggle with a decision. 'This is awkward for me as I mustn't blacken someone's character, and I don't know the lady's name, so she could well be a friend of yours.'

'That should be no problem,' replied Alison. 'We've only been in the village a few months, and there aren't many women that I know. If you tell us what the problem was, we'll have to decide if it sounds like anyone we've met – if not, it'll be somebody to avoid, that's all. What do you think?'

Broderick thought hard for a few minutes while they all drank their tea, then spoke up. 'I sincerely hope that what I say won't upset you or spoil any friendship you might have for the lady, as I'm sure you'd enjoy taking the magazine round, get to know some people, as well as the area, and it would be a real help to me too.'

'I think you'd better just spit it out,' jumped in Ted, 'and we'll not repeat anything, will we, love?'

At Alison's nod of agreement, Broderick took a deep breath. 'Well, for a start, she wanted to be paid for the work – I should have explained that there's no money for that – but, even if she'd been prepared to do it for nothing, I couldn't have used her...' Another pause, 'I'm afraid she carries an aroma with her... A very strong, and probably cheap, perfume. There, I've said enough. Except that, if you were to agree to do some distribution for me, I'd still take the copies to your Post Office, and I'd like you to avoid mentioning anything about this if you know the lady and she asks you what you're doing – perhaps say you were covering somebody's holiday or sickness – not let her think

I'd treated her differently. I know that's a lot to ask, so if you'd rather forget all about it, that's fully understandable.'

Ted and Alison looked at each other before Alison replied. 'Look, you've told us it's a couple of weeks before the next issue goes out, so we've got time to think about it. I'm pretty sure we know who the mystery woman is. We already try to avoid her, so we'll just need to think about how we'd deal with any confrontation. So, if you can give us a ring a day or two before handover, tell me what villages you'd like me to cover, and we'll finalise things then. How does that sound?'

'That sounds fine, but I can tell you now where I'd like you to deliver so you can check that out and see if you could manage it – OK?'

Ted and Alison were happy with that idea, so they set off to drive around the villages that Broderick suggested, but didn't stop for any more cups of tea as it was getting late in the afternoon and they wanted to get back home for their evening meal. However, by the time they'd arrived back home, they were all getting a bit too hungry to wait for Alison to prepare something, so they readily agreed when Ted said that they deserved a treat and he took them to the Red Lion in the hope of being able to get in for dinner.

Walking in, they were met by the sight of landlord Jim going around the bar to close down the windows.

'Everything all right, Jim?' Ted asked.

'Yes, it is now, just been clearing the air as usual.'

'Why, what's happened? Farmers been spraying the crops again?'

'No, just our usual fragrant, frequent afternoon customer scenting the air.'

'Sorry? Have I missed something?'

'Of course – you're not usually in this early, are you? No, it's just that one of our regular afternoon customers makes her presence felt in her own unique way – but it soon clears – except in winter when we don't really like having to open all windows.'

'I think that must be the lady we've just been talking about,' Alison joined in. 'It was suggested we avoid her, for various reasons, but we weren't given her name – can we guess that we're talking about Hattie?'

'Yes, it's Hattie, and it's no secret that she carries an aroma with her. Sometimes it's awful and no-one seems to know where it might come from. At other times it's a strong sort of scent and one suggestion was that she makes it at home and applies it by the bucketful! In either case, no-one wants to confront her about it! She's got a bit of a waspish tongue.'

'What about family?' asked Alison. 'Are they all the same?'

'As far as we know, there's only her mother – they live together down Parson's Lane in one of those wooden chalet places, but her mother is housebound, so we only see Hattie.'

'Right, I'm glad we've got that sorted,' said Ted. 'Now, how are we fixed for dinner this evening, Jim?'

'Depends on when you want to eat and how many for – we're fairly full, but there are gaps.'

'Well, it's Alison and me, at least, but what about you, Whacker? Going to join us, or off out into town with friends or a certain young lady?'

'Depends if Tina is working or not, Mr Parker,' replied Whacker, for once managing not to blush.

'She's just finishing checking the tables then she's free, so you can go in the dining room and have a word with her.' Which Whacker did, only to re-emerge straight away, smiling broadly, to say he wouldn't be joining his mum and dad as he was off to the pictures in Salchester, and obviously taking Tina. So, while Alison agreed a time with Jim, Ted quietly made sure Whacker was OK for cash, both for the cinema and for getting home if they missed the last bus.

Chapter 7

Ted Bailey still found it hard to believe that it was little more than a year since his first visit to Charlford Manor. Now, here he was with his workshop in a coach house, and living just across the stable yard with his wife and son in what had once been the servants' cottage. He still sometimes wondered if he would wake up and find it had all been a dream.

Whilst the move away from the hustle and bustle of a New Town had fulfilled his long-held ambition to live in the country, he had secretly wondered how Alison and Whacker really felt about it. So he'd been really pleased and relieved when they both also seemed to settle down fully and happily, even though more or less every aspect of their lives was different.

As far as work was concerned, at the time of the move the only physically big jobs in hand were a couple of chests he was making for an Oxford college – the final phase of a large order. He naturally hoped that further orders would come from the same group of customers, but he also had to make his name in the Salchester area by tackling whatever jobs came his way. The fact that the first new jobs were small ones within the confines of the manor didn't worry him at all – they allowed him to compare his costings with local traders and, for a change, there was no travelling involved.

First off, there were shelves and a notice board that Kelly needed in her kitchen – he had got Whacker to do the measurements, choose the materials, and cost the job, parts of the business that Whacker had never had to tackle before. This paperwork aspect of their business coincided nicely with the current phase of Whacker's college course, so that workshop and classroom complemented each other nicely. Ted made and installed the kitchen pieces himself.

The other local job was for Tony Philips, making bookcases for the manor house. Ted was able to get on with this fairly straightforward work in the sort of calm he'd always dreamed of; it had taken a little time to get there but he was certain that the result was worth the effort.

During his first few weeks at the manor, he would often be interrupted by 'Morning, Ted, sorry to butt in.'

This would announce Tony's appearance at the workshop door, usually bringing suggestions of perhaps a good place to advertise or mentioning someone he wanted Ted to meet. At first, Ted assumed it was all intended to help him build up his customer base, but he'd soon realised it also helped Tony to establish the presence and purpose of the organisation and hopefully attract new traders to the site and to the group.

Ted was happy to go along with things even though the interruptions sometimes caused him to delay the planned finish date of a job. While he did end up with some useful contacts, as time went by he realised that not all of these were worth interrupting a job for, and he eventually decided that the situation needed to be sorted out.

'Look, Tony,' he began, 'I know you mean well, but do you really have to bring all these people to see me – particularly the last bloke, offering an accountancy service when I've told you that I manage all my own paper work, thanks very much!'

'Well, he did ask for you by name, and it might have been for a cabinet job, so do you really want me to be deciding who should see you and who shouldn't?'

'That's fair, but—'

'And look at it from my point of view – all these people come calling unannounced up at the house and interrupting whatever I'm doing—'

'Yes, but—'

'But you're right, Ted, we've got to sort out a better system – any ideas?'

'Well, what's the situation with callers for Joan and Doug?'

'It's different for them – we had their own phone lines installed for them. But you said you didn't want one – is that still the case?'

'Yes, it sure is. I had enough problems dealing with the phone in Bracknell, so I only want to use the home phone – it used to make me jump if I was really concentrating on something. And on top of that, I'd rather be able to decide when it's a good time to have people come and see me.'

'Fair enough, Ted. I'll have a word with Reg and Julie and see if we can't come up with something to deal with visitors but, for your phone problem, I rather anticipated this and talked it over with Julie. She suggested you could have a phone that you can turn the ringer off and callers get put through to an answering machine.'

'Now why didn't we think of that?'

Gradually the interruptions and introductions died down and Ted thought they might have stopped; he was also coping happily with the telephone answering system.

Then, one day, Tony brought along the secretary of Salchester Chamber of Commerce who, after the usual introductory chat, invited Ted to join them. The Chamber was the sort of body Ted had always thought to be too august for the likes of a simple cabinetmaker and would consist of boring committee meetings and the like. But he soon discovered that most of its activities seemed to consist of chats between members before, during, and after, the monthly lunches – it was to one of these that Tony took him first.

The venue, just away from the centre of Salchester, was a rather splendid looking hotel that did little to ease Ted's feeling that he'd be a fish out of water. But, by the time they went in, about half the expected members were already there, and this allowed Tony to make introductions to the people he felt Ted would be comfortable with – in other words, he was able to avoid the pompous and the bores. Then, at their lunch table, Ted was placed between a florist and a jeweller; they did little more than exchange cards with him after accepting that he wasn't in the market for either of their products on a regular basis. Though the next day he was well impressed when a welcoming bouquet of flowers arrived at home for Alison, and that certainly confirmed her support for his membership of the Chamber.

All in all, that first meeting resulted in his ideas undergoing a pleasant change because of the warmth of the welcome he received. As part of the Chamber's aims to improve links and services to a wider community, his views on all sorts of topics were sought, and appeared to be valued. Naturally, many members were eager simply to enlist him to their own points of view on any contentious projects, but he readily fell back on the tried and tested response – 'I'll think about it, and let you know' – and their ready acceptance implied that they would be happy to have him as one of their members.

A couple of days later, he took a call from another member who'd been at the meeting.

'Hello, Ted, this is James, or Jim, Harding, city branch of the county building society. We met briefly at the Chamber do, but I had to leave early to meet a client and didn't get chance to have a proper word.'

'OK, James, what can I do for you?'

'I wonder if you can help me with a little project I have in mind – or perhaps suggest somebody who could?'

'Fire away, James, and I'll let you know.'

'Ah, well, it's not easy to describe over the phone and there'd probably be interruptions at a Chamber meeting, so I wondered if we could meet up somewhere – perhaps over a pint some lunch time – and I can explain it more fully?'

'Yes, that would be OK – I don't get into town midweek very often, but I'm meeting my son at the college the day after tomorrow and I could come in a bit early if that would suit?'

That did suit, and a meet-up was agreed in a small bar just off the main square. It had all happened so quickly that Ted spent a lot of the intervening time wondering what on earth could be so important – most of the jobs he did had a fairly long time from inception to completion. Perhaps the chap had broken something and needed it repairing quickly before his wife found out – he'd come across that situation before!!

Arriving a few minutes late, Ted was greeted by a face he remembered fairly clearly from the Chamber meeting – he'd felt at the time that the chap was looking for a chance to have a word, and he'd obviously been right.

'Thanks for coming Ted, and I do hope it's worth your trouble.'

'Always happy to help where we can. So, what's the problem – apart from me having forgotten your name, along with most other members', I'm afraid,' replied Ted, feeling less embarrassed than he'd expected in the circumstances.

'That's all right, Ted, I was just the same in the early days – apart from the ones that I knew through the firm of course.' And they shook hands and exchanged greetings as if meeting for the first time. James got the drinks and sandwiches in and they settled in a quiet corner of the very pleasant room.

'What can I do for you, then? If it's a big job, I'm a bit busy for a week or two, but I can have a first look for you.'

Before James could continue, a figure stopped at the side of their table – 'Well, well, Mr Carpenter! Does your good lady wife know you're having a cosy lunch meeting without her, I wonder? And what secret deal are you concocting away from the office, Mr Mortgage-man?'

'Why don't you just mind your own business, Hattie?' Ted was the first to respond.

'But it surely is my business to make sure you don't bring dishonour to the village so soon after we welcomed you there? But never mind, I'm sure you can explain everything and it will all be above board, so I'll wish you both a lovely day and be off to tend to my own affairs.' And with a broad smile she swept off out, leaving the two men rather open-mouthed.

James was the first to recover enough to ask 'Who on earth was that, and what was it all about?'

'That,' explained Ted, 'was Harriett Scattergood, known as Scatty Hattie, and she lives in Charlford. That's really all I know about her, except that she always carries a smell around with her – sometimes putrid and sometimes sickly sweet! And I believe she behaves much the same all the time – but she seemed to know you, James, referring to you as Mr Mortgage-man.'

'I'm absolutely sure I've had no dealings with her, but she could have seen me in the branch – and I think I've heard our tellers talk about her, though I never knew the details. What an odd person! Now, where were we?'

'You were starting to tell me about the job you need doing.'

'Oh yes. Well, it isn't big in the physical sense, and it might not even be in your line of work. In fact, it was something I thought I could do myself as a sort of hobby, but it wasn't long before I realised it'd be beyond me – at least to make a decent job of it.'

'OK, if you tell me about it, or let me see what you've done so far, I'll see if I can take it on – if not, I'll do my best to point you elsewhere.'

'Thanks, Ted. Well, a few years ago, I designed a board game and obviously hoped it would do well etc., but it didn't. It's nice enough, but people who know more about these things than I do, said it didn't offer enough interaction between the players. They suggested the sorts of things I'd need to introduce, but I just couldn't see a way to do that without spoiling the story I wanted it to tell, so I dropped it. I'd planned to make a decorative version of it at some time, to have on display at home, and wood seems to be the obvious material. I made a bit of a start on it but soon realised I just don't have the skills or the tools to make a proper job of it, so I wondered if it was something you could do – or perhaps recommend somebody? There, what do you think? And you won't hurt my feelings if you tell me to clear off!' he ended with a smile.

'Don't worry, I'd never do that, James. So, it's something like a chess board, is it? With similar pieces that would need carving? And it sounds like you want it open, as if ready to play – does that sum it up?'

'Well, yes, except for the figures – I use cast metal ones, the sort they use in war games.' And he sounded quite pleased that Ted had got the drift straight off. 'But is that the kind of thing you'd do? And, just as important, would it be expensive? It means something to me, but there's a limit to how much I could spend on it, of course.'

'Oh, as for the size of the job, no problem – physically a bit like the size of a cutlery tray for a kitchen drawer, and we do them all the time – but it sounds as if it'd be much more interesting.' Ted paused, looking thoughtful, then continued, 'I'm sure we can do it for you, but I need to think about it – I've got an idea that might help us both. Give me a couple of days and I'll get back to you – OK?'

'Yes, that's more than OK, Ted, thanks very much.' With that out of the way, James felt, looked, and acted far more relaxed. The rest of the lunch time passed very pleasantly and then James needed to be off back to the office, first giving Ted his home number as being the best way to get hold of him. It was quite a thoughtful Ted that went on to meet Whacker at college as arranged.

Chapter 8

The move to Charlford from Bracknell had taken longer than, and not gone as smoothly as, the Bailey family had hoped and expected. The individual delays were all caused by Ted taking on 'just another little job – can't let the customer down – might lead to more work in the future'. Once or twice, both he and his wife Alison wondered if these little hiccups were sent as omens, presenting reasons to call it all off and not tempt fate.

But, in spite of all their doubts, they really wanted to move both the family home and business away from the increasing bustle and noise of a developing town. So Alison did what she could to keep the home ticking over while spending hours most days wondering what to pack, or unpack. Eventually, after the third or fourth postponement, she had quietly disconnected the phone in the house whenever Ted was home; but this, of course, hadn't stopped people calling on him at the work unit.

Eventually they settled down one evening and discussed all the options they could think of. As a result, they started moving home and work stuff to Charlford bit by bit, trying to allow both places to operate as well as possible – Bracknell eventually to run down and Charlford hopefully to build up. When they at last reached their final morning in Bracknell, all they were leaving in the town was their house, lightly furnished and ready to be rented out.

The other person affected by all this was, of course, their son, Whacker, yet he had been given no real say in the decisions. It was approaching the end of term at school in Bracknell and he would leave after the last of the exams. Once settled in Charlford, he'd begin his apprenticeship as a cabinetmaker under his dad; then in the autumn he'd sign up for relevant courses at Salchester tech college.

Final stages of the family's staggered move left him facing the odd few days here and there on his own. While he didn't mind looking after himself, his mum would wonder if he'd eat and wash properly (*You know what mums are like!*). Assuming that her son would worry about getting to school on time, particularly on exam days, Alison had put schemes in place to deal with this. Firstly, she arranged for a neighbour to feed Whacker in the evening, then Ted installed a phone with an extra-loud ringer so she could call him in the morning.

But, there were two things that had kept Whacker happy through all the upheaval. Firstly, the fact that he'd start an apprenticeship with his dad and, secondly, that he'd be able to continue his friendship with the fair Tina, daughter of the landlord of the Red Lion in Charlford. This growing friendship – and his feelings for Tina seemed to be reciprocated – had been the source of some puzzlement, if not amazement, to all who knew him. Whacker had a lovely relaxed attitude to most things including, at times, his appearance, and he seemed to lack any drive or ambition apart from wanting to be a cabinetmaker like his dad. Tina, on the other hand, was always well turned-out, and had a positive attitude that gave the impression that she knew where she was going in life – perhaps they would complement, if they didn't irritate, each other.

Friends at school had been rather surprised that Whacker could so readily walk away from the other members of their band, The Acolytes, namely Slim and Boots. (*Yes, all three lads were known universally by their nicknames.*) They wrote and rehearsed songs but rarely performed to an audience, and even more rarely were they warmly applauded – it seemed that, sadly, the band just hadn't had the right sort of music, or the charisma, or whatever it was that made a band stand out from the crowd. The lads all realised that the band would have folded fairly soon when their educational paths diverged, but Whacker still felt bad that it was his move from Bracknell that had been the final definitive nail in the coffin.

Finally, to everyone's relief, the family's move worked out just as Whacker – and his parents – had hoped. He'd helped with the tasks involved in getting the new family home as they wanted it, then pulled his weight with similar jobs in the workshop. At last, when everything was as settled as could be expected, his apprenticeship got under way in earnest.

In the past, Ted had allowed Whacker to help on actual paying work only in simple routine tasks such as sanding and final polishing. Now he needed him to follow all the steps in a job, from noting the customer's requirements through to delivering the finished piece and creating the invoice. Ted expected that some of the stages would find Whacker wondering if cabinetmaking really was what he wanted to do – in effect, it was giving Whacker a very practical interview, and it worked. Whacker loved it all, particularly assessing the materials needed and then deciding the most suitable methods and sequences of construction.

Another aspect of the early days of his training was learning to handle the various tools that Ted had previously kept him away from (*there we go again, ending a sentence with a thingy*). In Bracknell, it had once seemed rather silly to Whacker that his dad wouldn't let him use tools that seemed to be freely available in the workshop at school. Now he understood that this had been mainly to meet the requirements of the business insurance cover, and he realised that the same control needed to be applied to accessing business documentation.

Whacker lapped it all up and often had to be pried away from the workshop at the end of the day, but his dad wondered how long that enthusiasm might last. Whacker would eventually realise that he was mainly just doing basic stuff on his dad's jobs until he got the chance to do a piece on his own.

Ted's meeting with James Harding provided just the opportunity Ted had looked for, but he said nothing until after he'd rung James with his proposition. This was that James would allow the task to be assessed, planned and carried out by Whacker, as part of his apprenticeship, while fitting it in with any paid work. Ted would oversee all stages of the project to ensure it was to the standard he would set for his own work. If James accepted it being done on these conditions, there would be no charge for labour and only for any really unusual or expensive special materials that James might require.

Naturally, it took James no time at all to accept the offer and arrange for the pair to visit his home to see the piece and hopefully agree a way forward. It was only after that agreement had been reached that Ted told his son all about it.

Thus it was that Ted and an apprehensive Whacker were welcomed into the Harding home one evening, introduced to James' wife, then taken into what was obviously his study. After offering them drinks that were politely refused – Ted didn't drink when he was driving, and Whacker was too young – James removed a cloth that had covered a small card table, to reveal a very interesting-looking playing board.

'I call the game Knight's Progress,' he explained. 'It follows the main stages that would often occur if a young boy were to become a knight in olden days.'

'Wouldn't a knight be a knight because his dad was one?' asked Whacker.

'Not necessarily, and not all knights had sons – many were killed in battle before they even had chance to marry. So, the game starts with each player having a playing piece to represent a young lad from a village who's taken to work in a nearby knight's castle and be trained to be a Page. Once he's reached that status, he's trained to be a Squire and then goes out on campaigns with his knight. The aim is for the player to become a Knight but, to do so, along the way he has to collect properties such as farms and a village that can support him when he eventually has a castle to live in. The players throw dice and move their playing pieces on this track around the edge of the board. Each space, as you can see, tells them what happens when they land on it, and so on. What I'd like is a nice version of the board, with matching property pieces – like these I made for the original game.'

What James brought out from a large envelope were pieces of card, shaped to lie flat on marked areas in the middle part of the board. They were labelled to say what they were, such as Farm, Village or Mill, and coloured to match the colours of the four playing pieces.

'Well,' said Ted, 'there'd be no problem making the basic board, we could surface it with a nice veneer and the property pieces could be made in different-coloured veneers. Any thoughts, Whacker?'

'I think it's terrific!' he enthused. 'But we'd need to use ply for the property pieces, perhaps topped with a veneer, Dad, if only to give them some strength to cope with being handled. And I reckon the playing track would look good edged with strips of inlay. That would only leave the lettering and illustrations to sort out.'

After a pause he continued, 'Your illustrations look good to me, Mr Harding, so perhaps they could be transferred somehow – I'll have a think about it and perhaps have a word in the art department at college to see if there's any suitable process out there.'

'That's wonderful, but is it sounding expensive with veneers and plywood and special processes and such?'

'Not at all, James,' replied Ted, who was delighted at Whacker's show of interest and confidence. 'All this is great experience for young Whacker, and quite different from the run-of-the-mill work we normally have. No, I think we can say it will come well within the price of a meal or something like that, as long as you're not in a rush.'

'No, Ted, far from it – the game has been sitting there for years, so a few more won't harm.'

'Speaking of it sitting there,' interrupted Whacker, 'I assume we can take it away with us at some stage.'

'Yes, of course – I'm pretty sure I've got copies of most of it, so I can put a full set together for you in the next couple of days, if that's OK.'

'A set of rules would also be useful, please,' added Whacker, then the evening ended with all parties feeling pleased with the progress and the prospects.

Back home, it took Whacker no time at all to tell his mum about it and how he thought he could tackle it. Ted let him get it off his chest and enjoy the moment, knowing that there would eventually be the less exciting stages of the task to be worked through.

First thing the next morning, Whacker wanted to go straight to the stacks of materials at the rear of the workshop and sort out what he fancied for the job, but Ted called him back with a reminder of the terms of the offer he'd agreed with James.

'Slow down, son, don't forget the paperwork. First off, you need to think about the customer's requirements, OK? Then write them down, and how we're going to meet them, so that both parties can understand and agree what's going to happen. That's going to be the reference point for the job – then you can add materials, timescale, costings and, if applicable, any payment stages.'

'But Dad, it's a freebie!'

'I know that, you know that, and so does Mr Harding, but we're going to use it as a proper exercise in your apprenticeship. At some stage the paperwork may be useful, perhaps even necessary, if you come to presenting it at college – OK?'

'OK, but how much do I have to write before I can do anything else?'

'Well, you note what we plan to do, then check that we've got the materials to do it and, if not, sort out how and where to get them, what they'll cost, and will there be any delays in getting them. I know we've got a fair stock of timbers that we brought down from Bracknell, and there's the stuff that was found here behind the carriage but, if we're short of anything, you need to get that sorted out before you can complete the plans.'

Understanding that his son felt a bit deflated, Ted let him go and rummage around to find some materials before getting down to the boring bits. As a result, Whacker spent the rest of the day with a smile on his face and, after a couple of phone calls to suppliers, was able to present his dad with a fair attempt at a job quotation. He'd listed costings for laminates, some glue and perhaps a carrying case, together with a statement to cover the unknowns of illustrating the track around the edge of the board. The only aspect totally missing was a timescale, but neither of them could commit to one and the customer had agreed with that.

CHAPTER 9

Week by week, Hattie Scattergood and Mrs Gilbert looked out for each other until they found they had enough time to sit for another cup of tea, again in the cathedral tea shop, but at a table in a corner where it was quiet enough for them to relax and chat more freely.

'How is the job-hunting going, Harriet?' was the natural opening from Mrs Gilbert. 'Any success?'

'I'm afraid not, but I've started looking properly – even went for an interview at Jackson's bakery out at Overton, but it was a five o'clock start.'

'Oh yes, I see that would have been no good, leaving your mother at home all evening.'

'Worse than that, it was five in the morning – the buses don't start till seven, so I just couldn't get there in time, even if I'd wanted the wretched job! But anyway, on the way home that day I found out about another so-called job and went to see about that.'

While Hattie paused to have another drink of her tea, Mrs Gilbert just had to prompt her to continue. 'Don't keep me in suspense, my dear! Did you get it, and what, and where, is it?'

'Sorry, it wasn't a real job, after all – just once a month taking copies of that Aspire magazine round to some of the villages – and they didn't want to pay me, not even petrol money if I'd got a car – and I haven't.'

'That's a pity, Harriet! But, look, I've got a couple of ideas – but they are only ideas.'

'Anything's better than nothing, Auntie.'

'Seeing all the tourists and other visitors we get in the city these days, I wondered if you'd thought about a job as a city guide? I don't know anything about it – where you apply or what you need to know, and so on – but it might be suitable for you.'

'I must admit I've wondered about that – not as a job for me, but as how these people aren't even taken to some of the places that I find interesting. So, yes, I'll bear that in mind, thanks.'

'The other thing would be very short term, but it would get you back into the job market – and all recent work experience would look good on your Sea View.'

Hattie spluttered and burst out laughing loud and long, and Mrs Gilbert stopped and had a look around as people at nearby tables turned to see what the commotion was all about.

'Oh, Auntie Viv! That's wonderful, you've really made my day – look good on my Sea View – that's a peach! Wherever did you get that from?'

'I don't know what you mean, my dear,' she replied, looking as bewildered as she sounded. 'Isn't a Sea View what you have to prepare these days to show what qualifications you've got and what jobs you've done? I hear them mentioned all the time on the radio.'

'No, Auntie, it's a CV – curriculum vit something – I reckon it's Latin for 'quals and jobs' or something like that. I haven't got one, but it sounds like a good idea – perhaps if I called it my Sea View it would grab somebody's attention!!'

'Perhaps it would, my dear, as long as it doesn't make them think you're as silly as I seem to be!'

'If they thought that, they wouldn't deserve me! But, didn't you say you had a couple of ideas for me? What else have you got up your sleeve?'

'This would be really short term, I'm afraid, but perhaps worth thinking about.'

'OK, fire away.'

'I don't know if you've heard, but Silver's in Curzon Street is closing down, and places like that often encourage their long-term employees to look for jobs well before they broadcast that they're closing – it gives them a better chance to find a new job, especially if other similar places are closing.'

'So why would that be an opportunity for me, Auntie, if the shop's about to close?' asked a puzzled-looking Hattie.

'Well, when they announce the closure, they still have stock to sell and the premises to sort out, and they'll need staff for that. If some of their people have already left, they'll want at least a few to keep the place going and that's where you could step in. Even if it was only for a few weeks, it would be something to put on your – piece of paper!!'

'You don't believe me about CV, do you, Auntie?' chuckled Hattie. 'But I see what you mean, and I'll pop round there when the Closing Down notice goes up, OK?'

'That's lovely, my dear. Now sit back while I ask you something else, and enjoy your scone while you think about it.'

'Sounds ominous.'

'I hope not, Harriet, but I want to ask a favour of you, and you must say 'No' if you can't do it or would rather not do it, and no need to tell me your reason.'

Fully intrigued, Hattie stopped chewing and just nodded.

'I'm sure I mentioned my son, Andrew – he lives in Shropshire. He'd planned to come on a visit with his wife and their little boy, David. But his wife, Jane, is rather unwell and not really fit enough to travel, so they've asked me if I'd like to go to them.'

'And provide some free home-care?' commented Hattie, quite waspishly.

'Come along, Harriet, this is my only child and, so far, my only grand-child, so of course I want to go and help – and be involved, as I think the term is these days. Don't be fretful about it, my dear, it's not like you,' showing how little she knew Hattie.

'Sorry, Auntie, I guess I'm just reflecting my own experiences – and you're right, you should go. But what's the favour you mentioned?'

'It's just that I don't like leaving my bungalow empty for too long. It didn't use to be a problem because my neighbour was very good about keeping an eye on things, but the new people next door seem so busy – often away for days at a time, and I don't know them well enough to ask them anyway.'

'You'd like me to do what, Auntie? See to the bins, move the mail from the door, open and close the curtains, put the lights on and off once in a while – that sort of thing?'

'That's exactly the sort of thing, Harriet – how did you know? Have you done it before for someone?'

'No, but it's what I'd ask somebody to do for me and my mum if we went away. So, yes, I'd be happy to do it for you if I knew where it was and how to get there – and if it didn't have to be to a strict timetable if a job comes along, of course.'

'I live in Glenton, and the bus service is quite good until about eight in the evening. I wouldn't ask you to be there later than that anyway. But random timing would be fine – if anybody was watching the place it would match my own activity.'

Hattie had listened to these final comments with a rising sense of concern – was Auntie Viv being watched, or was she a bit paranoid or, more interestingly, did the house contain some treasures? Would she – Hattie – be putting herself in danger if she took on what could amount to a security role? That seemed unlikely, but she decided to play it carefully, just in case.

'Perhaps I could come out to your house with you some time, Auntie, to get to know the journey, see what I'd be doing for you, and sort out how to contact you if needed. If we both agree it looks OK, then of course I'll help you.'

Details were agreed, and a couple of days later Hattie was taken by bus to the Gilbert home in Glenton. It was a standard, detached, two-bedroomed bungalow – one of several in a short cul-de-sac – homely but tidy, with only a few photos and certainly no valuable pictures or ornaments on display, apart from what looked a bit like a George Riley vase. All in all, it made Hattie even more certain that she'd never let Auntie Viv know exactly where she lived in case a surprise visit should follow. But anyway, both agreed on how Hattie could keep the place looking occupied when Viv was away.

As Hattie was leaving to return to the city, Viv pointed out a twitching curtain in a house overlooking the road.

'You'll doubtless be spied on by old Mrs Franks over there,' she said, 'but don't worry about it. As she's seen us together, she should keep her nose out. I'll give her a wave so she knows all is OK.'

Viv waved, but the curtain fell into place without an acknowledgement. Viv shrugged, but Hattie made a mental note that the curtain-twitcher might be a problem that needed sorting out – but she didn't say anything.

Hattie heard no more about the house-sitting plan, nor did she see Mrs Gilbert until, about a week before the planned trip away, she found her waiting as she got off the bus in the city.

'Are we off then, Auntie?' asked Hattie, wondering for the first time how on earth she was really going to cope.

'No, my dear, I'm happy to say – well, happy to say that Jane is not as poorly as she was, but neither is she fit enough to travel. It means I don't get to see the family just yet, either here or there, and our little plan is on hold, as they say – sorry to have built it up like that.'

'Well, that's OK, then – back to reality,' with a sigh of relief.

'But I'd still like to be ready to go when I get the chance – these days I sometimes find it's a bit too much having a houseful of visitors, and I'd be happier about making the journey to visit them, particularly knowing that you'd be keeping an eye on the bungalow – if it's still alright with you, Harriet.'

'Yes, that will be fine and, quite honestly, I was beginning to feel it was all a bit quick, so I'll be happier getting used to the idea more slowly.'

'That's how I feel about it now – last night I realised there were one or two things we'd not talked about. If you've got time now, perhaps we could go to the tea shop and talk about them – and I'll pay for the tea and a nice piece of cake each – how's that?'

That was excellent as far as Hattie was concerned and they were soon settled at a favourite corner table in the cathedral tea shop and enjoying the mini tuck-in.

'Now, my dear, something I didn't think of before is that, while I'm away, there will probably be bills to pay – how many and what they are will depend on when I go and how long I'm away. If Jane were to be taken ill suddenly, and more seriously, I'd like to be able to go at short notice, so I wonder if you'd be happy to deal with bills for me if we set it all up in advance – hoping it would never happen, of course.'

DEAL WITH BILLS!! Hattie saw those three words in capital letters! So, she was being set up for a confidence trick – what a long build-up! Thank goodness the tea and cake gave her time to consider her reply.

'I'm sorry, Auntie,' she said, very quietly, 'but you seem to have forgotten that I'm not what you'd call well off at the moment – if I ever have been, really. So, much as I'd like to help...'

Before she could finish, Mrs Gilbert, looking quite shocked, stretched across the table to take Hattie's hand and calm her down.

'Oh, no, my dear! I'm not suggesting you pay any of my bills with your own money! Oh, dear me, no. I would make the money available if you could just see that it gets to the right people when they present their bills. I'm so sorry, my dear – I really should have thought more about how to put it to you, shouldn't I?'

Feeling quite relieved, Hattie could only nod and return her attention to her cup of tea while she waited to see what the grand plan might be. At the same time, Mrs Gilbert was trying to think of the simplest way to spell out her plans to Hattie.

'Let me start again at the beginning – while I'm away – no – before I go away, I want to make arrangements for any bills to be paid that come in while I'm away. There, how's that?'

'Seems clear to me, but how does it involve me?'

'Well, most of them can be settled by cheques, but there are a couple that need paying in cash. Until I receive any of them, I don't know the exact amounts, and that's the problem. For the cash ones, I could draw money from the bank and leave it at the house for you to use when the bills come in, but I hate the idea of leaving money there in case there's a burglary. And I don't like the idea of leaving blank cheques in case they get in the wrong hands.'

She was beginning to look quite upset, and Hattie just had to interrupt. 'Don't upset yourself, Auntie, I'm sure we can work something out. Perhaps we could talk to them at your bank – they must come across this sort of situation all the time – people having valuables to take care of, and so on. The old colonel that used to live at the manor house in Charlford, they say he was forever using a safety deposit box at his bank – perhaps yours helps customers in some way. Have you spoken to them?'

'No, I haven't – hadn't even thought of it. I'm sure they have bigger things to worry about than my small account.'

'They do, Auntie, but the money that's in all the small accounts must add up to a lot – and if they didn't look after even their smaller customers, lots of that money could be transferred to other banks, and they wouldn't want that. A lot of banking success is built on trust and reputations – and I got that from somebody who knows, an ex-bank manager!' Of course, she was alluding to Jim at the Red Lion, and she secretly hoped Auntie Viv wouldn't find out Jim had not actually been a manager.

Mrs Gilbert decided nothing would be lost if she asked at the bank, but she wanted to take Hattie with her, partly for moral support – she was rather in awe of people who worked in banks. But mainly she wanted to make sure she understood any suggestions they made, and that Hattie would too. So off they went and were greeted by a very pleasant young lady wearing a Personal Banker badge on the lapel of her jacket.

On hearing the problem from Mrs Gilbert, with some input from Hattie, she spelled out the simplest of solutions.

'Why not have your mail redirected by the Post Office to your son's address, or have your friend do it for you, then send out cheques to pay the bills from there? For the ones that need cash, like the window cleaner, send your friend a cheque for her to put into her own account and draw the cash that way.'

'Now why didn't I think of that?' was the response from both enquirers, and they left the bank happier than at least Mrs Gilbert had expected. The Personal Banker was more than happy to see them go – particularly Mrs Gilbert's malodorous friend! (*Though we don't know if 'malodorous' would be part of her everyday vocabulary.*)

'I'm sorry to have taken so much of your time this morning, Harriet, but so pleased to have the problems solved. Now, can I help with any shopping or other errands you may have to do?'

'No, I'm fine, Auntie, thank you – in fact this morning's given me time to sort of pluck up courage for what I'd planned, so I'll get on with it while I'm still feeling confident – and no, I won't tell you what it is, no time, really – strike while the iron's hot! Bye, Auntie Viv, I'll be in again on Friday, so perhaps I can see you then and tell you all about it.' And with that, she left a bemused Mrs Gilbert wondering what on earth it was all about, while hoping it was a job interview and that her young friend would be successful.

Alas, Hattie was only partially successful. She'd gone straight to the city's tourist office and found out where the city guides were based. She had then found and barged into that office, demanded an interview on the basis of her knowledge of the area, and been very quickly sent away with a flea in her ear!

The partial success of this foray was that the man she'd seen in the tour guide office had been so nauseated by Hattie's aroma that he'd had to turn his back on her on the pretense of looking for an application form. In that moment, Hattie had spotted, picked up and pocketed, one of the badged armbands the guides wore – it had been poking out of a file in an over-full tray. ('That'll teach him to be more careful in his decision-making!!' was Hattie's gleeful thought as she went off on the rest of her interrupted shopping trip.)

At home that evening, away from her mother's disapproving gaze, Hattie very carefully modified the lettering on the armband to read, 'Ind (for Independent) City Guide', and felt very pleased with the results.

Next day, she positioned herself on the side of the cathedral square across from the official guide stand – actually nearer to the bus stops – and offered 'Genuine local tours to the really interesting places in the city'. If anyone in a subsequent group said that their guidebook disagreed with one of Hattie's facts, she'd ask them why they bothered with the tour if they already knew it all! Funnily enough, this brusque, down-to-earth approach had a lot of admirers and she reaped a steady, if small, income. She worked the hours she chose and didn't even think of applying for any more jobs, though she kept an eye on Silver's Gents' Outfitters to see if they really were going to close down.

Chapter 10

A few months after the Bailey family had moved to Charlford, the 5.30 bus from Salchester drew up at its final stop outside the village shop. Slim Bennett and Boots Clark got up, stretched – almost in unison – retrieved their bags from the rack, and shuffled forward in the tide of passengers pleased to be nearly home. Reaching the exit door, the two received a cheery 'Welcome to Charlford, and I trust you have a very enjoyable weekend!' from the driver, Graham Bartlett.

'Now then, Graham, what's this all about? You come up on the pools and leaving us, or something?' asked one of Graham's regular passengers.

'You wouldn't have seen me at all today if that had happened! No, this was just for our visitors from Bracknell – you remember Boots and Slim from when they came down and got involved when the manor was getting started again?'

'Oh yeah, the eco-light kids,' he laughed. 'Trust our Lion Jim to get it wrong – but no harm done, I guess, if you've come back again, lads. But where's your mate? I'm sure there were three of you.'

'Yes, that's who we've come to see,' replied Slim. 'Whacker lives here now. His dad's the cabinetmaker down at the manor. But this is supposed to be a surprise visit – did you know about it, Graham?'

'No, lad, it's a surprise to me – and it will be to Eileen, particularly if you're wanting to lodge with us again!!!!' and Graham burst into a really side-splitting laugh.

'Don't worry, Graham, we're at the Red Lion – rooms in the annexe, wherever that might be.'

'Well, when you know where it is, can you tell Graham, please?' asked an older passenger who'd overheard the exchange. 'We sometimes have friends wanting to visit and there's rarely room at the inn! Graham can pass the word to us all.' And off he went home, looking a mix of puzzled and pleased.

The lads had been equally puzzled by the mention of an annexe to the Red Lion – they couldn't remember anything that might have fitted that name the last times they were in the village, so were eager to ask. But, as soon as they set foot in the inn, they were met by the landlord's daughter, Tina, who bustled them straight into the residents' lounge.

'Sorry about this, lads,' she said, before either could speak, 'but you asked us to keep your visit a secret from Whacker and his family, so this is what we've arranged for your arrival —'

'But —' interrupted Slim, only to be shushed as Tina went on, 'You'll be staying in the stable rooms at the manor – we sometimes use them as an overflow – and Anna is doing dinner for us, that's you two and Whacker and me, in the manor this evening. So, if you're up for it, we'll take you down there in the car at about half six. Dad and I will get your bags up to your rooms, then you call in on Whacker at the cottage and invite him out to dinner at the manor! How does that sound?'

'Wow, that really is taking the secret to an extreme, and it's fine by me,' said Slim. 'But won't I be a bit of a gooseberry if you're still seeing Whacker, and I know Boots wants to spend time with Anna this weekend.'

'Good heavens, Slim, don't be such an old romantic! It's your reunion, and me and Anna are just trying to get it off to a good start – what do you think?'

'Sounds great to me,' Boots contributed, 'and terrific of you both to take the trouble. But if we're having a meal at the manor, what about Whacker's parents, won't they feel a bit left out?'

'Don't worry, we've thought about them, at least Anna did – her dad thinks we're just having a girly evening, so was happy for us to book him a meal here. Hope he'll still be happy when he finds he's sharing a table with Whacker's parents – Anna's planning again. Now, if you're happy with all that, you're welcome to have a cup of tea and a freshen-up here before we set off. When we get to the stable yard, you call on the Baileys, then over to the manor house for 7 o'clock.'

All that Boots and Slim could do was to exchange looks of bemusement at the cunning of the young females of the species. But the plans ran like clockwork so that, by half past seven, they were sitting down, with an equally surprised/shocked Whacker, to a meal in Charlford Manor that had been prepared by Anna – with a little help from Mrs Wilkinson, who also served them.

Boots and Slim had already brought the Baileys up to date on all their activities while Whacker was getting ready for the evening, so the chat around the dinner table was filling the gaps for each other. Most questions were for Whacker, as he'd made the biggest changes.

'It's not been quite how I'd expected it. College for just two days a week can sound great but, when you're new to the area, it's not easy to make close friends there. And the gaps between classes can make it difficult to keep the thread of a topic. On top of that, college and my work in Dad's workshop are almost like two different worlds – if you know what I mean,' he ended.

'What are you doing in the workshop, then?' Slim wanted to know.

'Ah, now that's special – Dad's given me my own project, but I'll show you that tomorrow.'

'You bloomin' tease,' cried Tina, who'd had no joy in trying to find out about this project during their times out together. 'And your dad's just as bad, he won't tell anybody – your mum knows, I think, but she's not saying, either!'

'Now, Miss Bossy Boots, I've said I'll tell all about it in the morning when I show the lads in the workshop – I want to hear what Slim's been up to – we hear all about Boots from Anna.'

The arrival of their puddings calmed the banter for a minute or two, then Slim responded. 'I'm very pleased to announce to the assembled masses that I am now an official newspaper reporter – part-time and underpaid!' he ended with a rare grin.

'That's great, Slim!' responded the Charlford three, almost in unison. 'But what about college?'

'College is fine, and I'm only at the paper during holidays and some weekends. But it's great to have a proper job – and you'd never believe how much goes on just to get it all looking right – that paper has such a history! Did you know the Echo was one of the first to report – '

'I know, signing the Magna Carta,' interrupted Whacker. 'Come on, Slim, the Bracknell Echo isn't Fleet Street, now is it?'

'No, but at least we wouldn't print that!'

'Print what?'

'The Magna Carta – It's as bad as saying 'The Her Majesty the Queen'!'

'Leave off, Whacker!' Boots already knew how much this work meant to Slim. He'd heard all about it – in detail – on the bus here, and he felt pleased for him.

'OK, Whacker, I admit it only started as a Saturday job, going in to the offices to tidy up – do a bit of cleaning, help reporters and photographers load up their cars – that sort of thing, but the trainee reporter had to leave when his dad got moved with his work. So they took me on full time for the rest of the holidays,' and Slim seemed to swell and thrust his chest out – but only a bit.

'That sounds great, Slim,' said Boots with genuine admiration. 'Just the sort of job to suit you, and less hairy than being in the police.'

'Oh, it's alright, but I just get the minor jobs,' he replied, showing rare modesty.

'Such as what?' Whacker really wanted to know how this job of Slim's compared with his own apprenticeship, of which he was very proud. He'd worked hard to get accepted for it, and the college work was as demanding as the practical training. Trust Slim to fall into a cushy white-collar number without really trying!

'Well, during the week I'm mainly round the office, handing out the mail, making tea, answering the phone, keeping the copier topped up with paper, but...'

Before he could get to any interesting bits of the job, Whacker couldn't help jumping in again. He was incredulous that Slim – the most efficient, competent, looked-up-to bloke he'd known – was doing the sort of stuff you'd expect any office junior to do!! 'You mean you're not actually doing any reporting?'

This mini outburst earned Whacker a sly dig in the ribs from Boots who, as usual, wanted things to be nice and friendly, and felt that Slim needed a fair hearing. Slim had, after all, stuck his neck out once before and suffered a thumping – that time on their first visit to Charlford when he was trying to help the police – so it was taking guts to spell out what sounded to be a bit of a trivial job.

Seeming not to notice the reception his tale was getting, Slim continued. 'Of course, I am sometimes but, for a start, it was no more than going to funerals and getting the names of the mourners, ditto for weddings.'

'Mourners at weddings? I think you need to look in a dictionary and get a better word for it than that,' laughed Whacker, and the slight tension eased.

'Ha bloomin' ha, Whacker! You know what I mean.'

'So, what else?' asked Boots. 'Any crime scenes or traffic accidents?'

'No, the proper reporters do that, but I reckon they find me useful.'

'What sort of training do you get?'

'Well, so far none, really, and I'm not sure what to expect. I've spoken to them about it at college and I'm hoping it can be set up as an official work experience or something – they'll know what to do. But till then, I'm mainly enjoying being there, part of the team, you know?'

'Before our friend here interrupted,' said Boots, 'you sounded like you were going to tell us about some proper reporting you'd done.'

'Well yes, and you wouldn't believe the impact it's had on me. One Saturday, there was this serious traffic accident blocking the roads out towards Bagshot, and a reporter couldn't get in to cover a flower show in Winnersh, so they sent me – just to get the names of the winners and so on. Anyway, I did that and took a photo or two – and it was all in the next issue – my first published work! But after that, I've been recognised in the street a time or two, greeted with smiles, and people have asked me how I'm getting on! And you know how I never found it easy getting to know people, so it's great!'

Led by Anna, Slim's little speech earned a mini round of applause, took their minds off Whacker's secretiveness, and got them discussing plans for the weekend.

Boots started with 'I really want to have a proper look at the city, mainly the cathedral.'

'Would you believe I've not been in there yet?' replied Whacker. 'So that suits me. What about you, Slim?'

'Oh yes, I want to get to the city, get a copy of your local paper,' – groans all round – 'and see where Whacker goes to try to learn something useful!!' Cheers from everybody!

'Are you girls up for that, or do you disdain our company?' quipped Whacker.

'Less of the 'girls' if you don't mind!' Anna said. 'And I'd like to see you stop me going in on a Saturday – what about you, Tina?'

'If we have to be sure they behave themselves and really do 'do' the cultural bit, we've got no choice, have we? Anyway, I need to call in at college to pick up a book for some revision.'

So that was the plan for Saturday settled to everyone's satisfaction, and conversation then turned to the usual teenage topics of music, fashion and sport. But it soon seemed to Slim that he was a bit of a spare part, so he said he'd like to go and try to see Eileen and Graham.

'What time is breakfast at the Red Lion?' he asked Tina. 'And what time in the morning do you need rousing from the dead, Boots?'

'Didn't you know?' she replied. 'You're having breakfast with the Baileys.'

That stopped everybody short, particularly Whacker. 'Does my mum know about this? She wasn't expecting them to even turn up, any more than I was!'

'Of course she knew – but your dad didn't, naturally! When she heard you'd be staying above the stables, she straight off said she'd do your breakfasts – could you imagine her watching you walk past her kitchen window, possibly in the rain, just to have breakfast at the Lion?'

'But I thought this visit was all supposed to be a bit of a secret and a surprise,' said Boots. 'It seems like nearly everybody was in on it.'

'Only the women folk,' replied Tina and Anna, almost in unison.

And, with that ringing in his ears and settling in his trainee-journalist mind, Slim set off to find Eileen, who had looked after him so well on their first visit, and wondering if his arrival would be a surprise to her too.

Chapter 11

The 10 o'clock bus from Charlford took the three lads and two girls to the edge of Salchester, and set them down at the gates of a fine-looking old stone building.

'Don't say they let you in here on a regular basis, Whacker,' chided Boots. 'A lot posher than Brakenhale!'

'Very nice,' joined in Slim. 'I perhaps wouldn't mind studying here, myself. What's the history, do you know?'

Before Whacker could respond, Anna ushered them through the gates and towards a more modern-looking annexe, and then explained, 'The original school dates from about 1600 and was all contained in the one building but, of course, you had to pay to attend in those days, and not too many people could afford it – much better these days. But this is where the real work's done now – labs, workshops, library, and so on. The main building's mainly staff rooms, chapel and, of course, the head's office.'

They all followed her into the new building and saw a set-up much as they were used to back in Bracknell, including the carpentry workshop where Whacker pointed out the workbench he usually used. As that was all the lads were interested in, they waited while Anna and Tina dealt with their books, then they all set off on the short walk to the city centre where the beautiful cathedral dominated the scene.

'What's the plan, then?' asked Whacker who, he felt, knew the city well enough not to need a tour!

'A coffee, then a tour of the cathedral,' suggested Slim, who really wanted to sit down and study the local paper that he'd seen on sale at a nearby kiosk.

'I suggest we do it the other way round, before the cathedral gets too busy,' Anna replied. As she had lived in, or at least on the edge of, the city all her life and was aware of general visitor patterns, they took her advice and set off across the city square.

Part way over, they were accosted by a young woman who looked vaguely familiar to Anna, but who addressed herself to Tina.

'Now, Tina, you don't want to be trying to act as guide for your friends. I can take you round and tell you things properly – and at a discount for an old friend's daughter.'

'Thank you, Hattie, but we can manage – we're not trying to see absolutely everything.'

'Don't you call me Hattie, young lady. It's Miss Scattergood to you, so you mind your attitude and your behaviour!'

The friends all stopped, open-mouthed, at the woman's abrupt change in attitude and demeanour; it was Whacker who recovered first.

'Look, Miss – whatever you prefer to call yourself – there's no need to be rude to people like that, particularly to my friend. If you're an official guide, I reckon you'll be lucky if we don't report you! And I'm sure they'd take into account the trouble you've caused in the past at the manor house! So, how about an apology?' and he really glared at her.

'You'll get no apology from me, you jumped-up thing! I know who you are, and I reckon you're no better than your mother – stealing the job in Kelly's Kitchen from me! And as for you, Miss Tina, I think your dad needs to hear about you and your gallivanting around with three young boys – you're no better than he is, having a young girl like you live with him at the Red Lion! I reckon Tom Grover put you up to annoying me!'

Then, just as quickly, Hattie changed again. 'But never mind, my dear, you and me can see through all that and be friends, can't we? Now, I can't stand chatting to you all day – must be off – people to greet!' And off she went, as if nothing had happened, leaving the friends looking at each other in shocked amazement!

'Are there any more like that around here?' asked Slim, totally taken aback and being far less aware of local society than even Boots was.

'No, she's a one-off,' replied Tina, recovering her composure. 'I don't know the full story, but she lives in a sort of wooden shack type of place on the edge of the village where she looks after her invalid mother. Eileen Bartlett knows more about them than I do – from when she was a district nurse, I believe. Anyway, let's forget her and move on, shall we?'

They readily agreed, and got into the cathedral just ahead of a coach-load of tourists and their official guide – no sign of Miss Scattergood, thankfully.

Making their way along a side aisle, admiring the stained glass and stone carvings, they arrived at a corner containing something covered in a protective sheet and cordoned off with a velvet rope and a sign telling them to: "KEEP OUT! – the Cope Chest is awaiting repairs". Whilst the others were prepared to carry on around it, Boots exclaimed, 'Of all the luck! That's just what I wanted to see! Don't say the trip's a bit of a waste!'

This mini outburst stopped the group in their tracks, but Anna recovered quickest with an angry 'So spending time with me was a side issue, was it, or just an excuse to be here?'

'No, silly, course not. I meant the trip here into the cathedral might have been a waste of time – at least as far as what I'd wanted to see here. I was hoping to have a close look at the bishop's cope – more than one of them, if possible – I'm doing a piece on them for college and these have a good reputation.'

As luck would have it, their semi-heated discussion had drawn the attention of one of the cathedral guides who, when told of their – or at least Boots' – dilemma, explained that the cope chest had been damaged and, until it could be fixed, the copes were in store. He had no idea how long the repairs might take and referred them to the Dean – 'Ask for him at the information desk.'

They all felt somewhat deflated, even though it was only Boots who had real reason, and they rather lost their initial enthusiasm for a full tour, so were soon on their way towards the exit. As they were passing the information desk, the same guide approached them and offered to introduce them to the Dean who was arriving to prepare for the next service. Boots was rather surprised that the Dean couldn't give him any idea of when the copes would be on display again.

'The problem,' he explained, 'is that our wood man is off sick, and we don't know when, or even if, he'll be fit to work again. Fortunately, we don't have any urgent problems at the moment but, if any structural ones turn up, they'll take precedence over the cope chest. I'm sorry.'

As he started to turn away, Whacker surprised himself by speaking up. 'If you're stuck for a cabinetmaker, sir, I work for one – perhaps he could help – if you're really stuck, that is, and if he's not too busy and – sorry, I shouldn't ...'

'No, young man, that's fine,' the Dean replied, smiling at Whacker's obvious embarrassment. 'Is he accredited to the church, do you know?'

'Sorry, sir, I've no idea – I've not worked for him very long – but I could ask him.'

'Well, look, this is really the Clerk of Works' area, so get your employer to contact him if he's interested – is that alright? Even if he's not accredited, there might be other work he could help with – perhaps even gain accreditation. And good for you for speaking up for him!'

Turning to the lady on duty at the desk, he asked for Whacker to be given details of how to contact the Clerk of Works, and then went on his way, wishing the group a pleasant weekend.

'Wow, Whacker!' exclaimed Slim. 'I'd never have expected that of you! The world of work has done wonders for your confidence – well done.' A sentiment that was echoed by the others.

'That wasn't confidence, Slim, that was putting my foot in it, in all probability – not even sure if I should tell my dad. I've no right to put him up for work like that.'

'What rubbish,' joined in Tina. 'I bet he'll be chuffed to death that you grabbed the opportunity, even if it comes to nothing. But it's a good way to find out how he'd feel about that sort of thing if it happened again.'

They all agreed on that, and on the fact that they really needed to sit down with a coffee to get their plans for the remainder of the day sorted out.

Avoiding the central tourist areas, Anna took them to a café situated above a baker's shop where they settled down with coffees and soft drinks while Slim opened the copy of the local paper, the Salchester Chronicle, that he'd bought en route.

'Come on, Slim,' semi-complained Boots, 'can't you leave the job alone when you're out with friends?'

'Sorry, but I just had to do a quick comparison – and look what I found! My boss would have me out on my ear if I did anything like this. Listen.' And they all did, as he opened the paper to one of the middle pages and read: '"Peter Smithers was given a heavy fine and points on his licence when he was found guilty of driving at 90 miles an hour in court today"!'

'What's special about that?' asked Whacker. 'Sounds like he got what he deserved.'

'Of course he did – and so would anybody "driving at 90 miles an hour in court" – get it? That's the sort of thing our editor goes to town on – not putting things in the right order. His favourite example is what he calls the definition of a biped – an animal with one leg, both the same, each side.'

The lads looked puzzled while Anna looked bored – not the sort of thing she wanted as part of a weekend with Boots! But it was Boots who asked for the inevitable explanation.

'Just re-arrange the words a bit,' obliged Slim, 'and you get "an animal with one leg each side, both the same." Obvious, really, and amusing on first hearing it, but it wears a bit thin with regular repetition. And that's part of the editor's problem – he thinks he's amusing and doesn't realise that he's not got enough to do – he's bored and boring.'

Slim looked to be getting into full flow, but Anna jumped in, picking up on those last words.

'Well, we've got plenty to do today, particularly if we're going to the gig in Skelford this evening, so what say we move on, show you lads the salt market in the quay area, back here for a bite of lunch, then check out the art show in the park?'

'Sounds good to me,' replied Boots, 'as long as we manage to avoid that woman that was pestering us this morning! Did anybody else detect that strong smell around her, or was it my imagination?'

'Not your imagination,' replied Tina. 'Any time she's been in the Lion, Dad has a job clearing the air. But nobody seems to know what the smell is. Some reckon she sometimes tries to cover it with a perfume she makes herself and just ladles it on – certainly nobody's bold enough to mention it to her!'

'Tina,' jumped in Slim, 'has the inn changed its name from Red Lion to just Lion? That's all I seem to have heard this time?'

'No, but there isn't any Blue Lion or White Lion in the area, so "The Lion" is the easy way, probably the lazy way, to refer to it. OK?'

'Yes, but my boss wouldn't like it!!'

'Not sure if we'd like your boss, either,' Anna joined in, with a laugh to take any sting out of it.

With that, they set off to fulfil the plan they'd agreed. They had a really pleasant day, even though the lads were a bit critical of one of the bands that played in Skelford village hall that evening.

Next morning, over breakfast with the Bailey family, Slim raised the subject that had been bothering him and Boots equally.

'I'm sorry to raise the question of money, Mrs Bailey, but it doesn't seem right that we're paying the Red Lion for bed and breakfast, but here we are having breakfast with you again, at your insistence. Boots and I are more than a bit confused.'

'Don't worry, son, it's all taken care of – yesterday morning was our treat, as long as you enjoyed it! But, for the rest, we have an arrangement with the Red Lion where we provide breakfast when it's more convenient for guests using the stable rooms to drop in here rather than go up to the inn.'

'That seems reasonable,' joined in Boots. 'But doesn't it tie you in a bit? And what about the food you'd need to have in stock if somebody unexpected turned up?'

'Again, it's all taken care of – Jim Parker only offers people breakfast here if it's really convenient, otherwise they go up to the Lion. But we've only helped out a few times – he puts stuff for continental breakfasts up there if they prefer that instead. As for supplies, we rely on Kelly, next door, especially if it's at short notice – and she gave me training to get the food-handling certificate. It's no big deal, and we're really pleased to have you here, so eat up, get off, and enjoy the rest of your stay!'

Much relieved that they weren't imposing on the Baileys' hospitality, Slim and Boots ate up as instructed, then followed Whacker across the stable yard and into his dad's workshop.

'First off,' Whacker started, 'don't touch anything unless I say you can, or my dad will kill me, OK?'

'Right,' they both agreed, 'we just want to see what you've been doing.'

'Well, for a start, Dad showed me all the background to a job, paper work things I'd never thought of, like drawings, measurements, customers' orders and such – I just wanted to get on and make something, or at least help Dad with something. But it all worked out when he got me a job that I can do on my own from start to finish, and I'm getting on great with it.'

'A doll's house, then, Whacker?' Boots couldn't resist.

'Ha, bloomin' ha, Boots. No, it's a display version of a board game.' He made it sound as special as it felt to him, and he almost thrust out his chest. 'And, no, you've not heard of it. This chap, from Dad's Chamber of Commerce meeting, used to be in the Army, and designed the game just to pass time in quiet spells on an overseas posting. It shows how an ordinary bloke in the olden days could work his way through the ranks, sort of thing, to become a knight. I'm making the board in wood, of course, and it's probably going to be mounted above a base, so that the playing pieces and the like can be stored in drawers underneath. There's a lot of fretwork for the design on top, and for pieces that are introduced during the game – I'm really enjoying it.'

For anybody watching, Whacker's enthusiasm went without saying – he seemed to have really found his vocation, and they didn't even try to stop him as he went into more detail about the piece he planned to complete.

But all the while this was happening, Slim was quietly looking around until, at a pause while Whacker turned to pick up another piece of his work, he just had to ask, 'What happened to the drum kit? I thought your dad said he'd set it up on that balcony thing, up there?'

'You mean the mezzanine floor – we tried it, but it was too hot in summer and miserable cold in winter – the skins kept needing to be adjusted. Not a lot of fun, really. In the end I checked with Tony and gave it to the college for the music department – they were really chuffed with it.'

'Does that mean you're not doing any music?' asked a rather incredulous Slim.

'Well, not really, not just now, but I'm considering giving the bass guitar a go. They suggested it at college, and they can lend me one, but it would mean going in more often for lessons and practice, so I'm not sure yet how I could fit it in.'

With that, he got back to showing them more of his project, and all too soon it was time to break up for lunch. Boots was called in to the manor house to join Tony, Anna and others from the Enterprise team. Slim had accepted an invitation to eat with Eileen and Graham Bartlett. To save Whacker from feeling a bit left out, Tina came down from the Red Lion for a relaxed meal with the whole Bailey family, a nice change from helping to serve her dad's customers.

After lunch, the groups re-formed according to age, with the older members sitting around for a chat, or even a doze, while the youngsters set off for separate walks that ended up in a particular nearby hay meadow. This was where the three Bracknell lads had first met Anna and her friends – the starting point for the major changes that had since happened in all their lives. Then, unusually for folks so young, they sat and reminisced.

Eventually, an evening chill began to be felt, so they drifted off to meet up with the elders of the day in the lounge of the Red Lion – another gathering that promoted an out-pouring of memories.

But this was all rather overwhelmed by the arrival of Slim's lunchtime hosts, Eileen and Graham, the latter wanting to set up a mini cribbage tournament! Eileen soon reined him in, and the evening settled into another session of reminiscences and plans for the future, the dominant one of these being instructions for the lads to meet up again – and not leave it too long next time!

But, at long last, and too early for most of them, the evening drew to a close. Next morning, the visit ended, and Boots and Slim headed back home to Bracknell in a bus driven again by Graham.

'Are you just making sure they go, Graham?' asked one old friend.

'No, pal, hoping I can get them to change their minds.' But, of course, they didn't, and everyone's lives returned to pre-visit normal.

Chapter 12

Like any good village pub, the Red Lion in Charlford is a hub in the lives of some sections of the community. In the past it would have been local farm workers on their way home from the fields and the milking parlours, but even they deserted it when the previous owner let the place go downhill. It then took some time for new owner, Jim Parker, to create an atmosphere that attracted the current habitués – the quiet card-playing, crossword-solving, serious discussion strata of local society. As you'd imagine, there were not too many of these in a village the size of Charlford, but the Lion's reputation gradually drew them in from the surrounding area, with one or two even venturing out from Salchester's outskirts.

It was during a pause for drinks between games of crib one evening, that Graham Bartlett again asked the question that was heard many a time in the village, namely – 'Are we likely to see the old Colonel's carriage being driven around the village again, Tony?'

'Could be,' replied Tony Philips, 'but, as I've said before, it's out of my hands. It'll only be driven on the roads when the restorers can assure somebody, somewhere, that it's roadworthy. But they're doing it as a favour to Loada and his ex-Met Police pal, so Loada can't push for it to be speeded up. Until it's proved to be roadworthy, I'm afraid it's in the restorer's yard doing nothing.'

'But have they re-painted it, and so on?'

'No – not worth the cost and effort until they know it can be driven out to be seen.'

'But it is yours, isn't it?' persisted Graham. 'And you've got a coach-house to keep it in and a yard to bring it out and show it off in, so surely you have a say in it.'

'Look, Graham, I know how keen you are to see it running and perhaps have a go at learning to drive it, so rest assured you'll be the first to know if the situation changes – OK? But it won't be coming to the manor to stay – just a visit perhaps for a PR thing. We decided long ago that we don't want horses, or any other large animals, in the stable yard now that we have a home and some clean trades being carried out there – sorry!'

'But–'

'If you want to put the money up front to try and move it along, Graham, that's fine by me, but it's not important enough to me to justify any expenditure – OK? Can we leave it now? I thought we were playing crib!'

'You're not using those coach-houses, then, Tony?' asked another chap at the bar. 'If not, you might find that Keith at the garage could be interested in renting one to store some of his so-called collection!'

'Oh no, we're not letting them go – one's still got spare stuff in it from the manor, plus odds and ends that Reg brings round, and we're looking to have a paying trade of some sort in the other one – if only to keep Ted from thinking they all belong to him!'

That closed the discussion and they settled down to start the next hand of crib but, before they could, Roger West looked up from his crossword to ask if anybody could come up with a six-letter word for an animal. This was a normal type of request and drew a typical range of replies: 'smelly', 'horsey', 'donkey', 'costly', until Roger spoke up to clarify it a bit.

'Right, you clever lot, the actual clue says, "Perhaps pesky six-footer". Now I reckon it's an animal with six feet, so – any better ideas?'

This attracted the same sort of ribald responses: 'Caterpillar – that's got six and some spare.' 'One and a half hedgehogs.' 'Three ducks.' Finally, Graham interrupted with 'How about, insect? Most of them are pesky pests and I think they all have six legs, don't they?'

'Thanks, Graham, sounds right to me and fits with another answer – have to check whether spiders come into it – they have eight legs, so what are they?'

'If you find out, Roger, keep it to yourself, will you?' This from Rob Wallace trying to concentrate on the same puzzle in his own copy of the paper and hoping at last to complete it before Roger did.

Up at the bar, although he made a point of not joining in, these were just the sort of evenings that Jim really enjoyed – they also eased some of the hurt of his wife walking out on him. At times like this he often thought back to her saying, as she often had done, 'These are not our sort of people, James. If you wanted a business of your own, why not a wine shop or a gentlemen's outfitters – but, a village PUB – I ask you!' Calling him James was, of course, her way of trying either to raise his standards or to reprimand him for lowering them.

At this point, almost on the dot of 8.30, in came Tony's business partner, Reg Harris, regular as clockwork on Tony's crib evenings. He always claimed he couldn't get away any earlier after dinner at home, but he'd confided in Jim that he needed to be sure he'd be too late to be conned into joining what he called the Crib Brigade. After greetings all round, and ordering a glass of his favourite beer, he asked Jim the standard question, 'Anything special on their agenda this evening?'

'No, Reg – same old, but Graham was a bit pushier about when they might expect the carriage to make an appearance. Tony gave him the standard reply – no room at the inn – though he did mention one of the coach houses still having old stuff in it from the manor house, and you adding to it!'

'Thanks for the warning, Jim, and I think that's the sort of prod I needed. You see, I've got an idea that I put to Tony a while ago but it was sort of pushed under the carpet in the grand scheme of things. I reckon that was partly because he wasn't too keen on it, but I want to raise the subject again, so that's a nettle I'll have to grasp one day – perhaps sooner rather than later.'

'Want to try it out on me first?'

'Don't suppose it'll do any harm – you bankers can be a cagey lot!'

'Ex-banker, if you don't mind, but you're right – you can treat this like a confessional if you like. They've got their heads down for another ten minutes, so you've got my undivided if you care to try me out.'

So, tentatively at first but gaining momentum as he marshalled his thoughts, Reg spelled out for the first time to someone else a pipe-dream, an idea, that had gradually developed over the past couple of years into a plan. He wanted to set up an auction house and perhaps see if he could qualify to become an auctioneer.

He was soon in full swing, telling Jim that he'd long had a general interest in collectable items and, probably unknown to Tony, had spent hours studying auction catalogues and trying to judge the prices various items would eventually fetch – it was a bit like a parlour game. Once or twice he found that his chaps, when they were out on the rounds to pick up scrap, had been persuaded to collect more than the usual old electrical items that they looked for. This had persuaded him to officially extend the scrap-metal business to include a house-clearance service. If he felt that any of the pieces they brought in were too good to go straight to the rubbish dump, he enjoyed placing them in local auctions and monitoring their progress.

At some stage, a friendly auctioneer had told Reg that he was getting knowledgeable enough to perhaps make a living in the trade – although that was meant simply as a friendly compliment, it got Reg thinking. He'd started looking seriously at the time and effort he put into taking items to auction, and what it cost him in fees and so on, to actually sell them.

'I guess you know, Jim, that City Auctions is mainly interested in fine art and antiques – and that's OK – but we're handling a lot of functional things and modern stuff. On top of that, even if you've got anything that they'd handle, City's not very accessible and you never know when they're open to take stuff – or even when the auctions are.'

'So, you fancy setting up on your own then, Reg – is that what you're taking some leading up to?'

'Sorry, Jim, but since that auctioneer's comment, I have been thinking seriously about it – and it all keeps going round in my head.' And he couldn't keep the excitement out of his voice and his expression as he carried on. 'We'd be selling a wider range of items and perhaps taking the auctions out to the people in village halls and such. But I had no real space to store stock, so the idea has just had to stay as no more than an idea.'

'But you reckon the time is right to spell it out, then? What's brought that on?'

'I guess you've heard Tony say that he found all sorts unwanted items of furniture and so on, stored in attics and spare rooms when he started work on the manor. Looks like even the fairly upper-class previous owners had kept stuff "just in case". Anyway, he'd simply shifted it all into one of the coach-houses, but now he's talking about having to get rid of it and make that space pay for itself.'

'So, you want to sell it through your own auction house, is that it? That should be great, shouldn't it?' asked Jim, wishing Reg didn't feel the need to tell him every last detail.

'Yes, but it's a bit awkward – Tony doesn't seem to have been to that coach-house for some time, and he probably doesn't know how much stuff I've been quietly adding to what he put there. I've just got to get him on-side with the auction idea before he sees how much there is there!'

'How much of what is where, Reg?' asked Tony who had just finished a hand of crib and arrived at the bar in time to hear the end of Reg's comments.

While Jim went off tactfully to get Tony's refill, Reg was left to deal with a potentially tricky situation. He quickly decided to keep it simple. 'Ideas in my head, Tony, the main one being an idea for a new Enterprise project. Can we have a chat soon, so I can spell it out?'

'OK, mate, but not now – new game starting – I'll give you a ring, OK?' and back he went to the table not knowing how very relieved Reg felt to at last have (almost) broached the subject. Reg thanked Jim for lending an ear, but couldn't say more as the bar got suddenly busier.

A group of walkers had come in, still discussing fairly loudly their sightings of flora and fauna, only to be shushed by Graham with a 'Can you keep it down a bit, folks, serious game in progress here.' To which Jim responded with an apology to the group, many of whom were regulars, and suggested they might like to rest their feet in the lounge, and he'd serve them there.

The offer was accepted by all except a couple who seemed new to the group and who moved closer to the crib players and watched the game in silence. In the pause before the next hand was dealt, Tony looked up and explained, 'It's crib, or cribbage to give it it's proper name. Do you play?'

'Oh, yes, we certainly do, and we'd fancy our club's chances against yours, any day! But no, seriously, our group calls itself a club but we only play amongst ourselves socially and no idea how good – or bad – we are. What about your group – are you a club?'

'Well, Graham here feels we're the village Crib Club but, like you, we only play socially. Although, for some, it's more competitive than that, isn't it, Graham?'

Graham had never been known for a subtle sense of humour, and he didn't like the idea of his beloved crib being treated lightly, so his response was milder than might have been expected.

'Very pleased to meet someone else who appreciates the game's social benefits.' And his face lit up with a real beam of pleasure at meeting fellow players. 'This crowd here would never meet up, let alone speak to each other, if it weren't for the occasional game of crib.'

'A bit like us, really,' the woman replied. 'My name's Sarah Paterson, by the way, and this silent lump is my so-called better half, Steve.' She gave her partner a playful dig in his ribs and went on, 'He's certainly the better player – he's a bookie, so all the mental arithmetic is second nature.'

'Hope he doesn't expect to play for money! No gambling allowed in here, thank goodness.'

'Oh, no – perhaps I shouldn't have called him a bookie – that's our almost private joke – actually he's a book-keeper or, as he prefers to call it, an accountant. It's all double-Dutch to me, I just do enough to make sure the house-keeping lasts the week.'

'Nice to chat,' interrupted Graham, 'but must crack on – I'm in danger of losing here – can you leave us some contact details if you have to go before we're done? P'raps see about a game between the clubs – just tell Jim at the bar and he'll pass it on. Cheerio!'

As Graham turned away to the crib table, Sarah gave her husband a quick dig in the ribs, and almost whispered, 'Steve, that's Graham!'

'Yes, love, he just said he was – no detective work needed there.'

'I know that's what he said, but he's the Graham – that drives our buses! Fancy that! I recognised him from the back of his head – and you never think of people like that except from where you know them – never think of them having a private life that could be at all like your own! Fancy that!'

'OK, love, but how about we join the others and give our feet a bit of a rest before we set off home – and find the landlord to leave our phone number in case Graham really does want to see about meeting up for a game.'

So off they went and did just that. Then they were long gone before the crib session ended, with the players the last to leave before Jim covered the pumps, switched off the lights and locked up at the end of another enjoyable, and probably profitable, evening.

Chapter 13

A couple of days after airing his auction ideas to landlord Jim in the Red Lion, Reg Harris at last got the phone call from Tony Philips asking him to drop in at the manor and tell him about this new project for Charlford Enterprise. Arriving ready to spell out more details and hoping to get a favourable response, Reg didn't expect the grilling he got!

'Right, Reg – Jim let slip that you want to set up an auction house and your ideas have gone a bit further and firmer than when you first mentioned it, way back. That right?'

'Yep.'

'And you're telling me because?'

'We're pals, and partners, and…'

'So, you want *us* to set up an auction house. Is that right?'

'Well, no – er – well, yes. Look, let's start again, OK? I'd like to look into the possibility of setting up an auction house and I think it could work as part of the Enterprise scheme, so I want to talk it over with you. There, is that better, SIR?' looking and sounding more than a bit miffed at Tony's initial response.

'Sorry, Reg, but I ought to have seen this coming – or something like it, anyway – from the way you keep quietly taking stuff to the end coach-house. So, how about you letting me ask about it in bits that I can understand?'

'Fine, fire away.'

'First off then, why do you want to sell the stuff this way instead of opening a shop somewhere or having a stall on the market? If you want to auction it, I guess you want the best prices, so what's wrong with doing it through City Auctions?'

'Well, for a shop, there's such a range of things to sell that it'd be hard to know what to call it – apart, perhaps, from Ye Olde Junk Shoppe! As for a market stall, I've never fancied standing out in the cold and wet, have you? With an auction there's the fun of the unknown – will it sell and, if so, how much for? I could sell better items through the City Auctions, like I do at the moment, but why pay them to do something I'd really love to do myself? And that still leaves the bric-a-brac, the odd household item, the golf clubs, the trouser presses – I could go on.'

'I take your point, but don't you need some sort of qualification to set yourself up as an auctioneer? I'm sure you would if you went to an auction house for a job, wouldn't you?'

'Probably, but not an auctioneering qualification – I asked Arthur Smedley about that at the City – and it seems that people go in with qualifications or experience in the line that the auction house specialises in, like ceramics or paintings.'

'OK, Reg, but where did all this start from? I know I loaded the coach-house with spare things from the house here and some I brought with me after the divorce, but I didn't mean that to be the start of a dump for all things we can't decide what to do with. If it was my heap of stuff that inspired you, then I'm sorry.'

'No, mate, far from it – in fact I'd not realised your stuff was there until I was nosing around to see what the electricians had been doing to the yard buildings. Since then, I must admit I've added a few bits and pieces picked up in house clearances – sorry! But no, to answer your question, I suppose auctions have always been an interest, and it got stronger when I started taking things to the City – better things that the lads brought in from their rounds, you know. I'd estimate a value and see what came of it, and I started to get fairly good at it – and here we are.'

'So, the main reason you want to sell stuff through your own auction house, instead of through City Auctions, is that you'd enjoy it – have I got that right?'

'Well, yes, but you make it sound a bit childish – I feel we could make a worthwhile business out of it. Profits for the Enterprise, probably one or two jobs for people – nothing wrong with that, is there? Come to think of it, not a lot different from somebody I know wanting to use his outbuildings to house crafts people!!'

At that, the atmosphere lightened and they both had a good laugh.

'You're not wrong, Reg, and, if you look at it like that, the costs of setting up and running an auction business would be a lot less than what it cost me to get the stable yard buildings up-dated.'

'Good, so can we start to talk business?'

'Not without a cup of coffee and Julie in attendance, I think. I'll give her a ring and see if she can come over.'

Half an hour later, with Julie having joined them to contribute to the discussion as well as record any significant points, a fairly formal meeting of the executive of Charlford Enterprise got under way.

'Well, folks, this auction business has got to be the same as any other business we consider,' began Tony. 'But, instead of an owner paying a rent, it's got to be profitable, which means it has to cover its costs and then some. So, I suggest we start by listing the costs we expect to have to meet. If they're too high, we might just stop there, OK?'

'Sounds good to me, but I can't imagine what we'd have to provide or do,' began Julie. 'Even if you can give us a list of things, Reg, we're not likely to have costs at our fingertips – but let's give it a go. And you'll have to start, Reg – OK?'

'Fine!' he said. 'Well, we'd need to start small, so I suggest trying it out in villages first – perhaps one a month for three or four months while the idea gets put around a bit. I reckon the costs for each one starts with location hire – village hall for about six hours – then staff for at least the same time. That would be somebody on the door to register potential bidders, a porter to handle and display the items, and a clerk alongside the auctioneer.'

'What's he for?' asked Tony.

'Mainly he notes who the successful bidders are, plus the selling prices of each item, but he can also help the auctioneer by keeping an eye on the bidders to make sure nobody gets missed.'

'I take it you're not planning to use volunteers, so that's looking to be quite a bill before we have any idea of what we might sell, if anything – and don't forget the auctioneer, Reg!'

'I hope that'll be me, of course, and at no cost! Oh, and there'd be somebody to collect the payments, give receipts and so on.'

'That sounds like the most complex part of the whole thing – could just one person do it? Records would need to be very tight for paying the people who'd brought the items in, don't forget!'

'Yes, but we could work up to that. To start with, I suggest we fill the auction with items we already own. That covers us in case the public don't bring much in, and it makes the money side easier to sort out – and don't forget that when our own stuff sells, it's all profit!'

'How do we make money when it comes to selling other people's stuff?' asked Tony, who'd never been to an auction in his life – probably wouldn't worry, either, if he never did in future.

'Standard practice is to charge the seller a percentage of the what the item sells for, but much simpler if we show it as a sliding scale of fees related to selling price – I think people would be happier with that idea.'

'OK, Reg, but I'd like to be clear about how you define what you're referring to as our own stuff – are you including things I've put in the coach-house from the manor house?'

'Only if you want them to be sold, Tony, and of course we'd list them as belonging to you. No, what I call 'ours', is the stuff we – sorry, I – put aside from house clearances over the last couple of years – the items I've been putting in the coach house.'

'So, you've actually bought them and the company owns them, is that right?' Tony asked. 'And they'll be on one of our books somewhere?'

Here Julie came in with, 'Yes and no, Tony. With regards to owning them and having bought them – when we clear a house, we just take out what the previous occupant didn't want any more and couldn't shift when they moved out. Mostly it's old carpets, sometimes curtains, and often old electrical appliances. We have an agreement with them that we clear and dispose of the items, then sweep the place out – and we charge for all that – that's the basic clearance service. Mostly, that stuff has no value and we get rid of it at the council tip but, if they reckon something does have a value and we agree, then we discuss it with them and come to an agreement on a value.'

'Right, and what happens then?'

'Well, the customer has options – they can put it to auction and get the proceeds, and if it's a big item or they're pushed for time, we can help with getting it there. Or they can keep the item and perhaps decide to take it with them when they move out, or they can sell it to us at a value that we agree on. So, the items in the coach-house are what we've bought and paid for from the owner, at the values we've agreed with them. Either that, or they're what the owner has said they don't want and we can keep. So, yes, it all belongs to us – to the company.'

'And customers have been happy with your valuations, have they, even when they're likely to be very much in your favour?' asked Tony, trying to be sure nothing would crop up that would cost the firm in cash and perhaps in reputation.

Here Julie just had to butt in again. 'Come on, Tony, most people we deal with are local enough to know our reputation is sound! Look – if it's a big item, like a piece of furniture, or something potentially valuable, like a painting, we get somebody from City Auctions to give an auction estimate. The client can then ask us to buy it from them at that price, and we've done that a couple of times. Often, though, they decide to keep smaller items, and sometimes go on to put it to auction themselves – whatever they do, if we don't buy it, we've ended our involvement with it. All fair and square – and fully documented, I might add, much to my frustration at times.'

'Do you know, I had no idea all this was going on while I was over here,' he said, 'getting on with renovating this place and dreaming of a life in the country. Well done the pair of you.'

'Team work, me old son!' joined in Reg. 'Never would have managed it without Julie's insistence on it all being recorded – for our own protection, if you like. The situation now is that, if we put a picture up for sale and some distant relative recognises it as having come from his old gran's living-room wall, we've got the records to show how we came to own it. All OK now, Tony?'

'I'll say so, and I'm impressed – and if the auction plan has been as well thought out, it sounds like it could be a winner, so, over to you.'

'Oh no, not as quick as that, my lad,' Reg jumped in again. 'We've only talked about how an early sale might work, selling just our own stuff. If we want the public to bring things to be sold, one option is to only accept stuff on the day, but that means agreeing an estimated value there and then, listing it, and perhaps producing an instant catalogue and, of course, hiring the venue for much longer.'

'Problem I see there,' interrupted Julie, 'is that everything's costing us more because of the longer hours, even if nobody brings anything in – don't fancy that idea, Reg.'

'OK, I take your point – it's more of a gamble that way. So, let's look at a situation like we have now – all the material in one place, under our control, ready to be taken, on the day, to the auction venue. But – hang on, Tony, I know what you're going to say – the place the material is in now is the end coach-house that's going to be needed for a more profitable enterprise. So that leads me back to our needing a location convenient for the public to bring their items to.'

'Gentlemen,' interrupted Julie, 'before we get into the realms of where and how to store unknown quantities of items, I suggest we get back to looking in some detail at the things we'll need that we can identify and put a cost to.'

'Good idea, Julie. Well, there are smaller items that we'd need, mainly on the auction day, but I'm sure they'll be available somewhere – things like books to register potential bidders, bidding paddles, labels to go on the lots, and so on. And, of course, there'll be costs of producing catalogues and advertising the events – more or less standard costs per event.'

'A fair bit for me to be getting on with, I think,' finished Julie.

'That's great,' Reg said, 'and we'll keep it simple until we get the feel for whether it's worth going further – OK, Tony?'

'Looks as if there'll be plenty to do, even just keeping it simple, but we can't let it run away with us – the whole thing's still very uncertain, to my mind. But thanks, and let's just keep each other informed of any new ideas or problems.'

With a promise to type up her notes of the meeting, Julie set off back to the yard in Salchester, while Reg took Tony along to the end coach-house to have a look at what they'd been talking about.

'It's quite some time since I've been in here, Reg, and you've certainly kept it neat and tidy.'

'Well, of course I had to, but I had my moments wondering whether to store it in date order or by category – finally decided date order was best in case we had to dig things out for disgruntled relatives of folk we'd bought from – you never know!'

'Has that happened?'

'Only once, so far, and it was understandable – we hadn't properly checked what was in an old gent's attaché case, only to find a full bar of medals that his dad had been awarded – very pleased to find the family and hand it back to a grandson. Right, what do you want to do now, Tony?'

'I really ought to be sorting through my stuff to see what to keep, what to chuck, and what might sell. That needs doing whether we go ahead with the auctions or not. So, I'll get on with that over the next couple of days while I give some serious thought to the auction idea and I'll let you know what I think as soon as I know myself.'

'Fair enough, Tony. Now, how about a bite to eat up at the Lion – and I'm paying?'

'Sorry, Reg, but I'm needed by the Wilkinsons on their latest course – I've got to be an awkward customer for some trainee waiters. Heaven help us all!!'

With that, they separated and Reg went off to enjoy a very tasty ploughman's lunch. Then, during his usual relaxed chat with landlord Jim, Reg got him up to date on the thoughts about the auction project, swearing him to secrecy, of course, and was pleased with Jim's positive response.

On his way back to the transport yard in Salchester, Reg detoured into Curzon Street to visit the premises of J Silver and Son, Gents' Outfitters. There, as reported in the local paper, the windows were plastered with signs saying that the business was having a "Closing Down Sale – All Items MUST Go". He went inside and had a good look round before finally getting back to the yard.

'Hope you don't expect my notes this afternoon,' was Julie's greeting, 'I've got a query on Charlie's holiday pay to clear up.'

'No, love, that's fine – but have I got something to tell you when you're ready!' and he busied himself making his own set of notes on what had happened so far today.

With such a tempting comment, it wasn't too long before Julie asked the obvious question, 'OK then, what's happened?'

'I called in at Silver's on my way back just now, to check up on the story about them having a closing-down sale –'

'And you at last got a decent suit, right?'

'Ha, ha, Julie, nice try, but no. Had a look and a word with Peter Silver and, wait for it, we may be in the running for renting the shop from them as a front-of-house for the auction business! There, what do you think to that?'

'But Reg, we don't even know if the auction idea is worth pursuing. I hope you didn't say too much or make any promises.'

'Come on, Julie, give me some credit! I only asked what their plans were for the building – they want to keep it and rent it out – and they gave me a quick tour. I said we'd want to keep stock there on a short-term basis, and assured them that there'd be no foodstuffs involved – it seems there's something in the terms and conditions of the business rates about not attracting vermin. So, what do you think?'

'Well, it's certainly well-enough placed for people to get to for bringing portable items in, but what about bigger things, settees and such – how much space is there? And isn't there an upstairs floor? If we need that as well, is there a lift to move heavy stuff up and down?'

'Better than that, love. First off, there's access from a service yard at the back for bulk items to come in and, if they need to go up or down for the first floor, there's a crane built in next to a back window upstairs! That's one of the reasons they don't want to sell the premises – the lift and window were designed and made and installed by some forefather of the family and it's part of their family history that they don't mean to let go out of their hands!'

'Sounds like a cracker, so let's see how the auction idea overall progresses. I'll be chasing the costs we talked about as soon as I finish here, though it looks more like a job for tomorrow.'

With that, each returned to the tasks they had in hand, tried to concentrate, and quietly planned for the next morning.

Chapter 14

With Whacker settled into his apprenticeship, and Alison happy with frequently helping Kelly, Ted Bailey at last felt able to put more effort into getting his business established in the wider Salchester area. He'd put out feelers within the Chamber of Commerce and could do little more than await enquiries from fellow members. But he did have one definite/possible opening, the one provided by Whacker, so one morning he set off to see if the situation was still the same.

Arriving at the cathedral without an appointment was, he felt, a bit tricky. He'd not even been inside the place and wondered if he might be put off by the atmosphere or anything. Finally he decided that, as nobody was expecting him, if he felt he couldn't work there, he could just turn around and walk out, no harm done. But if he was happy to give it a try, well, he'd say that he just happened to be in the area and called in on spec. And that was how it worked out and was quite OK when he was taken to see the Clerk of Works, who remembered Whacker speaking up for his employer.

'I'm told that it's a good young lad you've got there, Mr Bailey,' he commented, when Ted explained how and why he'd come along. 'I'm told he has nice manners and was part of a well-behaved group. Good to hear of youngsters taking an interest in the finer things of our culture.'

'Very pleased to hear it, Mr…? or are you a Reverend?'

'Oh no, sorry, it's just Mr Fisher, or David – I'm one of the hired hands, though this is also my place of worship. But you didn't come to chat, so let's have a look at the Cope Chest that needs fixing.'

They went from his office in the works yard, back into the cathedral and along to the still-roped-off area around the damaged chest, where Mr Fisher carefully lifted and removed the covering sheet.

'I can see what's happened here,' Ted said, as he tried to lift the lid. 'The timber's too heavy and the joints between the panels have weakened, allowing it to twist between the two separate hinges – that's why the far one has pulled away. So, first off, the panels need re-gluing, and I'd suggest strengthening the whole lid with reinforcing struts inside. Then I think you have two options – either replace both hinges or, perhaps, support them with a piano hinge. None of these are big jobs and won't spoil the appearance.'

'That sounds fine, Mr Bailey, and confirms my own thoughts on the matter, so could you let me have quotes, please. Assuming they're OK, I could give you the go-ahead within a couple of days – oh, and we'd need you to do the work on the premises, either here or in the works yard area.'

'No problem there, but my lad said something about being accredited to the church. Can you explain what that is, please? I've not done any work for any church before.'

'Don't worry about that for a single job like this – it's really just our name for the process of checking a person's suitability, honesty, reliability – the sort of thing anybody does the first time they put work to a new tradesman or business. It's important to us when we might need to give someone unaccompanied access to valuable items or vulnerable areas of the building but, as this job needs doing in our workshops, it's not necessary. But if you'd like to go through the process, it would help us to call on you until such times as our regular man returns to work. I'm afraid we're not sure if that's likely to happen, poor chap – sudden illness, and we're not sure about the prognosis.'

'I'd be more than happy to be considered for future work, and no problem in giving any info you need. Though for a reference, the nearest place I've done work for is Sandford College in Oxford.'

'That sounds fine. And we had a sort of loose connection with them – my predecessor took a post there, John Williams.'

'You'll probably recognise his signature then, on the references I can show you – small world, eh?'

And that started a whole conversation about coincidences in general and John Williams's current situation in particular, finally returning to Ted's move to Charlford.

'I take it you're in the process of getting established in the area, Mr Bailey!'

'Well, yes, and I must admit it's not as easy as I'd assumed. I guess I'd forgotten that my customer base in Bracknell built up fairly quickly because of Bracknell's New Town status and, of course, I knew the area fairly well. But now I need to find work for more than just myself – but that gives me a real purpose in getting out and about in the area. Speaking of which, I'd best be on my way and leave you in peace – I'll pop the documents you need in the post tonight.'

'That's fine, thanks, and if we can help with your search for clients, feel free to give me a call.'

'That's very generous and I might take you up on it. Tony Philips and his team are helping as well, and suggested I look in at the new indoor bowls site that's just been built. So that's where I'm off to now.'

So saying, Ted was soon negotiating the roads through a part of the city he'd not seen before until, suddenly, after a couple of industrial buildings, there was a sign for a car park. Next to it was quite a large, fairly square, single-storey building bearing loads of posters saying, "Salchester (CIS) Indoor Bowls Club – OPENING SOON – New Members Welcome".

After parking and paying, optimistically, for 3 hours, Ted made his way to the new building trying to decide how to ask about work without giving the impression that he was down on his luck!! He needn't have worried, as he was met at the door by a large genial chap who asked straight off, 'Hello, friend, have you come to join us?'

'I must admit I'd not thought about it,' replied Ted quite truthfully, 'but it certainly all looks very impressive.'

'Well, come on inside, have a proper look around and see if it helps you decide.' And with that, he stood aside to let Ted in, then proceeded to lead him around, pointing out the obvious, and not letting Ted get a word in until they reached the furthest corner of the completed but unfurnished building. 'There, sir, what do you think?'

'It's quite a structure. I'm really impressed with all this space under a single roof and no pillars – except, of course, where you have the side rooms. What are they going to be?'

'They'll all be labelled, of course, when they hang the doors, but that doesn't happen until all the work inside the rooms has finished. Anyway, starting from the far end, there'll be the toilets and changing rooms, the kitchen with tea counter, then the dining area and lastly the bar. Impressive, eh?'

'Certainly is – and when do you expect it all to be up and running – there still seems to be a fair bit to do?'

'Well, we could be playing in little more than a month, but a lot depends on some of the finishing trades – carpets, some furnishings and lighting, and the playing carpet won't go down till last – but the one thing out of our hands is the bar licence.'

'And you wouldn't want to be serving meals without a glass of wine or beer, would you?'

'Ah, meals – that's something to be decided on as we go along. There'll be tea and coffee, of course, and that's planned to start as soon as the main phase of building is over, hopefully next week. A wonderful group of volunteers, lady members and some members' wives, have set up a rota system so as to support people coming in to help with the final touches – and to show a welcoming face to potential new members. As for meals, we won't be expected to provide meals until we join a league and start entertaining teams from other clubs. It would be nice to do meals every day – at least at lunch time, if only for members who live away from the city – but we'd have to judge the demand.'

Before their discussions could continue, the outer door opened and a chap came in almost staggering under the weight a heavy sports grip. Seeing Ted and his guide he stopped and called across to them. 'Hi, Arthur, just brought these old woods in – where do you want them?'

'Oh, anywhere along there will do, Keith. I'm bringing my old set in tomorrow and I'll have to sort out somewhere proper to put them all. But are yours a donation or are they for sale?'

'Just a donation – their registration's well out of date, but if anyone wants to buy them as a starter set, put the money to club funds – not that you could ask for much. Anyway, got to dash – didn't have change for the parking meter!' And, with that, he let go of the bag, which hit the floor with a real thump.

'That sounded heavy!' exclaimed Ted. 'I didn't expect that!'

'Just a set of woods,' replied his guide, 'and you wouldn't want to drop even one of them on your toe, but come and have a look if you've not handled any before.'

The bag contained what looked like four identical balls that were mainly black, but with a couple of white discs on opposite sides, surrounded by sets of fine grooves that bordered a plain surface all around the middle. When Ted did as suggested, and picked one out of the bag, he was surprised at its weight – 'About three pounds, like a big bag of flour,' said his guide, 'but they feel heavier being so solid and, as I said, you don't want to drop one on your foot. But I hope it's not put you off.'

'No, in fact it's got me interested. But I didn't really come to find out about playing – you see, I'm a cabinetmaker, based in Charlford but not been there long, and I was wondering if a new place like this might offer me any work.'

'Ah! Now I'm not trying to put you off, but that's not in my area of interest. But I can put you in touch with the chap to speak to, or you can leave a card for him – or do both, if you like? Funnily enough, you're the second person to drop in from Charlford this week. The other one was a young woman looking for secretarial work, of all things – there'll not be much of that here, I'm afraid. Wouldn't have been with you, would she?'

'No, my wife seems quite content with looking after us at home, plus helping a small local company, thank goodness.'

'Pleased to hear it – this one would never have fit in here, even when we get the air conditioning installed and running, if you get my drift.'

'Oh no, not her again! I can't weigh her up at all – if it's the person I'm thinking it is – she floats in and chats, all smiles, but then, if she doesn't get what she wants, turns nasty then switches back to all sweetness and light and walks away! She's crossed our path a couple of times – glad she's not here right now!'

'That's the one all right – hope we don't see her here again.'

'Me too,' said Ted, 'but I'm bound to bump into her with living in the same village – never mind, I'm sure we'll cope. Anyway, must be off – nice to have met you, and thanks for the help.'

With that, after exchanging phone and address details, Ted headed back to the car and home, pleased with the contact he'd made and the one that he'd missed.

Arriving home mid-afternoon, Ted let Alison know he was back, then went over to the workshop to see how Whacker had fared without supervision, and was very pleased to find that all was well. The lad had finished the fitting of handles to a plan chest for a customer in Oxford and had then moved back to his own project – the board game for James Harding.

The main construction was going well. Having decided to keep it at the same size as the original, Whacker had used printed copies of the board as his template. The problem facing them now was how deep to make the board's base – he'd hoped to create a set of small drawers to store dice, playing pieces, instruction cards and so on, but some of these items could be fairly bulky.

'Do the rules help at all?' asked Ted.

'I've had a look, Dad, but it's hard to see if any of the pieces need to be more available than others. Once the game starts, it looks like players can progress at different speeds like in most board games, and the different bits – like the property pieces – don't seem to be needed in the same sequence for each player. I reckon the drawers are either going to be opening and closing all the time, or things will all have to be brought out at the beginning and used as needed. But I don't like that idea – the surrounding table would be quite a jumble. This needs lots more thought, and that's going to slow up progress on making the thing. Sorry! I really want to crack this and I know you don't want to let Mr Harding down.'

'Don't worry about the timing. Leave it alone for a couple of days and you'll perhaps see it in a fresh light. Give me a hand with a final polish on the plan chest, then call it a day, OK?'

Then, just before closing the door, there was a quick phone call from Tony Philips asking Ted to meet him, 'If poss, Ted, down at the end coach house at about 7 – work related.'

Unwilling to rush his meal, Ted arrived a few minutes late to find Tony sitting on a small stack of packages, engrossed in a study of a large illustrated book of birds. Ted obviously startled him with, 'Don't want to spoil your reading time Tony, but I've just rushed to finish my dinner' – though, of course, he hadn't.

'Sorry, Ted, I never used to look at books much – couldn't see the point once I'd left school, but there's some great stuff here.'

'And you rushed me here to tell me that?'

'Sorry, Ted. No, I'm really looking for ideas on how to display the ones I decide to keep – but that's the real problem – deciding what to keep. And I can't just keep looking at them all, or I'll never decide.'

'Can you split them up into categories like – I don't know – like history, travel, wildlife – that sort of thing, and decide which ones you like and don't like.' Not being much of a reader himself, Ted rather floundered to a stop, quietly wishing that Tony would keep this sort of problem to himself.

'To be honest, Ted, that's what I was hoping to do, but you sometimes have to have a proper look inside to decide, and that's usually when I get stuck into the book.'

'Is there anything I can do, now I'm here?'

'I'd hoped to have an idea on layouts so you can give me an idea of what size – or sizes – of shelving I'll need. That'll help me decide where to put them and how to sort them – or maybe I'll have to sort them first, but no idea how to tackle it, there isn't even a list of them!'

'You could have a word with Eileen Bartlett – unless she sees enough of them when she's working. She knows all about sorting books for the mobile library,'

'Good idea. I'm seeing Graham at the Lion later for a game of crib – I'll get him to ask her.'

'Are these the books that fell out of the coach last year, Tony – you've not been buying any more?'

'No, these are the ones, all right.'

'I assume you found out how they got there – and they really are yours now, aren't they?'

'They're certainly mine, I'm now happy to say. According to a chatterbox in their family's solicitor's office, it seems that the wife of the previous owner subscribed to a book club that specialised in these sorts of books – wildlife, travel, and that sort of thing. They said she used to be an active woman – rode to hounds and all that – until she had a nasty fall and was left bed-bound, or at least she was confined to the house. She wasn't interested in taking up any of the things you associate with a lady of leisure, things like embroidery or art or music – instead, she wanted to "feel a connection with the wider world", so she found this quality publisher and signed up to get books sent to her.'

'Wow, there's some years' worth of subscriptions there, I reckon,' said Ted.

'It's not as simple as that,' Tony went on. 'When she died, it looks like her husband just couldn't bring himself to stop the payment order – a bit like people not being able to dispose of a spouse's clothes, I guess – so the books kept coming. He didn't even open the packages, just dumped them in the carriage – along with a few more that were Christmas or birthday gifts from friends who didn't know she'd died! In the meantime, the publisher had been taken over by a firm covering more subjects, so we've got a wide range here and Heaven knows how I'm going to arrange them!'

'The books aren't still coming, are they?' asked Ted.

'Oh, no. The estate's executors stopped the payments, but then they couldn't find the books that had been sent – for a long time they thought the publisher was running a con trick! The solicitors were quite relieved when I told them we'd found the books – the family would be, as well, I guess. Then all of them probably started blaming each other for forgetting all about the carriage – not a happy family, I think. After that, it took some time to get the opinions of all the interested parties on what to do with them – they finally decided that we should just dispose of them as we saw fit. So here we are!'

Ted had been casting his eye over the nearest books and finally said, 'I think we'd be wasting time right now, trying to make decisions on shelving and bookcases – and how to marry them up with the ones I did for you last month, of course. I don't think I could offer any useful suggestions until you've got a better idea on how you want to arrange them – unless you sort them by size! So, if you don't mind, Tony, I'd like to be off – I want to take Alison out to town for the evening.'

So that's what happened. Then, a couple of days later, Eileen went to the manor to see how she could help Tony, only to find that both his daughter, Anna, and Mrs Wilkinson had opinions on the books.

Anna felt they should have a display in the entrance hall, but wasn't bothered about what the subject was, as long as it created a good background whenever there were visitors to the house.

On the other hand, Mrs W wanted quality reference books that might be studied by people attending the courses they ran for domestic staff – but she couldn't specify what subjects she wanted.

Then Tony wanted a set of books in his study, mainly for display, but also for ease of access to factual information such as world maps, notable historical figures, architecture, and cultural and political movements. None of them seemed interested in literature until she mentioned Shakespeare and Dickens – then they all wanted some!

Still with no clear guidance on how to select and arrange things to meet any of their requirements, Eileen got Tony to take her to the coach-house so she could at least see the books and hopefully create some ideas from scratch. But, before even that could start, Eileen was taken aback by a loud screech that greeted them when Tony opened and then closed the coach-house door.

'Tony!' she exclaimed. 'Surely you can do something about that racket! How you can expect anybody to work around here, I don't know! Haven't you got an oil can somewhere?'

It was a rather sheepish Tony that replied, 'I know there's one somewhere, and I mean to deal with it every time I come down here. Sorry, but it isn't always as bad as that! I'll go and have a look while you get started, OK?'

'No, don't. I really need you to be here so we can compare notes. But look – pass me that chair and I'll fix the door.'

'I can't have you climbing up on a chair, Eileen. And anyway, we haven't got any oil.'

'You may not, but I have. Just a mo'.' And she fished a little plastic bottle out of her rather large shoulder bag, climbed on the dining chair that Tony had moved for her, reached up, squeezed the bottle, and dripped some oil on the offending hinge.

'There,' she said, climbing down, much to Tony's relief. 'Give it a minute, then move it a couple of times and it should be OK. If not, send for a bloke with a new hinge!'

'Where on earth did you learn that little party trick?'

'Oh, that's from way back in my early days as a District Nurse. Some of our patients needed olive oil drops in the ear and they all had to have their own bottles. They had to be replaced after a month, and the old ones had to be ditched – but we sort of hung on to some of them.'

'But, olive oil to oil a hinge! What made you think of that? I'd have just put the old bottle in the rubbish bin.'

'It was a necessity and a fluke, really. A couple of us had to share a hotel room on a training course, and we found that the door to the bathroom really squeaked. It was too late at night to get the hotel maintenance guy, then the other girl found one of these bottles in her bag, used it and – hey, presto!! I've never been without one since then – but rarely needed it, I must say! Anyway, let's get on with some sorting – Graham wants me to meet up with some of his pals at the Lion by 8.'

Even with Eileen's help, sorting the books still wasn't easy – some you'd class as travel that also contained a lot about local flora and fauna, and so on. But they carried on, and had lost track of time when the door burst open – with only a small squeak! – and Graham burst in rather angrily.

'What are you still doing here, girl? We've got the people from Newton up at the Lion wanting to talk about their social evening, and I'm stood there like a lemon not knowing what you've arranged with the Skelford crowd! It's not good enough!'

Both of them were thoroughly taken aback, but it was Tony who came to the rescue.

'Look, sorry, Graham, it's all my fault – it's a bigger job than I'd realised, and I shouldn't have asked your wife to do any more than just give us some ideas. You go off now and ask Jim to get your party a round of drinks on my account, OK? I'll finish up here and follow you to give my apologies in person.'

So, Tony missed the heated debate between husband and wife on the walk up to the pub. It started with Eileen, through gritted teeth, saying a quite ferocious, 'Don't you EVER again address me as GIRL, particularly in front of others!' The remainder of the conversation is best left unreported.

However, Graham's interruption had come at a timely point – sufficient general sorting had been done for Ted next day to be at the stage where he could measure up and give Tony some basic ideas on the numbers and types of bookcases he thought would meet all the household's needs.

Whilst no-one said so, they all privately felt that the books would either never be looked at, or would be borrowed as needed and put back wherever it was convenient. This meant that Ted's suggestions for each location were generally accepted by all the interested parties. Once Ted had given Tony his costed designs and gained his approval, he could at last get on with the work.

Chapter 15

'Mum' began Whacker at breakfast one morning, 'you know that Scatty Hattie woman that was having a go at Kelly a while ago? Her proper name isn't Susan, is it?'

'No, it's definitely Hattie – short for Harriet, I believe. Why, has she been causing you problems? If so, you must tell your dad or Tony – they'll sort her out.'

'Don't go into Mother Hen mode, Mum,' he laughed, 'it's just that I heard Anna and Tina talking on the bus yesterday and I'm sure I heard Tina tell Anna she should get hold of lazy Susan. But they were talking about a meal for some of Tony's friends and I just couldn't imagine anybody wanting that smelly woman anywhere near food!'

Ted had walked in, overheard the end of the conversation, and soon put Whacker in his place about how he'd referred to Hattie.

'You might think of her like that, my lad, but you don't know her circumstances – so if you must mention her to anybody, just use her name – OK?'

'Sorry, Dad – it's just that I feel sure the girls know what she's like, but it sounded like they were thinking of having her to help them with food at a party!'

With a small nod indicating he was satisfied that Alison would deal with the situation, Ted gave her a quick peck on the cheek and went off to open up the workshop for the day.

'You've really proved that folk shouldn't listen in to other people's private conversations, my lad,' said Alison, trying not to laugh out loud.

'Come on, Mum, what's the joke? I'm supposed to be on my way to work by now.'

'Lazy Susan isn't a person, it's a dish or tray for serving food at big tables. It's round and stands on a middle point, like a wheel on its side, and it turns round so people can help themselves from it. I've never been in one, but I'm told they're used a lot in Chinese restaurants. You really shouldn't jump to conclusions on other people's

115

conversations, you know – but it's brightened my morning, I must say!! Now, be off before your dad docks your pay for being late.'

Going into the workshop, Whacker wondered if his dad would go on about smelly Hattie or let it drop. Fortunately, it was the latter, but Ted still had questions for him.

'How's the board game going, son? I don't want to pressure you, but it's the Chamber meeting this lunch time and I'd like to be able to say something positive to Jim Harding – he's usually there, and he's been very good about not expecting progress reports so far. What's the position?'

'Well, I now reckon it's starting to look good after Mum just gave me an idea. I've been thinking about all the bits that go with it – you know, playing pieces, information cards, money tokens, and such like. They've got to be stored properly or it's going to be a right mess – just look at all the envelopes and little boxes we brought away with us from Mr Harding's. But, apart from that, I'm sure the board itself will look better if it's raised a bit – at least when it's not in use'

'OK, so what are you thinking?'

'If the game's never going to be played, you know, just sitting there as a sort of conversation piece, as they say in the posh magazines, then we only need to make a decent wooden version of everything, plus a matching box for them to keep the bits in.'

'That's a good start, and I reckon he'd probably be happy with that, but surely we can do a bit better?'

'Well, a step up would be to have the playing board as the top of a box that has all the small pieces in it. Then if they wanted to play the game, they'd take the lid off the box and put it where they're going to play, then the playing pieces can be taken out of the box when needed during the game. And....' quickly going on as Ted started to speak, 'at least the board and all the pieces could be robust and in far better shape than the card originals. OK so far, Dad?'

'Fine so far, but don't take all day.'

'That's as far as I'd got until Mum just described this Lazy Susan device, so I've not thought it through properly yet, but...how about considering that the playing board stays on top of a box and all the pieces for the game live inside the box underneath it? They'd be in small compartments that sit on a turntable ready to be brought out when needed during play?'

'Right, the playing pieces would sit in little boxes on a turntable inside a bigger square box? And you get them out how – without spoiling whatever situation's already been reached on the board on top of the box?'

'You open the sides of the box! I know this is all a bit er, flimsy, Dad, but I'm actually thinking on my feet! You see, at the moment, apart from the board, it's just a collection of bits. So, to play the game and be able to bring in pieces when needed, they'll need either a big table or perhaps a main table plus a side table. I'm now thinking towards a version that looks good and can be played without re-furnishing the room, OK?'

'I see – or I think I do – the box would really be four corner pillars with removable side panels. It would have a solid top – the playing board – and a turntable carrying boxes of playing pieces inside. Well, my lad, that sounds very interesting and worth looking at in more detail. If we get the chance, I'll sound out Jim Harding on it – so carry on thinking that way, but don't commit any materials to it, will you?'

'Fine, Dad, but what do you want me doing today, particularly when you're out this afternoon?'

And then began the usual morning discussion, this time resulting in Whacker being tasked with sorting and noting the materials that had been found behind the coach last year, and considering if any of them might be useful for Jim Harding's game.

'If you end up making a rotating tray for it, for instance, you'll need a hard wood for a spindle as well as for the base for it to turn on.'

With this guidance in mind, Whacker really concentrated on his task and soon found what he felt would do the job – some wood that looked as if it had been a spoke for a carriage wheel, plus a brake shoe for a carriage. He then spent the rest of the morning labelling, listing and re-stacking the other pieces of timber, though his main project was never far from his mind.

Over a bowl of soup and a sandwich lunch at home with his mum, Whacker told her how what she'd said about the Lazy Susan had given him an idea that looked like it might work and solve a problem on his project. He was quite surprised by her cautious response.

'Won't it look a bit – I don't know – unfinished, with all these bits spinning round under the game board, and perhaps falling off, and people looking for them under the board and knocking more bits off if they nudge the table?'

'Hang on, Mum, it won't be like that.'

'I don't see why not. I've not read the game's rules, but if people are buying things and collecting money and so on, surely they'll have their hands in and out of the Lazy Susan all the time, and things are bound to get spilled out.'

'I see what you mean – I'd not looked at it that way. I'd best have another look at the rules and see if I've got it right or just missed something.' So, after lunch, that's what he did, across the yard in the workshop.

After about an hour, he was back in the kitchen at home, game rules in hand, excitedly exclaiming 'Got it, Mum! There has to be a King for the game – like a dealer, I reckon – and he's the one, the only one, that handles the money and the other items that go in and out of what you might call the kitty.'

'So, are you still using a Lazy Susan, or does he just have all the bits and pieces in front of him?'

'I like the idea of having all the pieces under the playing board, otherwise they take up so much space. I'll just have to work out how to limit access to the Lazy Susan. Anyway, thanks for the ideas, Mum.' And off he went.

Approaching the workshop, he was horrified to find the door open. Then, peering inside, he saw Hattie looking through the tool rack, fingering the cutting edges of his dad's wood chisels. She didn't see him, so he quickly and quietly backed out and nipped back home.

'Mum!' he whisper-shouted, 'that woman's in the workshop and she's handling Dad's chisels as if she's looking for a weapon! Quick, ring Tony while I keep an eye on the doorway!'

Alison did as he asked, but got no reply, so straight away dialled 999 and explained to the operator that an intruder in a workshop was handling very sharp chisels as if looking for a weapon.

Within minutes DC Loada Cole arrived quietly – he'd been at home in the village doing some paperwork – and went straight to the Bailey's kitchen door, arriving just as Hattie emerged from the workshop.

'Hello, Mr Policeman, you come to tell them how to keep their dangerous tools locked away safely when they leave the building open to the world?' she asked, with a really broad smile.

'What have you been up to, Hattie, entering private property without an invitation?'

'It was just a social call on a fellow villager – if necessary, to offer secretarial assistance, seeing as how his wife spends her time gallivanting around the villages delivering sandwiches – a job I should have had – instead of helping her husband in his business.'

'Come on, Hattie, you know it's not acceptable to go into business premises without an invite, particularly if there's possibly dangerous items around! Now, have you brought anything out with you – like chisels or hammers or drills?'

'Course I haven't – but shouldn't you be telling Mr Carpenter and his boy not to leave their stuff open to the public? I'm doing them a service not charging them with – I don't know, but there must be something they've done wrong here!'

'Is your husband around, Mrs Bailey?' DC Cole asked, 'he's not perhaps in the workshop needing help, is he?'

'Oh, no. Sorry, Mr Cole, he's in town at a meeting, and young Whacker here had just nipped across to tell me something – hadn't been away from the workshop more than two minutes.'

'I'm afraid that's often more than enough time for the criminal fraternity to take advantage. Can you go over and see if everything looks alright, Whacker, while I have a word with Miss Scattergood, here?'

Just then, Ted returned, saw the scene and feared the worst.

'What happened, love?' he asked Alison, 'is Whacker alright?'

'Yes, he's fine, Ted. In fact, I don't think anybody was actually in any danger, but Whacker got me to call the police, just in case.' And she went on to tell him all that had happened.

'That's all my fault, love. I really should have thought it through, you know, but I didn't see it as a problem for the pair of us and I couldn't see an easy solution. I'll have to go and apologise all round.' And he was turning to move off when Alison grabbed his arm to stop him.

'Ted!! What on earth are you talking about? What's all your fault? You weren't even here, and Whacker's capable of looking after himself – and the workshop – as he just proved!'

'Sorry, love, I'm talking about the stable door – or lack of it. When we fitted that one to keep Kelly safe, I should have looked into what we could do for ourselves at the workshop. Problem is that the door is so high and wide there's no easy way to do like we did for Kelly's Kitchen. But you're right, we couldn't have foreseen this, so I'll just accept it as a pointer that we've got to deal with the problem – we won't want to have the door being fully opened to get in and out in winter anyway.'

With that conclusion in mind, Ted went off in a calmer state to have a word with Tony, Whacker and DC Cole. He wondered if they could come up with a workable solution to the problem – how do you put a stable door into a coach-house door? The ensuing discussion saw the four of them move over to the workshop, go inside – and not re-appear for nearly an hour! When they did finally emerge, it was with broad smiles, shaking hands all round and slapping Whacker on the back before heading off in different directions, Ted going home to the cottage.

'And what was all that bonhomie about, then, Ted?' Alison wanted to know.

'Well, they inevitably saw what Whacker was working on – Jim Harding's game, you know – and so we were telling them a bit about how it's Whacker's project, and he's getting ideas and info from the college, managing it as a proper project, doing the paper-work – all that stuff. And I must admit the lad really did himself proud – quietly confident and treating us all more or less as equals! You'd have been proud of him, love – I certainly was – always have been, of course.'

'Me too, my love, me too...but now, what about your Chamber meeting – anything of interest?'

'Not really – main topic was about the possible effects on traffic of some planning request – nothing I could give a worthwhile opinion on. But I did have a chat with Jim Harding about his game, so I'd best get over to the workshop, let Whacker know, and then it'll be time to close down for the day.'

In the workshop, Whacker was sweeping up after some sawing he'd done, and was in a mix of pleased and apprehensive when his dad re-appeared.

'Right,' he said, 'I had a good long chat with Jim at lunch – told him what your latest thoughts were about keeping the game pieces accessible under the playing surface, and we had quite a discussion on it.'

'Thanks, Dad, and what does he think? Can I go ahead with it?'

'Afraid not – at least not just yet. He took on board – sorry about the pun – that you, well both of us, were trying to keep it compact, but he feels that it could be too complicated to use that way. But he does like the idea of the game board being the top of a box that can store all the playing pieces.'

'I know that would be simpler, but the box shouldn't be too deep, or it can end up looking like – I don't know – just a box with an ornate top. But you'd need to be able to get to all the bits when the game's being played – what did he think to our ideas on that?'

'He's aware of all that,' Ted said, 'I told him how we'd considered all the options – but he's going to have a word with his wife about it. He said that, since he first spoke to me, he's thought a lot more about the game and instead of just having a nice-looking memento in his den, he rather fancies trying it out again, so he's just got to check a couple of their tables that they might play it on.'

'But he doesn't want—' then the phone rang and Ted answered it.

'Hello…That was quick…Yes we were just discussing it… No, that's fine, Jim…Yes…yes…OK, we'll do that, and thanks for getting back to me so quick, Whacker can get on with it. Cheerio.'

'So, what can "Whacker get on with" then, Dad?' asked Whacker, sounding a little bit put out, as he fully expected his latest idea was about to be rejected.

'Well, contrary to expectations, he and Mrs Harding decided they rather liked the novelty of the idea of the Lazy Susan inside the box, with the game board as its lid.'

'OK, Dad, but it's going to be one big design task to keep all the loose pieces in one layer so that the box isn't too deep and no bigger than the board itself – but I'm really looking forward to getting stuck into it – yippee!!'

With that they closed the workshop, went home for dinner, told Alison and could hardly eat for talking all about it.

Chapter 16

The tentative knock on the office door in the yard of Harris and Philips – Haulage and Scrap Metals, was met with Julie Strong's unusually gentle response of 'Come on in Charlie, your money's nearly ready.' But it wasn't Charlie who came in, it was Reg Harris's wife, Lynda.

'Sorry to interrupt, Julie – I'll come back later.'

'No, hang on, Lynda, I'll give him a shout – I got his overtime wrong last month and he'll be in earshot, don't worry.' And he was, and quickly took the envelope and disappeared for his lunch break. 'Now, what can I do for you? I didn't get Reg's pay wrong, did I?'

'No – at least I assume not, he always just looks at the slip and mutters something like "Fine, should keep the wolf from the door for a bit longer!". And I never actually see it, so it'd never be me complaining if anything was wrong.'

'Good, so what can I do for you, and how about telling me over a drink at the Boatman?'

So they went, put in their orders, settled at a corner table, dealt with the pleasantries, and Lynda began with 'What's the situation with the Auction House idea, Julie? I wouldn't ask, only Reg seems to be getting quite obsessed – no, that's a bit too strong – but it's almost his only topic of conversation. But I didn't think it had been agreed yet – you know, by you and Tony. So I just wanted to find out properly what's happening – or would that be divulging commercial confidences?'

'Nothing to be really confidential about, but you do surprise me! We had a meeting about the idea, and I've done some basic costings on things we feel we can identify. I've given the figures to Reg and Tony, but the next step, as with any commercial idea, is for us to sit and chat and either make a decision or get more info – and that hasn't happened yet. But, between you and me, I think it looks worth going a bit further, and that's probably why Reg is straining at the leash.'

'Oh well, that's fine, Julie. I like the idea, myself, and would be more than happy to lend a hand either on the day, or even in the planning stages, if that would help – I could then perhaps keep Reg under control a bit – stop him running away with too many ideas!'

'There's a good chance you've turned up at the right time, then. Reg is off to see about shifting some stock at the wagon works near Oxford, then, on his way back, he said he might call in at Silver's, ostensibly to see if they need any of their fittings taken out. But you can bet your bottom dollar he's trying to find out more about their timing and if anybody else is in the running to lease the shop.'

'What do you mean – anybody else?'

'Oh, he does keep it close to his chest, doesn't he!! He's already chatted them up about the Enterprise perhaps being interested in renting the premises – though he didn't say if he mentioned to them that it would be as front-of-house, as it were, for the auction business.'

Over in the city, in Curzon Street, that was precisely what Reg was preparing to do, now that he'd got what he felt was a bit more than a tentative agreement to give the auction idea a try-out. Unfortunately, the first person he bumped into was Hattie who greeted him like a long-lost friend.

'Mr Harris! So lovely to see you again! Are you looking for anything in particular – a suit, perhaps? At the back there's a lovely grey with a chalk stripe that would really sit well and accentuate your fairly military bearing.'

'Thank you, Hattie, but no, I'm not buying, I'm hoping to see Mr Silver. Can you tell me if he's in?'

'How would I know?' Hattie again switching moods in a heartbeat. 'I don't work here, you know! – And I wouldn't, even if they paid me to! But it was lovely to meet you again, Mr Harris.' And, with a lovely smile, she turned and headed for the door, leaving Reg wondering what on earth to make of her, before seeking out a real shop assistant.

At the door, Hattie was surprised and delighted to bump into Mrs Gilbert whom she'd not seen for a couple of weeks.

'Hello, Auntie Viv,' she said, 'fancy meeting you here, of all places! I'm really pleased! Our paths don't seem to have crossed of late, and I've really missed our coffee-morning chats. How are you?'

'I'm fine, my dear, thank you – and how are you? I've looked out for you around the cathedral, but no wonder I didn't see you if you got yourself a job here after all! Well done!'

'No, Auntie, I don't work here, I just called in to see if there was anything I could get for my brother for Christmas, but all the shirts in his size have gone, and I know he's got more than enough socks and scarves – I send him some every year!!'

'That's rather like me and my son, but I thought I'd look in for fresh ideas. But now we've met, how about we have a cup of tea and a cake together somewhere and we can get up to date on family news? I can come back here tomorrow to have a browse.'

Back inside the shop, Reg at last found Peter Silver but was very disappointed to be told that the family didn't expect to be clear of the premises for a further two or three months, if that. They had been let down on a promise to take surplus stock at an acceptable valuation, so had decided to continue trading – perhaps even up to the end of the year. So Reg set off back to the yard with a heavy heart, but with a brain going ten to the dozen trying to see a way forward.

Meanwhile, in the bar of the Red Lion in Charlford, Graham Bartlett had called in for an unusual afternoon glass of beer.

'Not working today, then, Graham?' asked Jim. For once, the landlord was ready for a bit of a chat, there being only a couple of customers in the bar, walkers studying a map over a final cup of coffee before heading off out.

'No, Jim, early morning school run – had to have some of the older ones in early for a day visit to one of the colleges in Oxford. Can't see many of them being bright enough to get a place there, but a visit might inspire them. Mind you, it'd have scared the living daylights out of me!!'

'Me too – but, from what I've heard, it can set you up for life, no matter what subject you study. I didn't know that in my time – I just couldn't imagine what subject I'd do, what it would be like or what job it would lead to. Anyway, sorry to interrupt, Graham.'

'As I was about to say – when I was so rudely interrupted!' – and they both laughed – 'being finished early worked out well. I bumped into an old pal of mine and he's got a mate whose lad does some taxi work for the council, and he told him that he'd heard as how Marshalls have put in a planning application for a housing estate "on the edge of the village". What do you make of that then, Jim? More customers for you, I dare say, and perhaps one or two more passengers for me!'

'Come on, Graham! A friend of a friend who's got a mate whose son overheard? I'm not ordering extra barrels on that basis – and you ought to know better. Anyway, if it's the Dave Marshall that did some work for me here, I thought he was just a jobbing builder and wouldn't have the funds for doing something from scratch.'

'That's the one, I reckon, but he could be fronting it for a landowner – make it sound small, not attract adverse comment, then BAM, a couple of hundred houses taking out whole fields or woods – not a nice prospect.'

'Thanks, Graham, you've really cheered me up – made my day! We're now going to have convoys of heavy trucks bringing building materials through the village night and day, are we?'

'Come on, Jim, I'm pulling your leg! P'raps you didn't know, but there're no really big estates owning land round here. Whatever land Tony Philips got with the manor house, that's scattered over quite an area – all leased out to individual farms – so that'd never make up a housing estate. And I reckon all the other bits of land that join up with the village are owned by different farmers.'

'So,' said Jim, rather relieved, 'it's just a nice story to sell a few more copies of the local paper, I reckon. But we'll see.'

However, they wouldn't have been so sanguine if they had overheard a conversation that took place a couple of months earlier in the City Council Planning Department: 'What do you make of this, Charles? Marshalls are applying to build on the edge of Charlford "on behalf of the landowners, who wish to remain anonymous unless and until approval is granted".'

'That can't be our Dave Marshall, can it? For a start he ought to know it should go to County – and as for remaining anonymous! They'll be lucky!!'

'Bit of a funny one, though – be interesting to see what County has to say about it. I'll have it passed along.'

When the local paper came out the day after Graham and Jim's chat, the report of the planning application was there, but didn't name the target village, hence it was the main topic of conversation also in Skelford, Overton, and Newton.

While most people were puzzled about the possible location, just as Jim and Graham had been, Pete Newsome was sure it referred to the area around Parsons Lane, where Hattie Scattergood and her mother lived.

'What makes you think that, Pete?' asked Graham, getting tables and chairs ready for the evening's crib games.

'I don't think it, young Graham, I know it. Them houses was built for the workers on the Sanderson estate – before your time, of course. There used to be general farm workers, foresters, game keepers, a shepherd – oh, yes – and a blacksmith for looking after all the ploughs and other implements.'

'Where was the main house then,' someone asked, 'was it our manor house?'.

'There wasn't one – at least not around here. No, the owners had the land mainly for hunting and shooting, but farmed it enough to keep it in good fettle. Oh yes, I remember. There was a sort of big farm house, way out towards Charlbury. I reckon that's where the owners stayed when they came down – from London, I guess – and the estate'd be managed from there, and the horses kept there, too.'

For all that Pete could tell people about the estate, it seemed to raise more queries than there were facts. But the main questions were about why, and when, it had all stopped being a working estate – certainly nobody else seemed to know anything about it. But Pete Newsome felt he had the answer to that puzzle.

'I reckon it happened because of the fire – at least that's what my old dad used to say.'

'Come on, Pete,' said Jim, 'none of us knew your old dad – at least, I didn't – so tell us what he used to say. Either that, or buy yourself a drink and let the rest of us get on with making up our own minds about this mythical fire that ruined the mythical estate.'

This was a most unusual sharpness from Jim. But it was fully understandable considering that some lost bit of local history might have been unearthed, with the results coming to bite him and his livelihood.

'Keep your landlord's shirt on, Jim. I just need a minute to be sure I've got things in the right order – and I'll have another half, please.'

Sensing something of a revelation in the offing, the other customers closed up to Pete's area of the bar; a couple ordered drinks. Jim just hoped that Pete wouldn't start while the beer pump was making too much noise for him to hear any important details.

'Well, this were some time back, probably sixty or seventy years, and there were no more than eight or ten cottage affairs down what's now called Parsons Lane,' Pete began. 'They were all built the same – timber with corrugated tin roofs – and not very big, so they was all supposed to be warm enough in winter when the cooking range was on. Being in the middle of a big wood, all owned by the estate, they had more than enough fuel for the stoves, so they was banned from having any other heaters in there. BUT, one of the chaps wasn't at all well – couldn't keep warm – so his missus went out and got a paraffin stove, and you can guess what happened.'

'Gosh, Pete – was anybody killed?' asked one of his listeners.

'No, but it cost the estate dear. You see, there was no running water for the fire brigade to use, so they had to bring in a bowser.'

'How come there was no running water? There is now, isn't there' – from the same questioner.

'Do you want me to tell the tale or not?' asked a harassed-sounding Pete. 'Yes, there's water there now – the fire made the estate do that – but at the time, they all took their water from a couple of springs along their backs, springs that feed the Charl, if you didn't know already.'

'Come on, Pete,' encouraged Jim, 'ignore the questions and just tell us what happened. Was it just that they realised they'd need water if there was another fire?'

'That was mainly it, but the real problem was the drains. You see, the water bowser was horse-drawn, so it had to be backed up the lane.'

'Why's that then, Pete?' a different voice from the group.

'If you knew horses, you'd know they don't like going towards fire, so they tried to back it in but, with the sound and the heat of the flames, the horses couldn't be coaxed to do that, so the bowser had to be man-handled and pushed along the lane. Then at some point, when it was nearly where they wanted it, it went off course, dropped into a drainage ditch and went right through to smash the main sewer pipe. When the estate put water in, I reckon they fixed the drains at the same time – OK?'

'But what happened next with the estate? If they'd spent money getting the water piped in, surely they'd have kept it all going?' asked Jim.

'I suppose it depended on how interested they was. But they lost two or three of the cottages in the fire, and Dad reckoned the Council would have come down on them pretty hard about that and what might have happened if the fire brigade hadn't got to it when they did. He said the cottages stood empty for a bit before people started using them – I think that Mrs Scattergood's place is the only one lived in permanent, like; the others are rented out for holidays, I think. The whole lot's probably costing more money than it's worth. Anyway, that's me done talkin' – I'm off home for some tea. Cheerio!'

And away he went, having said more in the past half hour than he normally would in half a year.

Chapter 17

A couple of days after his visit to the cathedral and the bowls club, Ted locked up the workshop, followed Whacker into the kitchen at home, and was met by an exasperated-looking Alison.

'What's the problem, love? The cooker hasn't started playing up, has it?'

'No, Ted, it's you that's not playing fair. Anyway, let's have you and Whacker sitting at the table in two minutes, or you'll have a cold dinner. After you've eaten, we'll perhaps get it sorted out.' And she turned away to start serving their meals – at least the meal was for all three of them, so the problem couldn't be too bad, could it?

After an unusually quiet meal, with Whacker looking as uncomfortable as he probably felt, Alison at last started the conversation again, but still giving little clue as to what it was all about.

'Right, Ted, are you forgetting something – or just hiding something?' was her ominous start.

'I'm sorry, love, but you'll have to give me a clue – I've no idea what you're talking about. What about you?' he asked, turning to Whacker.

'Don't drag your son into this, Ted – it's just you.' Seeing his still puzzled look, she continued, 'What about recent days? Anything special happen?'

'Well, we had the sort-out with that Hattie woman, didn't we? She's not been pestering you here, has she?'

'No Ted, it's about you and what you're not telling me – or what you're perhaps too embarrassed to tell me in front of your son!'

'Of course there's nothing I wouldn't tell you in front of Whacker – why wouldn't I? He handled everything just as I would have done if I'd been here and – Oh gosh, I didn't tell you what happened in town the other day, did I?'

And he totally embarrassed Whacker by going down on one knee beside Alison and giving her a big hug and kiss on the cheek.

'Why didn't you just ask, love?'

'It's just that you were so absorbed in Whacker's project, and rightly so, that it seemed a bit selfish to butt in.'

'Sorry, love, you shouldn't have needed to butt in, I should have told you.'

'Hey, can we stop this "I should/you should" business, and just tell us what happened?' asked Whacker, ducking to avoid a playful slap from his mum.

'Right, folks. I'm more than happy to report, madam chairman, it's all potentially good news. Things went well at the cathedral, and I've just written up a quote for the job Whacker told …'

When he'd finished and they'd chatted a bit of the rest of the day, Alison asked, 'Did you want me to tell Kelly about the catering situation there?'

'I must admit I'd wondered about that, but I've no idea what she can do beyond sarnies and soup.' He paused before raising the real point he'd had in his mind: 'And I feel it'd be a bit of a stab in the back for Tony if she took a job and left here, all because we'd told her about it.'

'That's true, Ted, and we owe a lot to him – even just looking at how he got this cottage done up like we'd suggested. But, on the other hand, Kelly could find out about the bowls club thing on her own – or from a friend – really want it, but find out she'd been told too late and missed it. How would she feel about us if she knew that we knew but didn't tell her in time!'

'I know, love, but she's not our responsibility, is she?'

'No, but… I know – I'm out on the sandwich run with her on Monday so I can see if there are any signs of her looking to move on, or expand, or anything. We chat all the time so I'm sure something'll come up without me mentioning the bowls club.'

'OK, love, that sounds like a good idea but, in the meantime, I can see what the situation is when I go to the club next – I've got to ring one of the committee members about their display boards and so on, and I'm told he should be there on Saturday – you could come and have a look as well, if you like, love.'

'What about me?' asked Whacker.

'Yes, you can come too if you've not got anything else planned – in fact that's a good idea. You could lend a hand if it got as far as needing me to take measurements.'

'No, Dad. I meant what about me mentioning the bowls thing to Kelly – I could do it all innocent, like – if you wanted me to, then Tony couldn't blame you if she upped and left.'

Before Ted could respond, Alison jumped in quickly, 'No, Whacker, you certainly shouldn't do that.' Then, seeing his crestfallen expression, she went on, 'This is quite serious – it's about people's livelihoods – perhaps even our own if the wrong thing is said at the wrong time. But thanks for the offer and the thought behind it – I think you'd best forget we had this chat and we'll see what happens.'

'Fair enough, but you know I'll help if I can. Anyway, thanks for a lovely meal, Mum – I'm off up to finish my homework for college tomorrow.' And away he went to his bedroom for a couple of hours of geometry. (*Lucky lad!*)

The next day, Ted put together and posted the papers that David Fisher, the cathedral's Clerk of Works, had asked for. Then he chatted to Tony about finding a local signwriter in case he got any work doing a display panel for the bowls club, only to find that the best bloke was somebody he might easily come across at the cathedral, as he did all their work – small world!

Ted had now got so used to Whacker being around in the workshop, either helping him or getting on with his own project, that he sometimes felt a bit at a loose end when the lad was at college. Today was one of those days, when he was also mulling over the potential prospects at both the cathedral and the bowls club. As he often did, he spent spare moments in the rest of the day phoning and letter writing to let old customers know where he was, and that he was still available to work when they needed him.

In the manor house, after a light tea meal with his daughter Anna, in what he called his family room but Anna called his office, Tony Philips was surprised by a discreet knock at the door that was followed by the entry of both Mr and Mrs Wilkinson.

'Hello Mr and Mrs W – I was about to say it's a pleasure to see you, as ever, but you're both looking a bit serious. So, what can I do to help? – And do come in and have a seat.'

'We'll stand, if you don't mind, sir,' began Mrs W, usually the duo's spokesperson. 'I'm afraid there's no easy way to say this, so I'll say it straight off – we feel it really is time for us to retire. We do appreciate all you've done for us this past couple of years – providing a roof over our heads, a real home – and we don't want to leave you in the lurch, so to speak, but there's been so little work for us from Miss Hammond's agency this past month – and nothing in the pipeline, as they say – and we're sure that you and Miss Anna can manage very well without us getting in the way and so on...'

As she ran out of steam, she looked down at her hands, apparently waiting for a storm of protest or even of rebuke. Instead, she found Anna at her side with a comforting arm around her shoulder.

'Oh, Mrs W, you've never got in our way, have they, Dad? And you've both been nothing but real treasures to us. Just look at all you've taught me about catering and keeping house – you've both been absolute gems. I don't know what we'd have done without you, isn't that right, Dad?'

'Absolutely, darling. You've been such important parts of the household that I can't begin to imagine life without you here. BUT...'

He had to pause and gesture Anna to wait while he marshalled his thoughts.

'I always knew this time would come, of course. So, do you have any special plans – anything we can help you with?'

'Well, sir, you might not remember, but our visit to Charlford was intended to be the start of a series of trips to places we'd been when we were in service. There were some very nice places but, like with Salchester, we never really had the chance to explore them, so the plan was to do that now – and then perhaps see if we'd like to settle in any of them for our retirement. We'd like to do that now, sir, carry on with that journey.'

'That's an excellent idea, even though we'll sadly miss you. But when did you plan to start – and is there anything we can do to help?'

'We need to look at timetables for trains and buses and coaches to plan a route so that we don't end up doubling back on ourselves – and there's accommodation to look at, too. We've got some tentative ideas, sir, but needed to clear it with you before we went any further.'

'Well, that's fine by me, but do feel free to come back and talk things over – particularly if you change your minds, you know you'll always be welcome here.'

With that, after an extended exchange of good wishes, the Wilkinsons retired, leaving Anna – almost in tears – and Tony to contemplate a much quieter future. Both were deep in thought as they cleared away the tea things and washed up together. Then, forcing himself to brighten up for both their sakes, Tony surprised Anna by suggesting they both went up to the Red Lion for the evening.

'Find some cheerier company for the evening, old girl,' he said, earning himself a thump and at last a smile. They tidied up and set off, avoiding the topic that had so spoiled the scene at home.

It was so unusual for the pair of them to arrive together, and so early, that Jim had to be told the reason. As Tina wasn't helping him that evening, Anna went and joined her for a girly evening in the family's rooms upstairs.

'I was going to ask how you and Tina manage on your own, Jim, but of course you're always surrounded by customers in the bar and guests staying here, so I guess you're never stuck for company and you have the staff coming to clean and cook, don't you? Perhaps I should set the manor up as a hotel after all.'

'Thanks, Tony. That's my livelihood up the Swannee, then!'

'Sorry, Jim, you know I'd never do that – it's just the miseries talking. Let me buy you a drink and see if you come up with any ideas to sheer me up.'

'I can tell you something to cheer you up,' came the voice of DC Loada Cole, who'd arrived unnoticed, just in time to hear the final bit of Tony and Jim's conversation.

'Thank Heavens for that, Loada – include Loada in that order, landlord, if you please,' and Tony at last had a smile on his face, though he'd still to hear whatever Loada thought was good news. 'Don't say anything 'til Jim's here – he needs cheering up as much as I do after I've dragged him down with my own news.'

As Jim was then called away to deal with a query from the dining room, Tony told Loada about the Wilkinsons planning to at last move on.

'Sorry to hear that, mate – I know Mr W caused us a bit of a problem early on, but they've lent quite a touch of the good old days, so to speak. How's that going to affect you and Anna?'

'Too soon to know – they only told us this evening, and I don't know yet when they plan to go. Maybe it'll all turn out to be too expensive or something – we'll find out soon enough, I reckon. Anyway, here's Jim with those drinks at last, so what's the good news?'

'Well, it's about the carriage – it's been passed as potentially roadworthy! How about that then?' and Loada looked really pleased with the announcement.

'OK... But what does "potentially roadworthy" mean to the man in the street?' asked Tony.

'I think, and I wouldn't swear to it, but I think it means it's worth doing whatever work's necessary to get it fit to use.'

'That's a bit woolly, isn't it?'

'You could see it that way, but I understand it means they've checked the main chassis – that it won't fall apart under load – and much the same for the bodywork and the shaft and the braking mechanism. The next stage comes when the wheels and brakes shoes are fitted; they can move towards that now, but they've first got to service and prove the wheel hubs and bearings – that's the expensive work that they decided not to get done before they knew that the rest of the vehicle was passed as OK.'

'Pardon my banking background butting in, Tony, but this all sounds a bit expensive for a hobby,' was Jim's contribution.

'Don't worry, Jim, it's not really down to me, though the coach is still mine – in a way. Any stuff around the manor that's not personally mine – and Anna's, of course – has been signed over to the Enterprise. Now, in the case of the coach, that's been loaned, along with certain expenses and responsibilities, to Loada's friend Harry Collins and his group of coaching enthusiasts – they're the ones hoping to get it working and at least get some pleasure from it.'

'They must be real enthusiasts then, Loada?'

'Well, one of Harry's mates spent time with the Met in London, got pally with somebody in either the royal stables or the Royal Horse Artillery, and was given a private – probably off the record! – go at driving a carriage, and he got the bug for it. Anyway, long story short, according to Harry, there's now about half a dozen of them raising funds and so on, just to get driving experiences in coaches the size of this one.'

'Must think it's worth it – but what about the horses?' asked Jim.

'That's the problem – not many trained for this sort of work, and them that are, are usually in use for weddings and so on. BUT they think they may have an answer to the horse problem as well as some financial support.'

'Sounds good to me,' said Tony. 'I sometimes wonder if it's all going to fall apart and land back on my doorstep. So, what's the news?'

Pausing only to wipe some froth off his top lip, Loada went on, 'Any of you ever heard of ORE?'

'You mean the stuff you dig up and get metals out of?' asked Jim.

'No, it's the initials O R E – stands for Open Road Experience.' The blank looks persuaded him to continue. 'It's a company that uses old-fashioned, unusual and vintage vehicles to give people rides in the countryside along quiet roads through pretty villages and so on – you get the drift?'

'And they want to buy the coach?' asked Tony, suddenly wondering if he really wanted to part with it.

'Oh, no, it's not got as far as that – Harry's been in touch with them and found that they might be interested, but only in hiring the coach. They're talking about paying a retaining fee to have first call on it, plus a hiring fee each time it's used. But none of it'll go any further until they've seen and used it and sorted out routes they could use – so it's very early days, but all looking promising.'

'That's great news, Loada, and just the sort of thing I wanted to hear right now. Funnily enough, I was never very bothered about the coach, but it would be nice to have it around again, particularly if it was kept in one of the coach-houses. If these ORE people wanted to store it somewhere else, I'd really want to be kept in the picture, if you don't mind telling Harry that, Loada.'

'Sure thing – he's well aware of where it came from. They feel really lucky to have all this involvement.'

So Tony's evening ended with more optimism that it had started with, and he enjoyed mulling over Loada's news as he related it to Anna later.

Chapter 18

Hattie was passing the Red Lion on her way to get the morning bus into Salchester when landlord Jim appeared at the door, and called out to her, 'Miss Scattergood – can you come here for a moment, there's someone wants to speak to you on the phone.'

'Oh yes, and who's that – the Prime Minister, wanting me to form a new government?' She was about to carry on, when Jim called, 'No, it's a Mrs Gilbert, your Auntie Viv? It sounds like it's a bit urgent.'

Going quickly inside and picking up the phone, Hattie found her Auntie Viv sounding really desperate, almost panicking.

'It's alright Auntie, try and calm down and tell me what's happened and what I can do to help.'

'Oh, Hattie, it's Jane – my daughter-in-law, you know. She's had a bad fall and been taken to hospital – Andrew's away in Italy and there's only neighbours to look after young David. Could you please, please, come over and look after the bungalow while I go there and help out? I know it's a lot to ask at short notice and I wouldn't if I had any other option.'

'Yes, of course I will, Auntie. I'll have to nip back home and get the spare key you gave me but I should still get my bus and be there soon after ten.'

'That's wonderful, my dear. I probably won't be here, but I can leave you a list of anything that might happen – and I'll leave money behind the clock on the mantlepiece for you to pay the window cleaner if he calls while you're here.'

'Don't worry about me, Auntie, you just get yourself ready and go – and leave me Andrew's phone number, won't you? And take care and give them my love.'

Without pausing for a reply, Hattie put the phone down, thanked Jim, and set off at a run back home. Her mum registered no surprise at this sudden return; in fact, most events in Hattie's life, and their explanations, no longer raised any comment. And this was an occasion when the young woman was grateful for that, as she had no time for questions. She quickly collected the key from her bedroom, shouted a brief explanation – 'Off to Auntie Viv's – I'll try not to be late, Mum.' – and was out of the door and hot-footing it back to the village.

In spite of the hiccup caused by Auntie Viv's call, she still had just enough time before catching her bus to call in at the Post Office where, for a change, there was no queue.

'Hello, Monica, I've been called away to help a friend in distress, so I wonder if you could be so kind as to help my mum and me – in our hour of need?' She asked so sweetly that Monica almost dropped the parcel she was stamping for Mrs Little.

'Of course, I will if I can, Miss Scattergood.'

'Thank you so much, Monica. It's just that we're expecting some rather important documents any time now, so they're bound to arrive while I'm away helping my good friend in Glenton. And they probably won't go through the letter box, and might even need to be signed for. I think you know that Mother wouldn't be able to cope with that, so it would be really sweet of you if you could perhaps hold them here for me.'

'Yes, of course, Hattie. If they do turn up, I'll pop a note through your door to let you know.'

'Now that won't be necessary at all – and would probably really upset Mother – so please just do as I ask, and I shall call in each day to check if it's arrived.'

With that typical mercurial switch of character, Hattie swung out of the Post Office – leaving Monica Tillotson shaking her head in disbelief – and was just in time to catch the bus. Not knowing what state she would find the bungalow in, nor how long she might need to be there, Hattie bought some basic provisions in the city before getting the bus to Glenton where she arrived a good hour after Mrs Gilbert had left.

As she had expected, the main part of the bungalow was neat and tidy with no dirty pots to wash but, on casting her eye around as she checked that the windows and back door were all locked, Hattie found the dirty linen bin was half full. That wasn't a surprise, considering the unexpectedness and urgency of the cry for help, but it provided Hattie with the chance to do a bit extra for her friend. Unfortunately, Mrs Gilbert didn't have a tumble drier and Hattie wouldn't be able to leave things on the clothes line she'd spotted in the garden. So it would have to be a trip to a laundrette, if there was one in Salchester – she couldn't remember seeing one, even during her tours around the city's less touristy parts.

'Never mind,' she thought, 'if there's nothing else to do here, I can nip home, get it washed this afternoon, dry by morning, ironed and back here by same time tomorrow – no problem!'

Turning into the road at the top of Auntie Viv's close as she set off for home, Hattie looked to see if the curtains were twitching in the house opposite, and was surprised – and a little alarmed – to see a uniformed policeman approaching its door. Fully expecting the woman who answered the door to point an accusing finger in her direction, Hattie was shocked to see the man take off his cap, give the woman a hug and a kiss and go inside the house with her!!

'Food for thought there,' thought Hattie. 'I wonder what Auntie Viv will make of it? Or has she seen it before – be interesting to find out when she gets back.'

As she transferred from the Glenton to the Charlford bus in the city, Hattie was spotted by Ted and Whacker Bailey, pleased to be travelling by car and thus avoiding meeting her.

They were on their way to the cathedral where David Fisher wanted to meet Whacker so as to consider to what extent he could be allowed to carry out work without always being supervised. He started by asking about the practical side of his apprenticeship, then on to the college aspects.

'College is actually better than I'd expected, really. It's perhaps because it doesn't happen very often in the subjects I'm doing, so people often have something they want to know about my work in general.'

'Doesn't that slow you down a bit?'

'Well, it could, but it gives me a reason – and I suppose the confidence – to ask things for my own benefit.'

'Oh? What sort of things?'

'Mainly to do with my own project back at work. I'm making a sort of display version of a board game, and it's got lettering all over it – well, not quite all over like a newspaper, but in spaces round the playing track and on some of the game's pieces. Anyway, I couldn't work out how to do it without paying a signwriter, so I asked at college, and they took me along to meet people in the art department, and I hope I've got it sorted.'

'I'm pleased to hear that – we've got a slight connection with the college, and it's nice to know they're setting good standards.'

Then the interview moved along, mainly asking about Whacker's levels of experience in various aspects of carpentry that might be needed for work in the cathedral – none of the questioning would prove his abilities, but the Clerk of Works was actually assessing him as being honest and trustworthy and amenable to guidance, or not. The meeting ended very amicably and the pair moved on, as Ted had done the previous week, to visit the new indoor bowls club.

Immediately they entered the car park, Ted spotted a familiar vehicle already parked. 'Isn't that Kelly's car that she sometimes comes to the kitchen in?'

'Don't know, Dad – not really into cars yet.'

'Never mind, we'll soon find out.' And they did, because the first people they bumped into when they got inside the bowls building were Kelly with Eileen Bartlett – and the women saw Ted too.

'Don't tell Tony you've seen me here, will you, Ted?' asked Kelly.

'Why not? No reason why you shouldn't be interested in playing bowls – either of you young ladies. And in the winter, it'll be warmer and drier in here than it will be on a hockey pitch! Anyway, I'm here on business, and if you are as well, it's none of mine, OK?'

With that, Ted took Whacker along to the slowly emerging office where he found Arthur Taylor, the acting secretary to the club – the chap who'd asked him to call in. They'd not met before, so there were introductions – including 'Steve, my apprentice' (meaning Whacker).

'Right, Ted, we're going to want at least one trophy cabinet and eventually probably another one, so we need to consider places for them but, first of all we need Honours Boards.'

'Bit soon, isn't it?' asked Whacker, assuming you only received and displayed honours after you'd been awarded them.

'Normally you're right, son, but we want to display the names of our founding members – people who've given the support – not to mention the money – that's got us as far as this. And it all needs to be on display in time for us to honour them at our grand opening ceremony.'

They moved out of the office to see where and how big these boards needed to be, bearing in mind that further boards would probably be needed in the future to display names of competition winners and so on. All the time, Whacker was taking and noting the measurements they wanted, and making the odd comment here and there about the positioning of lights.

Returning at last to the office, Ted asked about the signwriting needed for the boards.

'Ah, no problem there. We're using the chap that does it for the city's outdoor club – and for the cathedral, as a matter of fact. And we may have the chippy from the cathedral offering his quotes for the display stuff as well, but I hear he's not too fit at the moment and perhaps not be available.'

'I understand that situation,' said Ted. 'I may be doing some of his work there until he's fit again, so we'll just have to see. Anyway, Mr Taylor, thanks for seeing us, and I'll get these quotes to you as soon as poss.'

Returning to the car park, they were met by Eileen wanting a quiet word with Ted.

'Kelly's quite upset and a bit worried that you saw her here, Ted. You can probably guess she was asking about the catering situation and she's worried that it might get back to Tony before she's decided what to do, so you won't say anything to him, will you?'

'No, why should I? And Whacker won't, either – once I've had a word with him. But let me come and have a word with her, just to reassure her.'

Sending Whacker off to have a look around the area, Ted found Kelly sitting in her car, looking almost tearful.

'Now then, Kelly, what's all the worry about? Like I said in there, what you were here for is none of my business – and if Tony got to know you were here and asked me about it, I'd tell him the same – he doesn't own us, you know.'

'I'm sure you're right, Ted, but it feels a bit sort of disloyal to go looking at other possible jobs when there's nothing really wrong with things at the manor, if you know what I mean.'

'Of course, love.'

'Anyway, I'm wondering if I could do both places – neither of them is what you'd call full time – provided I got someone to help, of course – and could work out how best to do it all.'

'I don't know what the timescale is for the catering side of things here, but have a real good think before you say anything to Tony. Would it help if I put Alison in the picture so you could perhaps talk it over with her when she's out with you on the delivery run next? I won't mention it if you rather I didn't,' he ended, quickly.

'Actually, Ted, now there's more than just Eileen knows what I'm thinking, I'd like another opinion, and Alison would be the best one – she knows so much about the sandwich side of things.'

'Right, love, I'll put her in the picture. And if she wonders why you brought Eileen and not her, what can I tell her?'

'Oh, sorry, Ted. I've known Eileen for ages – she used to live next door to my mum – and she was the one that brought me here, not the other way around.'

With that all settled and sorted, and Whacker told to let his dad do all the talking when they told his mum about seeing Kelly, Ted drove back to the workshop to sort out some quotes for the bowls club, dropping Whacker off at college for the closing classes of the day.

Later, over dinner, Ted mentioned to Alison where they'd seen Kelly and why she was there, emphasising that the young woman's aim was to see if she could work at both businesses simultaneously.

'I can't imagine what Tony will think of that idea,' was Alison's initial reply. 'It'd look like she was letting him down – and it certainly would be if she chose to leave here for the bowls place.'

'Well, like I said to her, love, Tony doesn't own us, you know.'

'OK, Ted, but it seems a bit disloyal. I mean, look at all the fittings and the like that he put in just for her.' She was quiet for a minute, then went on, 'And it wouldn't feel right if she left and it was empty next door and no vans bringing the bread and the fillings in the mornings – and I do enjoy those delivery runs with her.'

'I know, love, and I'm sorry to be upsetting you with it, but you needed to know – and Kelly really would appreciate any ideas you have that might help her make up her mind.'

'You're right, Ted. I suppose I've got so used to how things are, but if she did decide to leave, we'd have no near neighbours in the daytime and it'd be so quiet.'

'Hey, don't forget about me and Whacker across the yard in the workshop, and there's Joan and Doug down in the stables, and Team Tony in the big house – you'd find yourself spoilt for choice for somewhere to go for a chat or to try something new. Perhaps you could get Doug to teach you some leather-work so you could make a harness for me to rein young Whacker in when he starts getting big ideas about who's boss in the workshop!!' And this time it was

Whacker's pretend punch he had to dodge, and the atmosphere was eased.

Chapter 19

Jim Parker was at the Red Lion's reception counter, feverishly going through the local phone book, when he looked up and saw a woman coming in.

'That was quick – come on through and I'll get you started,' he said, leading the way through the reception area into the kitchen. 'You'll find whites in the locker room and your own stuff will be safe there. Best if you start on the veg – thank goodness it'll be quiet this evening. We've got a couple in at 6.30, then a four, and another two at 7. I'm taking no more bookings, but there might be one extra if the new resident wants to eat in.'

'She does – if it's no trouble,' said a voice behind him.

Jim turned and, sure as eggs, the speaker was none other than the lady he'd assumed was a replacement for his absent cook.

'Oh, no, Madam!' he stuttered and blushed. 'I'm so sorry! Oh dear! How unprofessional! Here, let me take your bag, we'll go back to Reception, and perhaps you'll let me start again.'

When they were back at their appropriate sides of the reception counter, Jim said, 'Hello, Madam, can I help you?' and was mightily pleased and relieved that she seemed quite amused by what had happened.

But Jim's problem was that he knew he knew her from somewhere, but couldn't think where, and even less could he think of her name – and the bookings book was buried under a heap of lists of supply cooks.

'Well I hope you can,' she replied, with a slight smile at his confusion. 'You should have a room booked for me – Mrs Clark – Pauline – Boots' mum from Bracknell. I rang last week.'

'Oh, of course! I'm sorry, Mrs Clark, I just didn't put the face to the name or the voice on the phone, and the bookings book is buried here somewhere… Yes, here it is, and we've got your room, and no problem. Er… except that my cook called in and can't make it this evening – her son got injured in a game of football. That's why you found me in a tizzy, trying to contact a back-up in time for dinner this evening – I was miles away when you walked in, sorry.'

'Please don't apologise, I can have a walk around to stretch my legs. But if my room's ready, perhaps I could book in and go up and leave you in peace to sort something out?'

'You must be tired from the bus journey – if you'd like to take a seat in the lounge, I can bring you a pot of tea, make my calls, then deal with your room and luggage. How does that sound?'

That suited Pauline, and she was pleased that, when Jim returned with a laden tray, he asked if he could join her – an agency had phoned to say a cook would be there in time for his dining room opening, so he was ready for a sit down and relax.

'So, what brings you to our fair village, Mrs Clark – come to see the Baileys now they've settled in a bit?'

'Yes, I am looking forward to seeing them and finding out how country life suits them, but the main purpose is to see something of Salchester. On last year's visits I only saw glimpses as we passed through and it looked rather nice, so I've read up on it a bit and want to have a leisurely look around. Oh, and after last year's visits and the fact that the Baileys have moved here, I feel a bit like I belong – so it would be nice if you could call me Pauline instead of Mrs Clark.'

A full blush appeared immediately as she realised how that might sound. 'Oops, I'm sorry, Mr Parker, that must have sounded really pushy, and I'm not – well only when I feel I'm being pushed... And of course you're not pushing me, so that didn't come out right either! Should I start again, do you think?' And the blush bloomed again.

'Well, Mrs Clark, I'm "Jim" to everybody, so you'd better be "Pauline" – until my daughter Tina hears me call you that, then she'll tell me to stop being unprofessional!!' and they both relaxed and the tension was broken.

'I don't want to turn business away, Pauline, but aren't the Baileys expecting you this evening?'

'Oh, no – they don't know I'm coming. You see, it was really only through John – sorry, Boots – knowing Whacker, that I knew them. But I want to call on them this evening or first thing in the morning – rather hoping that Alison will be free to come into Salchester and sort of show me around a bit. I know that's a bit of a cheek but, if she's not free, I plan to see Anna anyway – though she wouldn't want me to be dragging her around all day.'

Jim sat back, looked at her for a minute, then said, 'Would you really have started preparing the vegetables when I thought you were a stand-in cook?'

'Yes – why? I've got a food-handling certificate, if that's what's bothering you – I wouldn't do anything illegal!'

'I hope you wouldn't – it's just that I'm often struck by the confidence and independence of so many women these days – and I think it's great.'

'Now then, Jim, you're sounding like my old dad, except for the approval bit. No, I don't feel particularly confident, I just had to get on with things when I lost my husband – it was an accident at his works.'

'I'm sorry to hear that,' said Jim, who actually had been sort of probing a bit, 'but you seem to have done a good job on your lad – is it "Boots" or "John"? Are they even the same lad?'

'Same lad, but he's a good lad and takes after his dad. And it's through helping him settle in at the Cub Scouts that I got the food-handling papers – I must admit I don't know how much weight they carry in the real world!'

'Now she tells me!' laughed Jim, feeling really relaxed in her company. 'Anyway, let's get you settled in your room – and did you mean it when you said you'd be having dinner here this evening?'

'Oh yes, but I'd like it to be fairly early so I can try and catch Alison and Ted this evening.'

So, the time, the table, and the meal were agreed, and Pauline headed off to her room to settle in, relax and refresh, in that order.

At about the same time, down in the manor stable yard, Whacker had completed the daily sweep-up in the workshop and Ted was waiting to close down and lock up for the week, when the phone rang.

'You clear off home, lad, and tell Mum I won't be a minute,' said Ted, before answering the call. When he came home through the back door some five minutes later, before Alison could ask, he announced, 'There's good news and there's bad news – which does everybody want first?'

'The good news!!' was the chorused reply.

'That call was from David Fisher at the cathedral – they've approved my estimate for the cope chest and – if it turns out as well as my references imply – I'll get the accreditation, and not just for the cathedral, but for all the churches in the diocese!! How's about that then, family?' and he almost jumped for joy.

'That's brilliant, love, but what's the bad news? Don't say it was a hoax call?'

'No, same call, but David wants me in at the cathedral tomorrow to do the job then. It seems some big wig is in the area on Monday and unexpectedly asked to see various things, including the copes – they're in a store and they really want to have them back in the chest by then.'

'Oh, Ted – can you do it in time?'

'Oh yes – I've already got the materials, but I'll need you, Whacker, to give more than the usual hand – we'll probably have to shift it ourselves from nave to workshop and back again. OK?'

'No problem, Dad. Be nice to be seen to be doing something useful. But did you have any plans for the day, Mum?' he asked.

'I'd thought we could all have a look at Silver's to see if there's anything interesting left for either of you two in their sale, but it's not critical. I'll perhaps go in later on the bus, have a look round and come and see how you're getting on.

Anyway, that's enough excitement for now, dinner's nearly ready, so get washed and to the table, the pair of you.' And they did.

A short while later, having finished their meal, and washed and put away the dinner pots etc., they were just deciding how to spend the evening when a knock came at the front door. It was answered by Whacker who was beaming all over his face as he ushered in Anna, followed closely by Boots' mum, to see his mum and dad.

'What a lovely surprise, Pauline – have you just arrived, have you eaten, would you like a cup of tea?' said Alison almost in one breath, while Ted just smiled and offered her a seat. 'And what about you, Anna – called to see us too, or just on escort duty?' she added.

'Hello, Mrs Bailey – bit of both, really. Mrs Clark's got a question about Whacker's project, from Boots – and I'd like to know the answer as well, so I thought I'd tag along, if that's OK with everybody?'

'Well, blow me, son,' said Ted, 'I never imagined this little task of yours'd attract so much attention, particularly from the ladies, or I might have kept it for myself!' And he just about dodged the elbow from Alison.

'Ha flippin' ha, Dad. I reckon you only gave it me when you realised it'd be too tricky for your old hands!' He wasn't quick enough to avoid the light clout round his ears, but carried on. 'What's the query from Boots, then, Mrs Clark?'

'He says you were wondering how to use the original drawings – does that mean anything to you?'

'Sure does, and I'm not a hundred percent there. Let me get a couple of bits from the workshop and I can show you.'

'I think it'd be easier and less messy if we went over to the workshop to see it,' said Ted, 'if that's OK with you ladies.' It was OK so, after they'd had the promised cuppas, all of them went over, including Alison. She, funnily enough, knew least of all of them about what they were talking about as she rarely ventured inside the workshop and so heard little of Ted and Whacker's discussions.

Whacker brought out a print of the game's playing surface and explained that he wanted to use, as closely as possible, the inventor's originals of the drawings in the squares around its edge, but couldn't see how to transfer them. He'd explained the nature of the problem to his main tutor at college, who'd introduced him to the head of the art department, who'd suggested the cartoon method often used for large works of art that were to go onto walls and ceilings and so on.

Seeing all the puzzled looks, Whacker didn't wait for the inevitable question, but carried on. 'They'd do the drawing on paper, called a cartoon, then go over it with a pin or needle, pricking holes along the main lines. Then they'd put the sheet of paper where they wanted the finished picture to be, and rub over it with powdered paint, or even just dust and dirt. That would go through the holes so that the image would be there, clear enough for it to be properly painted over. But if it didn't look right for any reason, they'd just brush the dust off and start again. There! Lessons over for today, class dismissed!'

'Wow, that sounds good – will it be as easy as it sounds?' asked Pauline. 'Boots is sure to want to know all about it.'

'Well, like you see here, I can use one cartoon to make the same image in all the different squares where it's needed, but the real problem is working out how to use the method on plywood. It's got a smooth surface, so the powder might not stick, but if I dampen the surface, have I then got to paint the image before it dries out? And would the damp damage the surface? I only started looking at this aspect today, and it's just one of the many things to sort out by trial and error – very enjoyable, but it really means the job's not going to be finished in a hurry.'

That was the main part of Whacker's explanation, and Pauline felt she understood enough to tell Boots when she got home to Bracknell so, leaving the others to chat on a bit more, Alison took her back to the cottage.

'Right, Pauline, that's that part of the weekend's mission sorted, what else is in your plans?'

The two women were settled in the cosy sitting room of the cottage, each relaxed with a glass of wine. This was an unusual luxury for Pauline, as she kept no alcohol in the house at home, not wanting to encourage her son to drink before he was twenty-one.

'Nothing specific,' she replied, 'apart from having a look around Salchester. As I explained to Jim, I only caught glimpses of the city when we went through in the taxi last year, but it looked pleasant. Then I read a bit about it and want to see more – mainly in the cathedral to look at their embroidered fabrics.'

'So, it's "Jim" is it?' said Alison, with a smile that took any sting out of the remark. 'I know he's a nice chap and you did meet him briefly last year, but that's a bit soon, isn't it?'

'No, and it's me that started it – I'm "Mrs Clark" to absolutely everybody I come in contact with in Bracknell, even at work, but here I feel more relaxed and as if I belong, so I suggested he call me "Pauline", and he agreed, so there we are – OK?'

'Yes, and I'm very pleased that you feel sort of at-home here – Ted and I certainly do, and did so quite quickly. Anyway, do you want any company tomorrow? We were all going to go in together, but Ted's been called in to do a job in the cathedral – so he'll be going in early, taking Whacker, and in the van – so I'll be going in a bit later on the bus. I can fit in with your plans, if you like?'

Pauline did like, so next morning found them on the bus to Salchester confirming their plans for the day – firstly a visit to Silver's to see if there was anything still available in their closing-down sale, followed by a tea and a bun in Alison's favourite 'Olde Worlde' tea shop, then the cathedral, and the rest of the day for whatever Pauline wanted to do.

Chapter 20

The premises of J Silver and Son, Gents' Outfitters, didn't look as smart and appealing as Alison remembered from her one earlier visit. For a start, the windows were covered in notices, some advertising the closing down sale, others mentioning both Northfield Hospice and City Auctions – all very puzzling and quite messy.

Inside the shop there were obvious changes to the layout, the main one being the fact that there were three counters, labelled separately as per the notices in the window, each manned by an assistant wearing a sash carrying the same information.

Not being at all sure what the situation was, Alison asked at the Silver's counter and was told that, yes, they still had clothes for sale, but only for a couple of weeks until Northfield Hospice took over the premises – though the charity might inherit some of any remaining stock and perhaps put it up for sale.

For information about the plans of the other two organisations, she was referred to their sales counters. The Hospice lady said they'd decided to take the premises instead of handling donations only at the Hospice itself. In turn, the City Auctions chap said they would help to price items donated to the hospice and offer an occasional valuation service at the shop. They were also considering taking auctions out to venues in the local area, mainly for smaller items, whether coming from the charity or not, and this could be a convenient place for things to be brought in – but that was in the early days of discussion.

Realising this info might be of interest to Tony – having heard rumours of an Enterprise doing auctions – Alison collected all the leaflets available before joining Pauline, who had made straight for the remaining items of menswear. They each found a couple of items – socks and gloves – that would be gifts for their menfolk, and were paying for them when they were distracted by the raised voice of a young woman at the Auctions counter.

'I don't want to sell it, young man, I just want it valued – like it says on the notice in the window – so I don't have to prove I own it! But, if you must know, I'm looking after it for a friend and I need to know if it's valuable in case it needs extra protection. So – who's going to tell me its value?'

'Don't look now,' whispered Alison, 'that's Scatty Hattie from Charlford, and I don't want to get involved – she's an odd character. Let's see if we can inch out quietly.'

That, of course, didn't work. The Auctions chap had left the counter to ring head office, leaving Hattie to gaze around haughtily at the results of the rumpus she'd caused, so she immediately spotted Alison.

'Hello, Mrs Carpenter – buying Christmas presents on the cheap, are we? Aren't you going to introduce me to your friend?'

'Hello, Hattie. Are you causing trouble again?'

'Me? Never! In fact, I need to speak to your friend the village bobby to report some police misbehaviour – any idea where he is or if he'll be in the Lion this evening?'

'Sorry, Hattie, I've no idea. Why not try the police station here in the city?' said Alison, hoping to get away without introducing Pauline. 'But we're meeting someone, so we have to go now. Cheerio.'

They were lucky that the Auctions chap was coming back then, and they got away without further ado. If they had stayed on a minute or two, they'd have heard Hattie at her usual awkward best when the young chap reached the Auctions counter.

'Right, Madam –'

'It's Miss, if you don't mind, young man!'

'Sorry, Miss. Er… The valuation service is due to begin the week after next. This is the first week's tentative schedule for valuations of the different groups the house deals with – we suggest you come in on Wednesday when the Ceramicist will be –'

'Sarah Miss who??'

'No, Miss, that's the Ceramicist – the expert in ceramics – pottery, if you like, and then—'

'That's enough, thank you, young man. That's the person I need to see, so I shall be here mid-morning. Perhaps you'd care to inform them and make me an appointment. I'll bid you good day, and thank you for your help.'

As she turned to go, the young man interrupted – 'I'm sorry, Miss, but we can't make appointments, and this is just a tentative schedule, but you can ring and check on the morning, if you wish?'

'Oh, I'll not phone, young man, I shall come and see Miss Sarah here. But I must move on, so I'll wish you good day – lovely to talk to you.' And off she went, leaving the poor young chap open-mouthed and attracting sympathetic comments from the small cluster of customers who'd hovered and heard the exchange.

Meanwhile, Alison and Pauline's walk to the teashop in the fresh air helped clear away Hattie's awful aroma, and gave time for Alison to explain that Hattie was a real enigma in the village. 'She's constantly switching moods from sentence to sentence, usually carrying that awful smell, but really devoted to taking care of her invalid mother.'

As they sat enjoying their drinks and cake, the pair were rather disappointed with the results of their shopping so far, but soon put it behind them as they talked about what they wanted to do in the cathedral.

Pauline was mainly interested in looking at any embroidered items. Alison had already told her that the cope chest was still empty and being repaired that very morning by Ted and Whacker.

'But as soon as it's finished and back in place, I'm sure they'll be replacing the copes, so you might get to see all of them when that happens.'

'When we get there, can you get Ted to check on that, please, Alison?' asked Pauline. 'Even if it's late today, or early tomorrow, I'd love the chance to see them properly.'

In the event, they didn't have to wait to find Ted – a guide who greeted them as they went into the cathedral told them that the copes would be brought out of temporary store the following morning and laid out for display ready for the expected visit the next day, whether the chest was ready or not. Then, following his directions, they arrived at the workshop area just as Ted was coming out to get a tool from his van. He asked them to wait there a minute, then took them inside, and proudly showed them the almost completely repaired chest – far more interesting than Pauline had expected.

Leaving the men to their work, the two women did the standard tour of the cathedral, arriving back at the entrance just as Ted was handing over a message to go into the Clerk of Works' pigeon hole.

'That's great timing, ladies,' he said. 'I asked about the copes, and it seems that they're being looked at by the Dean and a couple of ladies from the Guild of Embroiderers to see if any repairs are needed. I had a quiet word on your behalf, and you can go in for a look, as long as you don't touch anything or interrupt them – is that OK?'

'Try and stop me, Ted! That's wonderful!'

So, all three followed the same guide through to a room that opened off one of the side chapels, where he knocked and ushered them in and left them in the care of the Dean – Ted waiting outside because of the dust on his work clothes. Pauline was overwhelmed by the sight of all the rich colours and patterns of the garments – and almost equally surprised by the signs of wear and fading on some of the older ones. She explained that she had always been interested in embroidery and felt that the items in churches were the absolute best and most interesting.

In reply to gentle questioning, she explained that she worked as a seamstress in a dry-cleaning company that also did work for the local hospital and a care home, and most of her work used a sewing machine. But the highlights of her job were when she was asked to work on items with embroidery.

'But I'd never be able to tackle anything like you have here,' she ended.

'If you're really interested,' said one of the women, 'why not see about enrolling in one of our courses? – that's the Guild of Embroiderers. I don't have any of that information with me, but if you give me your address, I'll send you some leaflets – new members are always welcome.'

'That would be great, thank you. And I'm sure my son would find it interesting – he's studying theatre design with a special interest in costume, but I can't imagine him doing embroidery, can you, Alison?'

Finally, thanking them, and leaving them all smiling at their own mental images of a young chap in a group of female embroiderers, they came back out into the nave. Ted went off to find Whacker, who'd been tidying-up in the workshop, while Alison and Pauline slowly drifted back to the cathedral entrance, thanked the guide, and went outside to enjoy the sunshine.

'I don't know about you, Alison, but I'm really ready for a spot of lunch, then feet up for the afternoon.'

'Couldn't agree more – let's see what the men can suggest as somewhere to eat before we go back.'

With Ted and Whacker both in their work clothes, a lunch in a nice restaurant was rather out of the question, so they found a bench in the park near the quay and settled for sandwiches, crisps, and drinks in cans and paper cups from a nearby vendor. Pauline was happy with this arrangement and told them she'd taken the liberty of booking a table for them all at the Red Lion that evening, as a thank-you for their hospitality and for showing her around.

'You don't have to do that, Pauline, we were coming into the city anyway today,' said Ted, and Alison agreed.

'OK,' she replied. 'It's not just a thank-you for this weekend, it's for, well, sort of giving me a reason to come here and to feel at home here.'

None of them knew how to reply to that, but Whacker was the first to say 'I think I know how you feel, Mrs Clark. Even on our backpacking visits before we came here for the bed and breakfast weekend, I used to feel as if this was a sort of second home.'

'That's settled then – the table's already booked for 7 o'clock for seven of us – that's not an unlucky set of numbers, is it?'

'No, but it's a lot,' said Ted. 'Do you really want to feed that many? We can opt out to give you more time with the others – you'll have had our company for most of the day by then.'

'That's very thoughtful of you, Ted, but it's all booked, and the others are all set up for it – that's Anna, of course, and her dad. I've also asked Tina so that Whacker's got somebody to talk to – and to get her an evening off duty!'

'It's really very kind of you, Pauline – thank you,' said Alison, hoping to conclude that particular topic.

'Well, actually, I'm being a bit selfish,' Pauline laughed. 'It's better than eating on my own!! But seriously, I'm feeling a bit unsettled in Bracknell. In the past two years I've had three sets of new neighbours, nice enough people, but none of them are on my wavelength – the town is getting so much bigger and busier, I can go for days without seeing anybody I know to speak to – apart from Boots, of course. And I'm really not looking forward to him going off to college. Sorry to put a damper on things, but I'm seriously looking around to see if I can find somewhere to think about moving to – and this area, so far, is top of the list.'

'Speaking for myself,' said Ted, 'I'm happy about our move as far as the people are concerned. As for work, I still have good customers this side of Oxford to keep us going while it builds up locally, so I'm very happy we made the move. And I've not yet had to quell a mutiny from the rest of the family!'

'You will if you turn up at the Lion this evening in your work clothes, so you'd best both be off home and out of the bathroom before I need it.'

Taking the hint, Ted and Whacker left, while Pauline and Alison chatted until they decided it was time to stir and get the bus home – so they did.

Dinner for the seven of the them that evening was a mix of thoughtful and jovial, making Pauline feel even more sure she would like to be part of a community like this one. When she actually said as much, Tony Philips slowed things down a bit by pointing out what he called 'very serious challenges to all residents of Charlford'.

'Come on, Dad, don't spoilt the evening,' responded Anna. 'I'm fairly new here and I couldn't name anything like that!'

'Well,' he went on, trying hard not to smile, 'you've not had much contact with Scatty Hattie, nor had Graham badgering you to start playing crib! Wait 'til they take the shine off your dream, Pauline.'

'Oh, we had a brush with Hattie in town this morning, thanks, Tony – she was flavouring the air in Silver's, then the chap at the Auctions counter got her attention, so we beat a hasty retreat. But if Graham's in this evening, Pauline can bite the crib bullet then, perhaps.'

Before anyone could steer the conversation back to Pauline's ideas on moving, Tony butted in – 'Sorry, Alison, did you say there was an auction counter in Silver's?'

'Well, yes, and another one for the Northfield Hospice charity shop – there were notices pasted in the windows and I picked up a couple of leaflets for Ted to give you. Sorry, but it all got a bit forgotten, and I think the leaflets must be in my shopping bag at home. Can I give you them in the morning?'

'Yes, that'll be fine, Alison,' he replied, a bit distractedly. 'It's just that Reg was supposed to be… Never mind, that's business, and tomorrow or Monday can deal with that. So, the thing now is to teach you a Graham-avoiding strategy.'

'Stop it, Dad,' laughed Anna. 'You know you enjoy a game most weeks, and Graham's a lovely man.

'Not a description that I'd use, love, but I know what you mean.'

They'd been enjoying their main courses, and now Jim came along to offer the sweets menu that was immediately declined by the ladies. Tony, Ted and Whacker were taking a strong interest until, one by one, they were dissuaded by the women in their lives, poor Whacker being hounded on two fronts – Alison and Tina.

Needing the table for a further booking, Jim offered them the use of the residents' lounge after he'd taken their orders for teas and coffees. Having caught the end of their conversation, he also told them that Graham and Eileen were in the bar if they wished to have a word with Graham about crib.

Once settled in the lounge, Tina took Pauline into the bar and introduced her to Eileen and Graham. As both of them recognised her slightly from her earlier visits, it was easy for Pauline to spell out her interest in finding out about crib and to ask if Graham could help her.

'You don't know what devil you've unleashed there, Pauline,' was Eileen's response, while Graham seemed to grow and glow.

'If you're here Monday afternoon I can give you a quick intro then, if you like,' he said.

'Sorry, but I'm going home Monday morning – what about tomorrow? I'm off into the city first thing, but I'll be here after lunch?'

'I'm afraid not,' Eileen jumped in. 'I've put a ban on cards on a Sunday – it's the one day I can guarantee he'll not have a pack in his hands and I can talk sensibly to him, or perhaps have a trip out.'

'Best thing I can suggest, then,' said Graham, 'is to look in your local library to see if there's a crib club or a league near you – but wait a minute, don't you live somewhere near young Slim who stayed with us on the lads' first visit?' Pauline's nod got him to continue. 'You could have a word with him – he took to it quite quickly, so should be able to help you learn the basics of the game.'

'That's an idea, Graham, but I think he's at college now, and I don't really know much about the family – we only met through the lads coming here. Ah, but Boots will know how to contact him, I'm sure – why didn't I think of that before!!'

That quick word with Graham and Eileen couldn't have been timed better, as their friends arrived then, and the four of them went into the dining room while Pauline made notes in her pocket diary. Returning to the lounge, Pauline gave the others the gist of what the Bartletts had said, particularly the suggestion that she should have a word with Slim.

'What about you, Whacker?' asked Ted. 'Do you know how to contact Slim?'

'No, Dad – he was always much closer to Boots, and rightly so. And it rather illustrated the old definition of a drummer – a guy who hangs around with musicians! But that was OK by me.' Alison, and even Tina, looked a bit taken aback by that, as they both felt that Whacker had played a significant part in the Acolytes and shouldn't put himself down like that, but it passed, and general conversations resumed.

Not being accustomed to staying out in the evening after a meal, Alison and Ted were soon feeling ready to head home. Tony could have stayed longer, but he asked if Whacker could see Anna safely home later, and set off with them – not before they had all expressed thanks to Pauline for a lovely meal and evening. Tony didn't say so, but he was really wanting to go home and see if he could get hold of Reg to talk about the information he'd picked up about Silver's.

Still in the Red Lion lounge, Pauline and Anna were having a chat about embroidery, Boots' career plans, and life in and around Salchester, so this left Whacker and Tina to private (*undocumented*) discussions.

When Jim came in to see how they were for more drinks, Pauline asked him about the times of buses into Salchester on Sunday mornings so she could have another look at things in the cathedral.

'Sorry, Mrs Clark, but there aren't any on a Sunday.'

'What about Roger West, is he on choir duty tomorrow, do you know?' asked Anna, explaining to Pauline that Mr West took turns in getting his daughter to and from the cathedral for Sunday services.

'Not sure, but I can give him a ring and check.'

'Before you do, Jim,' interrupted Pauline, 'church services can start very early, and I'd rather not bother than be tied to somebody's important timetable. In fact, I'd rather you didn't ask him – I can perhaps make a bit of time between buses on my journey home on Monday.' And the topic was left at that.

Soon, Pauline was ready to call it a day, and went up to her room after thanking them all for a pleasant evening in their company.

Next day, it being Sunday, breakfast was served a little later than usual. As the morning was bright and fresh, Pauline went out first for a walk along the road to the ford that her son had told her that he and Slim and Whacker had enjoyed visiting. Leaning on the handrail and looking down at the gently moving stream, she also found the sounds it made over the stones to be very soothing – well worth the cost and trouble of making the visit to Charlford, she felt.

Back at the Red Lion, after assuring landlord Jim that she had again had a good night's sleep, Pauline had just finished her usual light breakfast when she was called to the phone.

'Hello, John,' she greeted her son (Boots), 'how's it all going – are you still at the theatre?'

'Yes, and it's fine, Mum – hard work but extremely interesting. But how are you and, more to the point, how's Charlford?'

'Oh, I'm having a lovely time,' and she told him very briefly about seeing the copes in the cathedral, 'and we all had dinner last night. I've just had a walk to the ford and had a look at the Ambulance Field.'

The phone almost jumped out of her hand as Boots burst out laughing – 'MUM! What are you like? It's the AMBIENT field – and that's not the Acolytes, it's the Mystic Wizards' field at Charlbury – but never mind, just wait till I tell the others. Anyway, Mum, what are you doing today?'

'I'd hoped to have another look at the copes, but there's no buses on a Sunday, so I guess I'll just explore as far as I can on foot.'

In the background over the phone, she heard someone call for attention, so Boots had to say a quick goodbye and hang up. The short chat left Pauline feeling a lot less alone than she had been. She returned to her table and asked for another cup of tea, while she thought about how to spend the rest of the day ahead.

She had finished her tea, and arrived at no concrete plans, when Tina found her and asked, 'Do you still want to go into Salchester, Mrs Clark?'

'It would be nice, Tina, but I can't see how to do it without getting a taxi, and I'm not sure it would be worth the fare.'

'Right, well Dad can take you if you'd like – and he'd take Anna as well, if that's OK.'

'That's more than OK – and I think I detect the hand of my son behind all this. But what about you and the Lion?'

'Don't worry about the Lion – Dad can't be here every day, and the staff are great, but he likes me to be around when he's out, if poss. So, go on and enjoy the day.'

And she did. Then, on the Monday morning she went home – happy, but keen for another visit, as was landlord Jim in the now quieter Red Lion.

CHAPTER 21

Even before Pauline's bus had set off from Charlford that Monday morning, Tony Philips was on the phone to the firm's yard in Salchester and asking Julie to put Reg on the line.

'Sorry, Tony, but he's on the other line – and he sounds a bit put out about something. Do you want to leave a message or shall I just get him to ring back?'

'I just wanted to know if he'd heard about what's happening at Silver's – have you heard about it?'

'If you mean the City Auctions involvement, I only got a snatch of it but I think that's what he's talking about now. What's happening, do you know?'

Tony repeated what he'd heard, and what was in the leaflets that Alison had brought him earlier.

'Looks like our auction plans are up in smoke, and I'm not sure if I'm more upset than pleased, to be honest, Julie. What do you think?'

'I'm probably the same as you on this. It would have been interesting, might have made a bit of money, and would have perhaps cleared out your coach house, but it would have taken a fair bit of paperwork and a lot of staff support. Overall, I think it probably wouldn't have been worth our while – but that's me, seeing it mainly from the paperwork point of view. And I'm not at all sure how we'd have managed to get the staff it would need. Sorry, Tony, I know it'll be a disappointment to Reg, but I'll not cry over it.'

'I feel the same, and I'm not sure I'd have voted to give it a try once we'd got the costings etc. Anyway, get Reg to ring me when he's got a minute, will you?'

When Reg rang Tony a few minutes later, he sounded much happier than Tony had expected. He apologised for not getting in first with the bid to get the Silver's premises, but felt that things had actually turned out not too badly; Tony agreed with him as he spelled out what he'd tentatively agreed that morning.

On the auction front, City Auctions had said they might let him try his hand as auctioneer – under strict supervision – but only if they went out to the villages. Also, because these events would be for less valuable items, they would accept items from those in the Charlford coach house, provided that their ownerships were certified.

He'd then spoken to his contact at Northfield Hospice who told him that there were two main reasons behind the move. Firstly, they needed a bit more space, and the room currently used for handling donated items would meet that need if they could empty it. A separate factor, albeit a seasonal one, was that visitors' cars and vans often caused traffic problems for the hospice and its neighbours. They had grabbed the chance to move into Silver's premises to ease those problems and also make it easier for donated goods to be brought in and to be sold.

This hospice contact had also admitted, in confidence, that his colleagues weren't absolutely sure that the space at Silver's shop would be enough for them. This was mainly because they sometimes had gluts of the same sort of things, again a seasonal factor. If, or when, that happened they could be interested in renting space in the manor's coach house. So, all in all, Reg felt that it might not turn out too badly, and both Tony and Julie were spared the problem of telling him their negative views on trying to run the auctions themselves.

Elsewhere, things weren't going so well for Hattie Scattergood who was still looking after the home of her friend Mrs Gilbert/Auntie Viv. Not being at all sure how long Auntie Viv would be staying at her son's in Shropshire, nor how she would let her know when to expect her back, Hattie had decided to visit the bungalow at least three times a week – on Mondays and Wednesdays, and then later as she saw fit. On each visit she planned to carry a partly-filled shopping bag, hoping to give the impression to any random watcher that someone was in the home and that she was shopping for them.

Having more or less arranged to take Auntie's George Riley vase to be valued this Wednesday morning, she decided to take it home with her today (Monday), so it was well wrapped in towels as she left the bungalow. On turning out of the close, she was accosted by a uniformed policeman – the very one she'd spotted a few visits ago.

'Excuse me, Madam –'

'It's "Miss", if you don't mind, officer, and –'

'Very well, Miss, could you tell me what you have in your shopping bag?'

'If it's any business of yours, it's the property of my friend and I'm looking after it for her while she's away.'

'Do you mind showing it to me, Miss?'

'I certainly do mind! Particularly out here in the street – and with your fancy-woman probably watching from behind her curtains!'

'In that case, Miss,' he went on, a slight frown being his only response to Hattie's comment, 'I'll have to ask you to accompany me to the Police Station where we can look at what you're carrying – and hear your explanation.'

'Are you arresting me, officer?' she asked indignantly, though she was starting to feel a little worried.

'No, Miss, just asking you to help with our enquiries.' He muttered into his radio thingy and a police car appeared almost immediately, implying that she had been watched for some time, and had probably been expected.

Hattie tried to think – had she actually reported him after she'd seen him being greeted with a kiss and taken into the nosy neighbour's front door, or had she just thought about it? Was that why she was being accosted now? (She wasn't to know that he didn't respond to the taunt about the fancy woman because it was his sister on a visit to their mother.)

At the Police Station, she was taken into an interview room, given a seat and even offered a cup of tea – which she declined, not trusting them not to poison or drug her! Nothing was said about why she was there until a policewoman came in and took the seat across the table from Hattie ready to ask questions.

Hattie had already decided not to mess about on this occasion – she knew she'd done nothing wrong, and the sooner it was sorted out, the sooner she could get away and forget about it. Above all, she was hoping that nothing would happen to affect her friendship with Auntie Viv.

The policewoman allowed her to tell her story without interruption, then simply asked if she could prove it – but of course she couldn't, not just like that, anyway. Hattie explained that it could all be sorted out with a phone call to Auntie Viv but, unfortunately, she didn't have the son's phone number. She explained that it was at home in Auntie's note under the biscuit tin in the kitchen – but, for some reason, the police just weren't interested in letting her go home to get it!

At this point they insisted on looking into her shopping bag, and there – wrapped in a small bath towel – was the vase!

'And this "friend" asked you to take this vase for a walk, did she?' asked the constable who'd brought her in, earning a rebuking look from the woman who'd asked all the questions so far.

'If you must know,' Hattie replied, 'I'm taking it to City Auctions to have it valued so that I'll know how much protection it needs.'

The looks passing between the two officers indicated that they'd heard that tale more than once before, but the woman treated the statement seriously enough to point out that the auction house didn't do valuations on Mondays.

'No, I'm taking it to the new place in Silver's old shop in Curzon Street for somebody to look at it on Wednesday – Sarah Miss somebody, they said – and I've got an appointment, so I'm taking it home now so I'll have it ready for then, OK? – Can I go now?'

'No, Miss Scattergood, it doesn't work like that. We need proof of what you're telling us – or proof that this vase is actually yours instead of this absent friend's.'

'OK, let me get Auntie Viv's son's phone number and you can ask her yourself.'

'Get it from where?'

'From her phone book in her bungalow or from the note she left me when she asked me to look after the place.'

'And where would that note be – in your bag, perhaps?'

'Course not – I wouldn't want to risk losing it – it's at home.'

'Right, at last we're getting somewhere. Let us have your home phone number and whoever answers will be able to give us your friend's number from that note – right?' she asked.

'Well, no, actually – we haven't got a phone at home.'

'Look, Miss Scattergood, if you think this is funny, I should point out that we've got genuine criminals out there that really need the attention that you're getting just now. We don't honestly believe you're a bad 'un, so we're doing all we can to sort this out so we can all get on with some real work. So – who can we contact who can give us the information we need to prove that you're telling the truth?'

'OK – you could try Eileen Bartlett. She used to be the District Nurse that looked after Mum until I came back – she knows where I keep a spare key, and she wouldn't worry Mum. I don't know her number but Loada Cole – sorry, DC Cole – or his wife could go and see her if she's in – though she might be out on duty with the Book Bus.'

'Local name for the mobile library, I guess,' said the policewoman, 'so it's probably quicker to check with them first – can you do that, Jack?'

After the PC left to do that, the woman seemed to relax a bit and tried chatting with Hattie about the usual things – weather, traffic, shopping – but Hattie was becoming too uncomfortable as the situation seemed to be getting far too serious.

They were both relieved when the PC returned with the news that Eileen had been located at home and would go and get the letter and bring it in. Hattie was again offered a cup of tea or coffee, which she accepted, and was then left to await Eileen's arrival, hopefully bringing the key to her release.

Meanwhile, Kelly's delivery round was somewhat reduced today – the staff of one of her larger clients had all been called to a meeting at their head office – so she'd taken advantage of an early finish to again visit the indoor bowls club. Things had moved on apace since her previous visit; the playing surface was now carpeted and there were fewer signs of workmen's tools and equipment.

This time she was met and escorted by a different club member who assumed it was her first visit. Commenting on the serving hatch and the kitchen equipment beyond it, Kelly asked if they were serving refreshments and was told the situation. This was the same as before – the club was still looking to employ some-one to take on the job, initially for light refreshments, but ultimately to provide full meals, at least for matches with visiting teams.

This firmed up her interest, but she said nothing, not even about her current work or experience, deciding she needed to give it some more thought. But she did ask more questions about bowls in general and the club's plans in particular, and was shown around and given information just as all prospective members were.

On coming out of the building, she set off back to where she'd left her delivery van and was dismayed, shocked, annoyed – and all other feelings you could imagine – when she found the tires had been let down and someone had tried, unsuccessfully, to break into the rear compartment where her sandwiches were normally carried. Not having a good enough pump to tackle the job herself, she called her rescue service; they were snowed under with calls because of disruption on a coastal route, but promised her a response within ninety minutes.

Instead of waiting in the vehicle, she went back to the bowls club, found the secretary, told him of her catering experience and asked for the job application details – almost all in one exasperated breath – then sat down to calm down and to think about things.

Ted Bailey was also in town at the same time, calling in the favour that Jim Harding had said that he owed him in payment for making the display version of his board game. Ted was hoping for some serious information, advice, and perhaps even some help, in solving a problem that had arrived in the post that morning.

He had told Jim over the phone that the mortgage provider for the family's house that they still owned in Bracknell – not Jim's company, happily – insisted that Ted used a specific letting agent if he wanted to rent the house out. Ted wasn't happy about that, as he explained when they met in Jim's office at the building society.

'A chap I know owned a house out towards Sandhurst and used that agent when the house was taken by a family from a foreign army. Fine, no problem about the property or payments. He met the agent in the house after hand-back, and happened to open a drawer in a bed-side cabinet – would you believe there was a pistol and ammunition in there, even though the agency had claimed it had all been thoroughly cleaned etc,'

There was an immediate silence to confirm that such a situation was definitely not acceptable to Jim or his company, so Ted went on. 'But can they insist I use that agency – more or less as a condition of my mortgage cover?'

'I've not come across that sort of persuasion before, but banks and building societies do have agents that they prefer to work with, simply because of the degree of trust that develops over the years.'

'What do you recommend I do, then, Jim – as a mortgage provider or as a friend?'

'Let me see what they actually say, first. Then, if I can have a look at your paperwork, I might have some suggestions.'

Ted had expected, and actually hoped for, this response and had brought a folder full of papers that he handed over. Then he sat back and waited while Jim studied them muttering only the occasional 'Right, that looks OK', 'Yes,' 'That's good', before uttering a final 'Ah!'.

'Is that a good "Ah" or a bad "Ah", Jim?' Ted asked when Jim handed the folder back.

'Neither, really – but, first of all, you took out that type of mortgage when you were employed, is that right?'

Ted nodded, so Jim carried on – 'Well, your status now, and the fact that you owe so little, means there are better products available to you. But that doesn't affect the company's insistence on using that letting agent though, and I do find it a bit odd.'

'So, what should I do?'

'At first glance I'd say you have three options. The first is to go along with what they ask you to do and use that agency – they can't be all that bad. The second is to speak to them about re-arranging your mortgage to better suit your current situation and at the same time sort out the agency situation.'

As Jim paused, Ted prodded him to move on – 'What's the third option?'

'Well, it probably sounds a bit pushy, but you could clear that mortgage and re-mortgage with us – we can offer a more suitable product and you'd not be dealing with it at a distance. But our Bracknell office would need to confirm that your choice of letting agent was acceptable.'

'I think we'd probably like to do that, Jim, but wouldn't you need to inspect the house to value it?'

'Don't worry about that. I know Arthur who does most valuations for that branch, and he knows the area very well. He'll have a ride around on his bike, probably stop outside, and he'll perhaps even go so far as to prop his bike up on a lamp-post and check there's no obvious damage – windows broken, that sort of thing – but I doubt if he'll go as far as taking his bike clips off.'

Ted was more than happy with that, so Jim gave him details of his mortgage suggestion to take away and discuss with Alison.

But, before letting him go, Jim just had to ask, 'Have you considered selling the Bracknell house and buying a home around here?'

'Well, yes, but for two things – first I need to be sure the business has a sound-enough customer base in this area, particularly now I'm also employing my lad. The other thing is that I want to live within easy walking distance of the workshop, like now.'

'That really does limit your choices, then.'

'Yes, my wife and I have looked at properties as we've walked around Charlford, and the only place we'd fancy living is in The Crescent – where DC Cole lives. We've asked about properties there, but it seems that they are all rented from the council, so we have no chance of getting one. I must admit, on that basis, it must sound as if the move here was all on a bit of an impulse, but we don't regret it. Anyway, if I can rent out the Bracknell house, it'll give us a bit more financial security.' And away he went with plenty to study and discuss with Alison.

Meanwhile at the Police Station, Eileen had arrived and was taken to the interview room where Hattie was still waiting, and the letter from Mrs Gilbert was opened and read by the policewoman.

'It doesn't say anything in here about getting this vase valued or even taken out of the house,' she said, rather accusingly.

'No, and it doesn't say anything about washing the breakfast things she had to leave when she set off in a hurry to catch the train (*bit of a fib there, Hattie!*) – or about taking home and washing and ironing the sheets and pillow cases so she'll have a nice clean bed to come back to.'

'You're saying you took these things out of the house without her express permission, are you?'

'Course I am – it's what friends and neighbours do – not that you'd have experienced anything like that in your line of work!'

'Sorry to butt in,' Eileen butted in, 'but now you've got the phone number where Mrs Gilbert's staying, why not just give her a ring and clear it all up?'

So the policewoman did, and Mrs Gilbert confirmed the arrangement she'd made, and approved what Hattie had done for her, even going so far as to accept what Hattie had planned for the vase. She then asked her to tell Hattie she'd be coming back home the following day, and to ask if Hattie could come and see her for a cup of tea and a hand-over.

Hattie insisted on speaking to Auntie Viv to confirm this. 'I'm sorry about the police being involved here, Auntie,' she said, 'but I was worried about the vase when I heard that it might be quite valuable.'

'Don't worry about it, my dear, but it isn't all that valuable – if you put me back to the police lady, I'll ask if PC Franks can look after it and bring it back when he next visits his mother.'

After handing back the phone and repeating Auntie Viv's request about the vase, she learned that PC Franks was the chap who'd brought her in, and his mother was none other than the woman whose curtain she often saw twitching as she went to and from Auntie Viv's bungalow – small world.

With this all sorted out, Eileen hurried Hattie out of the building before she could make any more enemies in the local constabulary. They set off to walk to her car, which Eileen had left it near the new indoor bowls club. She still quietly hoped that bowls would be a game she and Graham could take up together – and get him away from crib occasionally!

On the walk to the car park she just had to ask, 'Hattie, are you getting somebody to come out and look at that smell in the cottage?', hoping Hattie wouldn't flare up at her.

'What smells that?' was the totally unexpected reply.

'Well, it's a sort of farm-yardy, sewery smell, you know? If it's not dealt with it can get into your clothes and follow you around.'

'I can't say I've smelled it, but then again I can't really smell much at all – I sort of taste the smell of things at times. It happened when I was a kid and some girl at school pushed me over and I'm told I hit my head and lost the sense of taste and smell – but taste has been coming back slowly. Is this a bad smell – a really bad smell?'

'Yes, I'm afraid it is, and it looks like it comes from under the house. When I opened the door to come out, the mat under the table seemed to lift as if there was a hole in the floor and the air puffed in. I should get the council to come and have a look at it – it's their responsibility, or the water board's.'

'Thanks, Eileen – and thank you for helping me today, and I'm sorry if I've been a bit rude to you in the past – I just get so annoyed with things at times.'

'Don't worry about it, Hattie. Look, I want to go and find out a bit more about this bowls club – are you coming in with me and I'll see if we can get a cup of coffee before we set off home.'

'Oh, no. I don't want to go in there again, thank you. I went in to ask, quite politely, if they had any secretarial jobs, and they almost laughed me out of the place so, thanks, but I'll wait out here if you don't mind.'

'Come on, Hattie – after what we've been through just now, I certainly need at least a cup of tea, and I can't leave you waiting here. They won't be having a go at anybody who goes to see about perhaps joining, and that's what I'm here for.'

Rather unwillingly, Hattie followed Eileen through the club doors and was relieved to find that her new friend had been right – they were welcomed with open arms (at least Eileen was!).

Then, just as they were about to be taken on a tour around the place, Hattie spotted Kelly in close consultation with an official-looking chap, and she flipped. Looking round for a weapon, she spotted and picked up one of the woods (*that's bowls, to you and me*) that were set out on a rack for people to try and perhaps buy. She was really surprised at the weight of it and could only swing it under-arm to throw it in Kelly's direction.

Eileen caught sight of the throw, shouted Kelly's name, and was relieved to see her spin round out of the way as the heavy missile thudded into the floor not too far from where her feet had been.

The shout, the thud, and the cries from some of the watchers drowned out Eileen's apologies as she half carried, half dragged Hattie outside where she sat her down unceremoniously on a convenient sack of gravel.

Hattie burst into tears and this immediately turned Eileen's anger into an unexpected compassion. Here was a young woman living with, and caring for, an invalid mother, and suffering from an affliction that, coupled with an argumentative personality, pushed potential friends away. And when she did find a friend, in Mrs Gilbert, and tried to help her, she was picked up by the police and almost accused of theft. No wonder the poor girl flipped in there on seeing another young woman apparently being offered a job that she'd been denied.

'Poor Hattie,' thought Eileen, 'I'll have to try and help some way – perhaps sit in with Mrs Scattergood some time, and certainly try to stand up for the girl in the Red Lion.'

Chapter 22

While Ted Bailey was collecting information concerning the family's house in Bracknell, the three principals of Charlford Enterprise, Tony, Reg and Julie, met in the manor house to discuss the situation regarding the two unused coach houses.

'It's a bit of a blow not getting Silver's shop as a base for the auction business,' began Reg – understandably, as that had been his idea – but Julie disagreed.

'I think that project could have been more trouble than it was worth – apart from you doing the auctioneer bit, Reg,' she added hastily. 'A worst case could have seen us with all the hassle of setting it up, plus the cost of the premises, and then getting little or no sales income. I'm sorry, but that's how I see it – probably influenced by realising all the paperwork that would have been involved.'

They were both surprised when Tony laughed. 'Sorry, you two, but I'm right in the middle. I'd really hoped by now to see something happening to create an income from the coach house, if only from seeing the stuff in there being moved out. But, I've had some interest from the feelers I put out at the Chamber – though neither of what has come in so far has been acceptable. Keith Tillotson wanted to set up a paint spraying shop – no way; and Hillier's are looking for somewhere to enlarge their carpet store. The problem with the carpets would be the access for the manufacturers' lorries and the machinery they'd be using to load and unload carpets – and perhaps even cutting them.'

Further discussion was interrupted when the phone rang, and Tony took a call from DC Loada Cole. Julie took the opportunity to get some coffees while Reg thumbed through his notebook looking up his contacts at Northfield Hospice and City Auctions, thinking of ways to keep alive the idea of village auctions with some involvement for himself.

When the call had finished, Tony tidied up some notes he'd made, leaving the other two to wait, both of them wondering if the call affected them and the business, and if the news had been good or bad.

'Right,' said Tony at last, 'that was Loada, as you guessed! To say that the carriage has been passed as roadworthy,' smiles all round, 'and his pals are having it completely tidied up ready to be decorated – by that he thinks they mean it'll just have a coat of basic paint or varnish to protect it.'

'That's great, isn't it, Tony?' asked Julie, who had not really been involved in the carriage saga before.

'Well, that part of it is, but we both – Loada and me – feel we need to put the whole thing on a more professional, or even legal, footing.'

'What do you mean?' she asked, ever wary of anything related to the firm that might be less than legal.

'Well, for a start, we've got to settle on referring to it as a coach – it's for carrying people, like a stagecoach - and not a carriage that you take goods around in.'

'What about a railway carriage?' asked Reg, with a grin.

'Don't go muddying the waters, Reg – it's a COACH!'

'OK, back to reality. I actually owned it because it came with the house etc but, as it wasn't of any real personal interest, I sort of felt it became Enterprise property – a bit like the stuff I put in the end coach house. But we, the three of us, never talked about it before I loaned it to Loada and his mate – I was just leaving it to them to see if it was worth being fixed to make it roadworthy. Now, these restorers have got it to its current state as a favour to them but, in reality, I reckon that it's me – or maybe perhaps our Enterprise – that's benefited. So I feel a bit bad about not contributing to any costs, while getting the full benefit of the work. See what I mean?' and Tony did look a little troubled by it.

'If it now does have some value,' was Julie's contribution, 'I agree with you that something needs to be put down legally to confirm its ownership. That'll provide a basis for anything to do with it in the future – insurance and repair costs and so on – is that what you mean?'

'That sounds fine to me,' said Reg who also had had no involvement with it before. 'But hang on a minute, Tony –

wasn't the coach long gone before we even talked about setting up the Enterprise?'

'You know, Reg, I think you're right – yes, it was gone in the early days of Ted's visits and we only set up the Enterprise just before he finally moved in.'

'Well, you only got me involved after Ted was here,' said Julie, 'so that seems to make the coach your very own asset – or problem – Tony. And easier to establish ownership, I imagine. You know, we don't really own much, do we, except for the things in the end coach house, and they really belong to the yard's house clearance arm. So, yes – decision made, coach is yours, job sorted!'

'Actually,' continued Tony, 'I've just remembered that I've got the letter somewhere from the solicitor confirming that the coach was included in the sale of the house. Do you remember, the estate came 'lock, stock and barrel' – so you're right, it is mine! Blow me!'

'So, the Enterprise isn't involved at all – is that what you're saying, Tony?' asked Reg.

'I'm pretty sure that's the situation. But look, let's think about this – if we compare the coach to Ted or Kelly, they pay me rent, and the Enterprise only gets involved if we supply support such as accounts and advertising, and we get a commission on that – right, Julie?'

There was a nod of agreement, so he carried on. 'So, for the coach, the situation would only become the same if Loada and his pals owned it and paid me rent. As they've put themselves out to get it to this condition, it seems right that they should own it and benefit from it.'

Obviously still a bit troubled by the whole situation, Tony sat deep in thought for a few minutes while the other two knew better than to interrupt.

'Right,' he said, eventually, 'I don't know what you'll think of this, but I feel like getting Loada and his pals to form some sort of legally identifiable group that I can give the coach to, and for them to operate it as they choose, but paying me a rent for the coach house any time they choose to keep it here.'

'That's a bit harsh, isn't it, Tony?' asked Julie, 'it's surely just a hobby thing.'

'Hang on a minute! I did just say I'm giving them the coach! If the ORE thing goes ahead and they want to keep it here, then the retaining fee they've talked about could go towards the rent. Of course, the lads would still be putting effort and probably cash into the thing, but that's what people do with a hobby, isn't it? Look, I'll talk to Loada and his pals and see what ideas they've got. But I'm quite happy for them to have the coach and it would be nice for the village if it were kept here. I'll talk to them – and keep you informed – OK?'

With that decision made, the meeting went on to discuss items affecting the transport and scrap business. Tony had been drawn gradually into its decision-making processes when he realised that he did still have some money invested in the firm. After that had happened, his interest in the world outside Charlford Manor had re-emerged.

That evening, the main topic of conversation in the Red Lion was, unsurprisingly, the further details of the planned housing development, illustrated by artists' impressions printed alongside the layout maps that were published in that afternoon's edition of the Salchester Chronicle. It still didn't say where the estate was hoped to be built but, as it had been given the name 'Parsons Close', people were assuming it was going to be in, on, or near Parsons Lane, right here in Charlford.

The ensuing discussion included speculations about the impact on the bus service, the Post Office, the shop, the garage and, of course, the Red Lion itself. There were also vivid imaginings of how a Parsons Close name-plate might be vandalised to read things such as Parson's Nose and Parson's Too Close.

The latter suggestion was answered by 'Not likely if Hattie's still around there!'. This remark raised the question about the Scattergood home and how it would be dealt with if the development was planned for where they all assumed it would be. All-in-all it was chatter such as one would find almost anywhere when insufficient information is available for an informed debate.

Elsewhere, Eileen was at home telling Graham about her afternoon's experiences with Hattie, and how she felt sorry for the girl and her mother.

'Now don't go getting too much involved, love,' he admonished, 'or, if you do, please don't bring it home with you – I mean that smell, of course – it fair turns my stomach if she gets too close on the bus.'

'Oh, I agree with you there, but I feel I've got to try and do something. You know, when I went in their house to get that letter, Mrs Scattergood just didn't move a muscle, let alone look round to see who was there. She just sat staring out of the back window as if she was totally unaware of me. I wonder if she's more ill than Hattie realises. I can't do anything officially, and I wouldn't want to spoil Hattie's trust in me, but I feel I really ought to find out what the doctor's practice is treating her for – I'll put some feelers out.'

Graham again warned her to be cautious, but this was Eileen on a mission and he knew – or hoped – she knew what she was doing. To change the subject, he asked about the vase that all the fuss had been about, and it transpired he knew nothing about George Riley, nor about the City Infant School, so this is what she told him.

Over sixty years ago, George Riley was a young man in the first term of his first job, teaching at the City Infant School – usually referred to as the CIS – when the school was almost totally destroyed by a fire, believed to have been caused by a faulty paraffin heater.

That day, George was away for a final interview to confirm his position at the school. It seems that he felt strongly that he could have averted disaster if he'd been there, and forever blamed himself for the loss of the six young lives of children who had been in his class. George suffered a total mental breakdown and was never fully restored to health but, in his convalescence, he developed a skill as a potter. In all his works, mainly vases and bowls, he incorporated the letters CIS somewhere in the intricate decorations. The pots became very collectable in the local area, though not so much when further away from the background story.

As a result of the fire, the whole school building had to be demolished and the City Fathers – or some such august body – decreed that nothing should be built on the site for the next sixty years. It was put on record that they arrived at this figure to represent ten years for each of the six lost lives. The decree also said that anything built on the site would have to be for the good of the community, not be driven by profit, and would have to include CIS in its name. Rumour now had it that at least two former pupils of the school were among local bowls players who had put up money to help get the new venture started, as it seemed to meet all the criteria.

'So, there you are,' Eileen eventually ended. 'I've had a look at the bowls club and it looks good – rather swish, really. They're open for anybody to join and will give free tuition, so I wondered how you'd feel about going along with me and giving it a try?'

'It wouldn't have to clash with a crib night, you know, love!'

'Oh, I know that alright – but just think about it and we'll have a proper look when it gets going – OK?'

As that put off the decision for a week or two, that was definitely OK as far as Graham was concerned, and they finished their meal with no more discussion about either Hattie or bowls.

In the Bailey household, serious discussions were always put in abeyance during dinner, though this gap was often filled by Whacker being asked detailed questions about either his day at college or his progress in the workshop – not fair, really, he thought.

Today, Ted and Alison had decided that the future of the Bracknell house, and its mortgage, really was a topic for the lad to have a say in, but it was still put aside until after the end of the meal. So, when all pots were cleared, washed and put away, they took their coffees and teas into the sitting room and Ted again went over the salient points of his meeting with Jim Harding at the building society.

'So,' he concluded, 'what do you both think of the idea of selling up in Bracknell? Let's start with you, Whacker.'

'Why me, Dad? It's yours and Mum's – you're paying for it.'

'I know, but it's been your home all your life – Bracknell's really where your roots are – would you be happy for us to let the house go?'

'Well, yes – we could use the money to buy a boat!' and gave a really cheeky grin.

Ted and Alison just couldn't help but laugh with him, then Ted had to ask, 'Where did this idea come from? You don't know a thing about boats, do you?'

'No, but some lads at college have asked me if I'd like to go sailing with them – and I don't know if I ought to go. What do you both think of the idea?'

'Well,' Ted replied, 'if they're a responsible crowd and experienced and know what they're doing and so on, I don't see why not. What about you, love?' he asked, turning to Alison who was looking more than a bit worried by the idea.

'I must admit it's nothing I've ever fancied doing – but don't let that stop you. I'd be happier if it was an official college thing – it isn't, is it?'

'No, Mum, but these are all senior lads and well thought of – I think. But if I do decide to give it a go, there's one or two things I've got no idea about at all and I don't want to look a complete idiot. Can either of you help?'

'I doubt it, but give us a try,' said Ted.

'Right, well I've heard that a sheet is a name for a rope – but I don't know if every rope is a sheet – any ideas?'

'I don't know about sheets, either,' said Ted, 'but be careful that these chaps really do know what they're doing. If they're not qualified instructors, I'd not be happy for you to go.'

Alison agreed with that, so Whacker said he'd check, then went off to see if Tina had finished her shift at the Lion.

Alison felt that the decision about the Bracknell house really was hers and Ted's to make, but neither of them felt strongly enough to decide either way. It felt simpler to wait and see what came of the building society's valuation and mortgage offer, so they left it at that and went for a walk. Reaching the village, they strolled along to the ford where they stopped and stood, as they often did, leaning on the hand-rail and watching the gentle flow of the water.

After a couple of soothing minutes, Alison spoke up, quite gently. 'I don't want to go back to Bracknell, Ted – I'd really miss this.'

As she turned to face him, he thought he saw just the hint of a tear in her eye. 'I know, love,' he said, quietly, 'and so would I.'

Chapter 23

Whacker was with Tina in the Red Lion beer garden, talking over the idea of going sailing, when she asked when it was planned for.

'It's next Saturday – is that OK? Nothing special happening, is there?'

'Only your pal and his mum coming for the weekend!' she replied with a happy smile.

'Now come on, miss – which pal? You know I've got thousands – plus all my admirers!' and he stood firm to accept the gentle thump he knew was coming.

'It's Boots and Pauline – arriving Friday, leaving Tuesday, I think. And you should have seen the big smile on Dad's face as he took the booking on the phone. I reckon there's something in the air there, don't you?'

'How would I know?' he asked, 'I'm not fitted with women's intuition – and it's none of our business – oops, I can see that it's yours, of course. Did you say anything to him?'

'Course not – he'll tell me in his own time – that is, if there's anything to tell, but they got on like a house of fire that weekend she was here – and I like her and I think it's about time Dad had a life beyond the back of the bar here.'

'What if they're just coming down for Boots to see Anna? Isn't that a possibility?'

'That's a bonus for Anna, of course, but they already meet up for a day in Oxford most months.'

'Didn't know that!'

'You blokes just don't talk about important things, do you?' she laughed.

'Hang on a minute, miss – sailing's important, and I was talking about that – and I've decided not to go. Couldn't mess up the chance for a chat with Boots – wonder what he's doing in music these days?'

'You likely to have a session together?'

'I don't think so – he'll be wanting to spend time with Anna – probably won't even bring his guitar.'

'That's a pity, you sounded quite good together – but I wished you'd played something more mainstream, or at least a bit livelier.'

'Like what – not Rock and Roll, surely!'

'No, but what about R and B?'

'If I'd still got the drum kit, we could call ourselves that, "R & B" – Rhythm and Boots!' – seeing the smile and raised eyebrows, he went on – 'And you expect me to give up a chance to go sailing if you're going to look at me like that!!'

'Well, are you – giving up the chance to go sailing so as to meet your old pal Boots?'

'Of course I am, silly! And I think he may want to know about how I'm dealing with the artwork on the board game, so there's plenty to chat about – should be good. Will you and Anna make up a foursome to have a spell in town?'

'Try and stop us! So, expect to be torn away from your boys' toys – speaking of which, how is the board game coming on? Will it be done in time for the Apprentice of the Year comp?'

'No, and I'm not in line for that anyway – you have to be in your final year, I think, but there's all sorts of trades in the mix. I'd not get a look-in, and I'm quite happy about that, thanks.'

Tina was about to try and persuade him to not put himself down so much when they were approached by DC Loada Cole. 'Sorry to butt in, folks, but I'm looking for your dad, Whacker – he's not at home and the workshop's all closed up – any idea where I might find him?'

'Sorry, Mr Cole – him and Mum were still at home when I came out – they're probably having a walk somewhere – I'll tell him you want a word when I see him – is that OK?'

'Thanks, lad – I'll be here for an hour or so – got some good news to celebrate, plus I'm off duty for a couple of days!' and off he went, into the bar to start celebrating!

'Wonder what that's all about?' mused Whacker. 'Some work for us, with a bit of luck.'

'I must ask,' said Tina, 'how do you balance doing work for your dad with doing the board game? Haven't you got an end date for that?'

'Yes and no, as far as a date goes. Mr Harding knows the game comes second after paid work, but I really don't like it taking too long – it can look like I'm not bothered about it, but I really am and I'm really enjoying it. Once I can sort out how to do the artwork, it'll really move along and it'll start to look special.'

'How are you getting on with using stencils for the lettering?' Tina had been pleased to know that the college had really helped Whacker there.

'They're fine, thanks. I've got the pens and ink the art department recommended and it's easy-peasy – it'll be just as easy for the pictures, once I find ...' and he went off into a brown study, leaving Tina hoping that it was just a thought that had struck him.

'Wakey, wakey,' she eventually said, and was more than a little relieved to see a beaming smile appear.

'Sorry, love,' he began. 'I don't know if I should class this as genius, or stupid for not seeing it before, but I reckon I've cracked it – how to transfer the pictures to the board as easily as it is doing the lettering.' And he just had to stop for another big smile.

'Come on, then, spit it out!'

'Well, I'd been thinking all along that I had to use the cartoons the same way as artists do. But just then I suddenly realised that they use dust or powder to transfer the image because they may need to move it or modify it when they see what it looks like. But I want these images to look exactly like the cartoon and I put them exactly where they're needed, so that means I don't have to use powder and risk it blowing away – I can use paint or ink to mark the image outline, like I do with the lettering stencils– then I only have to join the dots!!'

'And that's a big breakthrough, is it?'

'You bet it is, my girl – I can really crack on with it now. Just wait till I tell my dad!'

'What's this you want to tell me?' asked the familiar voice behind them as Ted and Alison came into the beer garden from their walk by the ford.

'Two things, Dad – first off, DC Cole is in the bar and is looking for you, but the important thing is that I've sorted out how to do the images on the game board. Now, can I get you both a drink to celebrate my breakthrough?'

'Very kind of you, Whacker,' replied Alison, 'but you're too young –'

'Don't worry Mrs B, I'll organise it and use his money,' Tina teased, and went off to do just that, followed immediately by Ted going to look for Loada.

Alison took the seat next to Whacker and told him of the decision she and his dad had reached.

'We're not going to sell the Bracknell house just yet – we're going to rent it out, and put the money on one side until such times as we might want to do something different. We're leaving our options open – OK?' That was fine by Whacker and, in turn, Alison was happy when he said he'd decided not to go sailing – yet!

Meanwhile, in the Red Lion bar, Ted was pondering the request Loada had just made – for him to see if, and how, he could make inter-changeable destination boards for the coach when it came back to the manor.

'Sorry, Loada,' was his immediate response, 'but I can't say either way with any confidence until I've seen it again and studied it. I'm fairly sure something can be done, but the question is whether any options would be acceptable to ORE. Let me know when I can see it and, in the meantime, I'll be thinking about it – OK?'

Of course, that had to do for the time being and Loada was quite happy that he'd raised the question and could now really relax. His offer to get Ted a drink was gently declined when Tina came in and told him about Whacker's round. Ted moved away, looking forward to enjoying it quietly with his family, when he was accosted by Kelly.

'Ah, there you are, Mr Bailey, I'm so glad I've found you. Is Alison with you? I'm sorry to barge in on your evening out, but I've just looked for you at the cottage and I'd really like to have a quiet word with you both.'

'We're really popular tonight, aren't we?' he said, to no-one in particular. 'The stable yard must have been like Piccadilly Circus. Alison's out in the beer garden with Whacker – will that do for you?'

'I'd really like to ask your opinions on something a bit – er – confidential, if you don't mind.'

Tina had been quietly hovering and, seeing Ted nod his agreement, she suggested they go into the residents' lounge while she went and told Alison, getting Kelly a drink on the way back.

When Alison joined them, looking a little worried, Kelly was quick to reassure them both that nothing was wrong, but that she needed to make a decision fairly quickly, and she'd appreciate their help with it as it might affect them to some extent.

Taking their nods as agreement, Kelly said 'You know I went to the bowls club, and I really liked the idea of working there, but it's a bit too uncertain how it'll go. Anyway, I talked it over at home and my dad came up with something I'd never thought of. You see, he sometimes works on the turnstiles at the football ground in Oxford and told me that most of the refreshment booths there are what they call 'concessions' – they pay the club for permission to trade at the ground, and then keep what they make.'

'Yes, I know about that,' said Ted. 'The risk is taken by the trader, but the club probably puts a clause in to ensure they get a bigger share of the profit on something like a Cup match.'

'That's right, and that's what my dad suggested I try to do for the bowls club – notices saying something like "Katering by Kelly's Kitchen" might even lead to other things. What do you think, Mr Bailey?'

'I don't know, Kelly. The idea is good, but the club's not even open yet, so you can have no real idea of turn-over. I'd see it as quite a gamble compared with running your present business – but it sounds as if your parents like the idea.'

'Well,' she hesitated, 'my mum and dad both think – and I agree with them – that I should at least talk to the club about it. The thing is that the club does tell all applicants what the demand for meals might be on proper match days, and it looks like it could be quite profitable. The unknown, of course, is the rest of the time, so that's what I wanted to talk over with you both.'

'Go ahead, love,' said Alison, 'you know we'll help as much as we can.'

'Thanks, Alison. Now, my dad suggests I try to get the concession idea accepted, while keeping the sandwich business going, at least for a start. I obviously couldn't do it all on my own, so I'd need to employ somebody. The two of us would have to be very flexible – perhaps doing the sandwich run a bit earlier – then one of us goes over to the club for the bar, with the other getting there as soon as possible on days when there's a mid-day meal to prepare.'

'Oh, Kelly,' interrupted Alison, 'I do hope you're not pinning your hopes on me being that other person. I'll help as much as I can, but that would be too much for me to take on.'

'No, Alison, I wouldn't ask that of you. My aim would be to employ somebody but, until I could get the right person, I'd plan to start the sandwich prep a bit earlier and perhaps ask if you could do all the deliveries on your own. How does that sound? And, of course I'd pay you properly, and it would only be until I got somebody that could do more.'

'I'd really need to think this over and get Ted and Whacker's support, but you might as well put it to the bowls club and start looking for your employee at the same time. You've obviously got hopes and plans to build up your business, so you're going to need proper help soon, anyway.'

They all sat silently with their thoughts for a while, then Kelly thanked them for their help, said goodnight and set off home. Ted wanted to carry on talking a bit more about what they might have let themselves in for, but Alison suggested they re-join the youngsters and take their minds off Kelly's problems – so they did.

Still at the same table in the beer garden, Tina was trying to explain to Whacker the benefits of being able to play crib.

'Slim said how it had helped him when he worked at the till in a charity shop, and I'm sure it must help in other things.'

'Look, Tina – I reckon anybody would need mental arithmetic to serve behind a shop counter. But in my line of work you can't be relying on that – you've got to be accurate and show your calculations – see? Isn't that right, Dad?' he asked, in a fervent appeal for a way out of being pushed into one of Graham Bartlett's seemingly never-ending games!

'I agree with Tina, if she's trying to encourage you to learn the game – we used to play it at home when I was a lad if my Uncle Fred came to stay. Your mum and I could play it at home now, but she's not interested, are you, love?'

'So, come on Dad – or you, Tina – what's it about, and how do you play it? But not too loud in case Graham overhears and takes over!!' He laughed to take any sting out of the remark, as he rather liked Graham for his down-to-earth approach to life.

'Well,' said Tina, 'I've watched a lot from behind the bar, but I've only played a couple of times, so perhaps you should tell him, Mr Bailey.'

'Right,' he began, 'it's a game for two players – though you can play as pairs, I believe – and each is dealt just six cards, then each chooses two of his cards and puts them face down into the crib – hence the name of the game – and the crib stays there until they've played their own hands – OK so far?'

The nods got him to carry on. 'The aim of the game is to collect points for various things and each player records his own score on a board using little wooden pegs. You start by playing cards in turn, putting them face up in front of you and saying out loud what the values add up to. OK? You get points if you play the card that gets the total to fifteen or to thirty-one. OK?'

'Half a mo, Dad – is that your own total or do you add up both hands?'

'It's the total of both hands so, as well as trying to play your own card that gets to fifteen or thirty-one, you don't want to help the other player get there. So, if you're leading, you want to start by playing a four or smaller.'

'Couldn't he play a Jack or a Queen?'

'No – sorry, I should have said that all picture cards count as ten – and aces are one. Anyway, you play on until somebody takes the total to thirty-one – but not more than that – then you start again and play until you've both played your four cards.'

'That doesn't sound as if it takes long, Dad.'

'No, but that's just the start. Now the players take it in turn to count up any points in their hands. You get points for pairs of cards, or sets of three or runs, and cards that add up to fifteen. Then the dealer turns up the crib and counts any points that that holds. Sorry, a bit I forgot – I'm not sure when it happens, but the top card from the deck is turned up at some time and it's also counted along with your own hand to get points. Look, Whacker, I'd forgotten more than I'd realised, but it's a good game and worth getting to know a lot better than I can tell you. I'm sure that Graham would give you a simple intro without expecting you to join his group – then you could get me up to date!'

'Thanks, but I don't know if I dare risk that before I get this board game finished – Mrs Bartlett gives the impression it's taken over her husband's life!' The others seemed to agree, so it was left at that and, as far as this group was concerned, the evening drifted along to a gradual relaxed ending.

Chapter 24

Following all the discussions at the Red Lion, the topics were tackled in one or more of the usual various ways – information sought, a lot of head scratching, and decisions made or put off.

One topic that was dealt with quickly was Kelly's interest in the catering opportunity at the indoor bowls club. Her proposal to buy a concession had been well received and given serious consideration by the club committee; as a result, she was offered a short-term trial contract that she accepted straight off. She could hardly wait to tell Alison and Ted about it and was knocking on their door the same evening.

'It's far better than I'd expected in terms of working hours,' she explained. 'The club manager will open up in the morning and handle drinks and light refreshments during the morning playing session. That means I only have to be there early enough to prepare and serve any lunchtime meals that might be needed – they'd be for a club match and/or any meals I choose to offer. Oh, and I'd take over handling the club's light refreshments as well, of course. I'd stay on if a later meal was booked for an evening match but, if not needed, the manager would be there to run the bar and light refreshments from mid-afternoon until he closed the club at night.'

'So, have you agreed that, and signed up for it?' asked Ted, wondering still if Kelly would be able to cope straight away.

'No, but I hope to – but I needed to talk to you about it first, if that's OK, Alison?'

'Of course it is, but have you got time to join us in a cup of tea or coffee – we're about to have ours – or is it a very quick one?'

'I'd love a coffee, please, I'm really ready for one, but I'll try not to take much of your time.'

With that, the three of them settled round the kitchen table, and Kelly came to the nub of the matter, which was to ask if Alison could help a bit more with the sandwich business.

'As I said the other evening, until I can employ somebody, I wonder if you could handle the deliveries on your own and also perhaps help with preparing the sandwiches? I've worked out that I'd need to be away from here by 10.30 at the very latest on days when I'd be doing a cooked meal for a match – and I'd like to make that the regular time, if possible. I can come in to make a start a bit earlier, but I can't do too much before the supplies get here, and you know they're not always reliable – so that's why I'd probably need help with the sandwich prep. I know it's a lot to ask, but it would only be until I could take somebody on properly – and I'd pay you the same as them. I'm sorry to have dumped this on you and also ask you for a fairly quick answer, but I need to reply to the club's offer before somebody else beats me to it.'

Since Kelly's first approach on the subject, the Baileys had agreed on a reply, subject to Kelly's answer to a question from Ted.

'What are you doing about employing somebody, Kelly, and what do the prospects look like? We've not had chance to look at the job adverts in this week's Chronicle.'

'Unfortunately, it seems there's a lot of demand for the sort of person I'm looking for – there's so many cafes and so on catering for visitors. But I've been in touch with Jenny Matthews, who runs the cookery side of some courses at the Tech College – they keep changing their minds as to whether it's Cookery, Catering, Hospitality, or Domestic Science!'

'And…?' prompted Ted.

'Sorry – it turns out that she's got a connection with the bowls club, fortunately, so she's had a word with them, and the college has agreed to put me, and the club, on the list of suitable places for work experience. This'll be for the students that are serious about careers in catering or hospitality. It sounds promising except, of course, for fitting in with their exams, plus college and family holidays. But if I get somebody really keen, it should be OK. Sorry it's not clearer, Alison, and I won't take it badly if you feel I'm asking too much of you.'

This wasn't quite the response they'd hoped for, but Ted and Alison had decided that they'd do whatever they could to help. So they pressed on, telling her that there needed to be a time limit on it, and that Alison could help only for the duration of the club's trial contract, unless Kelly got an employee in that time. It was a pity that the contract was to cover the winter bowling season as they all would have preferred it to be in better weather, but winter appeared to be the club's busiest time. Anyway, Kelly went home a fairly happy young woman.

Next morning, Ted was putting the finishing touches to the last piece of work in an order from his favourite Oxford college, and wondering where the next big job might come from, when he took a call from David Fisher, Clerk of Works at the cathedral. Quickly finishing his task, he closed the workshop – Whacker was at college – left a note for Alison who was out on Kelly's delivery run, and set off.

David had asked him to visit a chap called Tom Willett, at an address on the other side of Salchester. Tom was the man who normally did all the woodwork repairs at the cathedral, and his expertise was needed right now.

Arriving at the semi-detached house, Ted's knock was answered by a middle-aged woman he assumed to be Mrs Willett. Hearing that Ted was from the cathedral, she warned him of her husband's mood swings and possible attitude, then reluctantly let him into the front room. The man he'd come to see was smaller than Ted had expected and was sitting in a wheel-chair.

'Come in and say what you're after – and if it's money, we haven't got any!'

Before Ted could begin, Tom Willett went on – 'Come on, man, don't stand there gawping – what's your business?'

Ted said that he'd come from the cathedral, and that David Fisher and staff sent their best wishes.

'Oh, yes? And you've come all the way out here just to say that? I bet they want to know how long it'll be before I kick the bucket and they can give their carpentry work to some young whipper-snapper like yourself, do they?'

'Well, no, actually, Mr Willett. They want to know if you can take on a job that's just come up – and they sent me to offer help if you need it.'

'And who are you, then?'

Ted's description of himself and his business brought the first sign of a thaw in Tom Willett's attitude. 'Got yourself an apprentice then, have you? Teaching him proper and paying him proper?'

'Yes,' said Ted with a smile, 'I've no choice – he's my son, so my wife makes sure I treat him well!'

'That's all right then, but you must see that you teach him wood-carving – that's what I'd have done if we'd been blessed with a son. Anyway, what's this job and why can't you do it?'

Ted repeated the explanation he'd been given over the phone, namely that a riser in the steps up to the main pulpit had been badly cracked and probably needed to be replaced for safety reasons, as well as for the look of it. David Fisher had said he remembered Tom telling him that there was a trick to getting into the steps after he'd re-built them, so he'd know the best way to fix them.

'Well,' Tom said, 'that's true enough, and if I tell you how to get the piece out, can you get it here and then take it back and fit it when it's done?'

'Of course.'

'And who's going to pay you for all your time? Don't expect anything from me!'

'Don't worry about that,' said Ted, not being too happy about the man's sudden changes in attitude, 'I'm just hoping to get Brownie points.'

'As well as some of my jobs that don't need me like this one does, I reckon!'

At this, Mrs Willett just had to intercede. 'Now then, Tom, there's no need to be like that. Mr Bailey's only doing what the cathedral asked. He's playing fair, if you ask me, and I reckon you should as well.'

Ted didn't say anything, but wished the man would decide what he was going to do. In coming out on this errand, Ted had expected to get nothing more out of it than his efforts being appreciated by the cathedral people, and that perhaps later he might be considered if other jobs came up that Tom Willett couldn't cope with. Right then, Ted was torn between feeling sorry for the man, and being annoyed with him.

'Sorry, Mr Bailey,' Tom said eventually, 'but it's so frustrating to be depending on people all the time and not having control of stuff. And you're right, love,' he said to his wife, 'I shouldn't look a gift horse in the mouth and I shouldn't assume the worst in everybody.'

With the other two looking relieved, Tom Willett made notes to guide Ted on how to get into the steps, pressing Ted not to leave the notes lying around.

'There you are, Mr Bailey, and I do appreciate what you're doing for me – blame the earlier outburst on the frustration. I realise you've put yourself out for me, so is there anything I can do for you?'

'Don't worry about that, but I wonder if I could just ask if there are any poor payers that might want to put work my way?'

'Well, there are no bad 'uns, though one or two are a bit slow. A regular one of the slow ones is Dave Marshall, but he does put some good work my way. Not sure if I'll be able to handle much for him for a while, so I could put him on to you, if you'd like – as long as you remember to count me in if there's bits that I can do.'

'Oh, I'd be more than happy to do that, Mr Willett, thank you.'

And with that exchange, and goodwill restored between them, Ted left the Willetts and drove to the cathedral. Using Tom's notes, he soon liberated the damaged steps, saw them on their way to the Willett home in the care of a member of the cathedral staff, then returned to his desk in his workshop to chase up some more work.

Over their meal that evening, Ted was telling the family about the episode when he suddenly remembered the name Dave Marshall that Mr Willett had mentioned. Could he be the chap that was reported to be behind the plans for the housing estate that everyone thought was coming to Charlford? Not wishing to raise false hopes in the family, Ted kept those thoughts to himself, but was open to discuss any other subjects.

The main topic centred around Whacker, who was reassured by both parents over his concerns about the following day. As part of his training, not just in their work, but in the wider world of business, he would be going as Ted's guest to the Chamber of Commerce lunchtime meeting.

Progress on James Harding's board game had reached the point where construction could begin, but the designer's approval on a few points was needed before Whacker could go ahead. Ted had cleared Whacker's paperwork for the job and agreed that now was the time to meet the client and gain his approval – or otherwise

At the Chamber meeting, although he felt more than a bit uncomfortable in the suit, with collar and tie, that he'd worn at the Brakenhale prom, Whacker soon relaxed in the warmth of the reception he enjoyed and in the un-starchy atmosphere. He was also surprised at the interest shown in his project by some of the members, so he was pleased and relieved when Mr Harding kept the enquirers at bay after the meal by taking him and his father to a side room to talk about the game board.

'First of all, sir,' Whacker began, 'I'm sorry we had to go back on the Lazy Susan idea after you'd kindly agreed to it. I'm afraid we soon realised there would have been too many movable parts – all at risk of failure – and, as my mum said, too many dust traps.'

'I think my wife will thank your mother for that contribution to the design process,' said James. 'So, where are we now?'

More relaxed after that agreeable response, Whacker went on more confidently. 'I just want to confirm that we've agreed that the board should stand alone, and the playing pieces, et cetera, should be in a separate box. And the box must be small enough to be stored in a cupboard or drawer, and then to be put on a side table when a game is played.'

'That's right, young man, gives me a choice of displaying the board on its own or actually using it. So, what else did you want a decision on?'

'The property pieces – you know, representing a village or a farm and so on. When you'd played the game in its original form, they were pieces of card that lie on top of the board. For this version, I feel that they'd look better if laid into spaces cut to fit them; I'd make them either to match or to contrast with the board itself, using the same thickness of ply as the top surface of the board.'

'Yes, I seem to remember you saying something like that, and it sounded fine, so what do you need a decision on?'

'Well,' he began, rather tentatively, 'I wanted the pieces to fit snuggly into place, but then realised that they could be difficult to lift out at the end of the game. So, the options seem to be to either make them a looser fit or put something on their upper surfaces to help lift them up and take out – I made up a sample for you to have a look now and see what I mean.'

Whacker delved into his old school briefcase and produced a full-sized piece representing a farm, nestling into a shaped space on a piece of ply. 'See what I mean?'

When James couldn't get even a fingernail between the piece and the board, he said, 'Well, young man, you can certainly make things to fit, but I think I'll have to ask you to make the spaces a bit larger or the pieces a bit smaller. I don't like the idea of having handles on top – I might decide to leave it on view with the pieces in place, and handles would make it look odd, I think. So, any other points to clear up while we're here?'

Whacker got all the approvals he needed as he went rapidly through samples of his lettering and the transferred drawings. James also approved of Whacker's suggestion that, from each side of the board, the grain of the surface should go towards the centre of the board to give the impression of ground rising towards the castle on a hill.

Now came the final – he hoped – point to be decided.

'All along, sir, I've been visualising the finished piece lying flat on a table top.'

'Yes?'

'When I went to pick up a sheet of ply from the bench the other day, I suddenly realised how difficult it can be unless you slide it to an edge and get your fingers under it, like we normally do in the workshop. I'm sure you wouldn't want to do that with the game, sir, so we need to decide how to do it and I've got a few suggestions.'

'Fire away, young man – I'm really impressed by the thought you've put into this project, aren't you, Ted?'

'I'll let you know when I hear what he's got to say about this – he's not mentioned it to me.'

'Right, gentlemen. The first, and easy, option is to cover the underside with a layer of felt – it will slide easily to the edge of any polished surface without scratching it.' Their nods of understanding encouraged him to go on.

'The next option is to cut a rebate round the edges of the underside of the board so you can get fingertips under to pick it up – probably with felt under the rest of the base so you can either slide it or lift it.' Their less enthusiastic nods made him press on quickly to the final idea.

'But what I feel is the best option is to have decorative feet under the corners to raise the board a little from the surface – easy to lift, and it won't look as if it's supposed to be part of the table top.'

After a moment of thought, James said, 'I think you definitely left the best till last – but what ideas do you have in mind for what the feet should look like?'

'Well, I discounted a claw shape – too many bits to either break off or scratch a surface – and a traditional column base probably needs to agree with an architectural style associated with the game, but I couldn't find one. So I suggest a simple ball – or a flattened ball. That would be easier to fix to the board and would have a big enough surface area to attach small felt pads underneath. There, that's it, Mr Harding.'

Chapter 25

It was early morning when Scatty Hattie came knocking at the side door of the Red Lion. As usual, it was Jim who answered and, as usual, was very polite in asking how he could help the young woman.

'I'm really sorry to trouble you, Mr Parker – and so early – but I've only just been given this important letter from the council and I need to ring my brother and the phone box is filthy and I don't think I'll have enough change and I'm so sorry to trouble you but I'd be – ' All in one breath!

'Do come in Hattie,' he interrupted, 'and of course you can use the phone – I'll connect it through to the lounge for you – and take your time. Give me a shout if you have any problems, I'll just be in the kitchen.'

So, a very grateful Hattie was left alone to try and relax and tell her brother simply what the council letter said, namely that they'd written to their mother twice before and had received no response. Under the circumstances, the letter said, they would attend the property in Parsons Lane the following Friday to deal with the sewer – and force access if necessary!

As ever, her brother was the fount of common sense, and gave her clear, simple guidance on how to deal with it, so that Hattie was calm when she ended the call and knocked on the kitchen door to thank Jim for his help.

'I owe you an apology for being so demanding, Mr Parker,' she began.

'Don't worry about it, Hattie – you're welcome to ask for the phone any time – particularly if you need any help for your mother.'

'That's very kind of you, Mr Parker, we really appreciate it – I just hope you can be as understanding and forgiving about something else I need to explain.'

'Look, Hattie, I know we sometimes don't agree on things in the bar, but everybody's entitled to their own opinions, so don't feel you need to explain your view or apologise for them.'

'It's not that, Mr Parker, it's the smell' she said, and blushed.

'Oh, and what smell is that?' was Jim's best attempt at a non-insulting reply.

'I'm sure you've noticed the smell I'm told I carry around with me. You see, I haven't got a sense of smell – well, not properly. I think I lost it when I was knocked over at school and hit my head. I can taste things a bit but – anyway, it's an outside smell that sticks to my clothes, but we now know what it is and it's being taken care of, but I feel awful about it and I want to apologise for it... And I'd like you to pass that on to anybody else who's noticed it, and tell them that I feel awful about it.' she concluded, almost in tears.

'Well,' he said, 'I must admit it's been a bit less than fresh once or twice, but don't worry about it.'

That seemed to calm the young woman who, with her phone call a success and her apologies accepted, left to get on with the rest of her day, leaving a rather puzzled landlord in the Red Lion. She'd never been apologetic about anything before, nor had she been so effusive with her thanks for the odd times he'd helped her with phone calls – he just hoped that he'd not been elevated to the status of 'new best friend'. But Jim certainly didn't plan to mention the incidents to anybody, as he didn't want any distractions today, of all days; he was busy making sure that everything was as good as it could be for when Mrs Pauline Clark arrived for the weekend.

It had been a fairly short-notice booking, made over the phone by Pauline for herself and her son, Boots – she now knew better than to try and refer to him as John when mentioning him to anyone in Charlford! With a bit of shuffling of rooms for a group of first-time visitors, Jim was putting Pauline into what he felt was his best room – Boots was more than happy to be in the Annexe (the manor stable block) and thus be near to Anna. Now, with both the normal duty manager and back-up chap ready to man the pumps at the Red Lion, Jim hoped to spend more time over the weekend with his special guest.

Someone else looking forward to an appearance that he hoped would lead to a pleasant weekend, was DC Loada Cole – the coach was about to be returned, at long last, to its coach-house in the stable yard at the manor. Ted Bailey had said he would be there to look at it, ready to design destination boards for the coach's anticipated use by the Open Road Experience (ORE) people. Loada was particularly pleased that all he had to do was to look on, smile, and approve Ted's suggestions – he hoped.

As Loada neared the stable yard entrance, imagining what it would be like to arrive in the coach instead of on foot, he was approached by a chap who looked vaguely familiar. But then, when the man asked after Ted Bailey, Loada stopped trying to place the face and assumed that this was the ORE guy, arriving a bit early.

'If his workshop's not open, I've no idea where Ted could be, sorry,' he replied, 'and it doesn't look as if the coach has come in yet.'

The 'You mean he comes to work by coach??' response was accompanied by eyebrows that could not have been raised any higher.

'I guess you're not the man from ORE, then.'

'Sorry, could we start again, please? We seem to be on different tracks. I'm looking for Ted Bailey to see if he can do some work for me, and this is the only location I was given.'

'Well, you've come to the right place, and this is definitely one morning when I'd expect him to be here.' And, sure as eggs, right on cue, along came Ted from the direction of the manor house.

'Ted,' Loada called, 'chap here wants you to do some work for him – don't let it get in the way of the coach too much, will you?'

'Don't worry about it,' replied Ted. 'I think you'd best go and see Tony to get the latest info.' Which, looking quite puzzled, was exactly what Loada set off to do.

Hoping to find himself discussing a more normal, preferably profitable, subject, Ted gave his full attention to the chap who'd been looking for him

'Yes, sir, I believe you were looking for me – how can I help?'

'I'm Dave Marshall,' he replied, reaching out to shake hands. 'I believe my uncle mentioned me to you.'

'Ah' replied Ted, rather slowly as the penny dropped. 'I guess that means that Tom Willet is your uncle, then – he did mention you, but he failed to say that you're his nephew.'

'So, what did he say – nothing too harmful, I hope?' was the smiling reply.

'Not really, he said you were a slow payer, but that at least you did bring work for him! I can cope with slow payment, as long as the work is worth doing and I do get paid for it.'

'That's good to hear. The thing is, my situation's the same as with most builders, so I guess you'll know that I can only pay after my client has paid me – that OK with you, Mr Bailey?'

'Yes, that's fine. So, you being here – does that mean you've got some work you can put my way, or is it just a fact-finding mission?'

'Bit of both, really – and it's a bit tricky.'

'Well, to roughly quote your uncle – don't just stand there, let's hear what you've got to say. But perhaps over a cuppa in the workshop would be best, yes?'

So in they went, and Ted got on with the necessary with kettle, mugs and ingredients. This gave Dave Marshall the opportunity to do what he'd hoped for – to have a good look around to assess Ted's working set-up and probable capabilities – and he was quite pleased with what he saw.

'Right, Mr Marshall,' began Ted, 'or should it be Dave, if we're to have a working relationship? If we are, then I'm Ted.'

'It looks like you could cope with what I have in mind, Ted, so I hope we are going to work together – and on a project that should be starting soon. I guess you'll have heard of the small housing development planned for the

Parsons Lane area?' Ted's nod got him to continue. 'Well, Tom Willett – my uncle Tom – would have done the bulk of the interior carpentry work on the estate for me, so I need somebody to mainly take over —'

Before he could continue, Ted just had to interrupt – 'Can you explain what "mainly take over" means? When I saw him, I got the impression that Mr Willett couldn't actually handle anything much bigger than a cutlery drawer.'

'Sorry, Ted, but I'm just being a bit wary of getting it wrong... Look, this is the first development of this size that I've handled, and that goes for the landowners as well, so we're all being a bit tentative and limiting ourselves on what we commit to. I'm sorry if you need things to be more settled, but they aren't – not just at the moment.'

'OK,' said Ted, 'you carry on and I'll try to keep questions to the end.'

'Right. Well, for a start, I've already got chaps I've worked with before for the structural timbers – the roof, floors, staircases and so on – and the windows and doors are being bought in, complete. But all the rest – built-in cupboards, wardrobes and such like – they're to be made to meet customer requirements, and that's the stuff I'd want to bring to you. Then,' he carried on quickly before Ted could interrupt, 'out of that, I'd like you to use Uncle Tom for whatever you need and that he can cope with. How does that sound?'

'Wow, that sounds a bit grand. But doesn't it leave you a bit vulnerable to some outlandish requests for fixtures and fittings?'

'Oh no, Ted, the customers only get to choose from a limited range of designs – designs that the architect will put together to go with the overall outer spec and to stay inside the budget for the price range of the houses.'

'I assume I get to have a look at these designs before I commit to joining the team?'

'Of course, Ted. It'll be a couple of weeks before they're ready, but I know there'll be nothing outlandish because we have to keep each property to a reasonable price.'

'And how do you plan separating out the bits for Tom to do? If I pass bits on to him, how do you know who to pay for it – I don't think it would work having him on my books as an employee, would it?'

'Not surprised you asked that cos I'd wondered about it, myself. But it seems that one of the landowners has a background in some branch of industry and has come up with a scheme for numbering the parts used in each house. Then, if we put the numbers on work sheets, that means they can be traced from start to finish and show who worked on them. Must admit I had a bit of a job selling the idea to some of the other trades – one chap thought it might mean a disgruntled customer coming after him to fix a dripping tap a few years after the job's done! Happy to say there's no fear of that – the numbers don't go beyond completion, and certainly not to the customer. But it does make sure the right people get paid for the work that's done – and that includes Uncle Tom, OK?'

'That's fine,' said Ted, 'but where do you expect him to work? We can sort out a regular work space for him in here, if you like?'

'Yes, I'd hoped you could do that – it's near the site and I can get him here when there's stuff for him to do – I reckon he'll be happy with that. It's a nice place to work, here, isn't it? What other trades are there?'

'Down in the stable block, there's a saddler and a woman who works in wool. Then, across the way, there's Kelly's Kitchen – she does a packed lunch delivery service around the villages.'

'But what about the other two places along here – old coach-houses, weren't they?'

'Yes, they're much the same as this – the end one is storing second-hand stuff waiting to go to the hospice charity shop, I think. Next door's currently empty, and is going to stay that way, according to the news that came in this morning, but no-one knows how long for.'

'If it's going to be empty, who do I see about having it for a while?'

'That's Tony Philips, round at the manor house, but if you can tell me what you have in mind, I might save you the trip.'

'Well, once we start on the estate, it'd be an ideal store for me – really handy for the site.'

'Ah,' said Ted, 'I'm not sure he'd go along with that – he won't have loose stuff like sand and gravel around, nor the sorts of machines you'd be using to handle it.'

'No, Ted, nothing like that – it'd be the windows, timbers, white goods – all the sort of thing that needs to be kept clean, dry and, above all, safe.'

'Where is it all now?' asked Ted.

'A few bits for the first house are on order, but the thing is, if we have the right storage, we can order in bulk and get better prices – keep costs down.'

'You'd best have a word with Tony, then. Do you want me to introduce you, or do you know him already?'

'We bumped into each other a couple of times a few years ago, but I'd like you to come along to make sure he gets the full picture. Then I'm off for another look at the site – you can come along if you like.'

Ted did like, and was pleased when Tony approved of the builder's plan for bringing the middle coach-house into use, and at a profit. So, it was a happy Dave Marshall that walked up to the village with Ted and showed him the intended locations of the first four houses to be built along Parsons Lane.

'Looks like all the current buildings are to go then, Dave?' queried Ted.

'Yes, they've had compulsory purchase orders on all of them but they're not being enforced until the plots are needed. I've been told that only one has been permanently occupied, but it's going to be cleared any time now ready for us to get to work on the whole site.'

Ted realised that the building that Dave was talking about was the Scattergood home. He was sure that no-one had mentioned anything about Hattie and her mother having to move out – perhaps the villagers had felt they might jinx the move if it was talked about! Anyway, it was none of his business, so he said nothing.

'What do you think of the site then, Ted?' asked Dave.

'Sorry, Dave, but I don't really know what to say – I've not been in here before and I didn't realise how big the copse was. And it's hard to imagine how it will look with houses, gardens, and a paved road instead of some of the trees, and the lane and this couple of shacks. I always think these artists impressions, that you see in the local papers, make the whole place look so much bigger than it actually is.'

'I tend to agree with you, but they're trying to show a front view of both sides of the road at the same time, and it's not easy! Anyway, I'm not here to do any more than just keep the area in my mind's eye, so, if you've seen enough, shall we call it a day and repair to the local hostelry and seal our future deal with a small glass of something?'

'Thanks,' said Ted, 'but it's too early for that for me, but another coffee would go down nicely.'

Dave agreed, so they went to the Red Lion, found that they were the first customers, and ordered two cups of coffee from the duty barman.

'Jim having a day off,' asked Ted, 'or just having a lie-in?'

'It's the full weekend off, at last, but he still can't get away – he's having a coffee in the residents' lounge if you really need to see him.'

Before Ted could reply, Jim appeared, mug in hand, to get a coffee refill.

'Morning, Ted – and isn't it Dave Marshall, the builder of houses and the bringer of more customers to my bar?'

'Yes, to all that, Jim,' replied Ted, while Dave and Jim shook hands, 'but we're also after some info – at least I am.'

'What's that then?'

'I wondered if you'd heard anything about the Scattergood family – perhaps moving out? I'm sure you hear all the gossip over the bar.'

'Sorry, chaps, that hasn't been mentioned at all, though I guess her house is near where you're going to put the new ones, so something's bound to be mentioned sooner or later

– perhaps if you popped in a bit more often, Ted, you'd keep up to date!' and Jim dodged quickly away from the mock punch that Ted threw.

Chapter 26

It was Thursday teatime and Jim Parker was pacing around his family rooms in the Red Lion like a cat on hot bricks, wishing he'd not had that second – or was it his third? – cup of coffee. Pauline would be here soon and the last thing he wanted to do was make it obvious that he'd been counting the minutes since she made her room booking for the weekend. Then, at long last, the in-house phone rang and he grabbed it, almost knocking over the bedside table.

'Hello.'

'Just checking if Room 3 is ready,' was the coded message from Reception, indicating that Pauline Clark had arrived.

'Just finishing – I'll be down to collect the guest's luggage,' was the agreed response in case anyone could overhear them.

He rang off, checked his hair in the mirror, hoped he wouldn't start blushing, and headed down to reception where he found Pauline studying a Salchester visitor leaflet.

'Good afternoon, madam, can I take your case and show you to your room?' he managed, without stuttering.

'Yes, thank you,' she began, before turning and realising who it was. 'Jim, I didn't expect you to be here – didn't you say you were having a long weekend off?'

'I did, indeed, and I am – in order to be at your service to transport you wherever the whim takes you, hopefully to show you the delights of our fair city and picturesque countryside.' He finished with a mock bow to cover up the seriousness behind his little speech.

'But what about the inn? Shouldn't you be here all the time looking after things?'

'I'm sorry, Mrs Clark,' he almost stuttered, 'that was too presumptuous of me. Yes, I'm usually here, but I do take time out occasionally and I'm well backed-up by Mike, who just booked you in, and Steve who's his number two. So having time off is quite normal – I just presumed – I'm sorry…'

'Gosh, Jim, it's me that should apologise – it's really kind of you to offer to show me around, and I never expected it – that's mainly why I'm here a day early, to get around while the buses are running.'

'Yes, you mentioned that when you phoned to book, and I remembered how Alison Bailey took you around on your last visit. I don't know if you've been in touch with her recently, but she's now doing a lot more to help Kelly with her sandwich deliveries. If she's not as available as last time, I'm here to offer my services as a guide and/or companion.'

'Thanks for that, Jim, I'd rather taken it for granted that Alison would be available again – whatever will she think of me, not even being in touch?'

'Don't worry about that – she'll be pleased to see you. So, do you have any specific plans – things to do or places to visit? And what about Boots?'

'Oh, he doesn't need me to look after him!! Actually, part of the timing of this visit is down to him and Anna – they want to look at a couple of colleges that are running the sorts of courses they want to take. They think that Fridays and Saturdays would be good times to visit, and Tony is going to take them.'

'I hope you've not had too much of your lad's company on the way down – Tony's invited us to have dinner with the three of them this evening, and I said I'd let him have your answer. Would that be OK with you?'

'That sounds lovely, Jim, but I haven't brought any clothes suitable for dinner at the Manor! I'd love to go, but will I be OK dressing casual, like this?'

'Don't worry about that, he's taking us to a nice little restaurant in the city, and there's no dress code. If you're up for it, I can give him a ring and confirm timing.'

'Yes, that sounds fine – thanks. You know, I hardly know Tony, even though Boots and Anna are so close and spend so much time together – it'll be nice to get to know him a bit better.'

With that all agreed, Jim showed Pauline to her room, rang Tony – and at last relaxed!

A couple of hours later, as he and Pauline were about to leave the inn, Jim suddenly remembered that he had to tell Mike about something that might crop up later, so he called him over to the reception counter.

'Mike, if the Pritchards turn up and want to store their trailer safely overnight, use the spare key and let them into the garage. But don't give them the key, just lock up after them, OK? There's stuff of mine in there that needs keeping safe. I'll sort it out with them in the morning.'

'That sounded a bit cloak and dagger, didn't it, Jim?' asked Pauline, as they set off in his car.

'No, far from it,' he replied. 'Just a family coming to help somebody move house, so they're bringing a little trailer – probably for stuff they can't get in the removal van. They were bothered that it might get wet – or even stolen, I suppose – if it was left out overnight. They'd hoped to be using one of the places down at the manor, so I was just setting that up with Mike in case they get to the manor after Tony leaves. Mind you, they weren't certain they'd get here today – something to do with possible hospital appointments'

'Is it somebody local that's moving?'

'No idea – it's not a name I know. Probably somewhere in Salchester – and were perhaps told about the manor through Reg and Tony's house clearance business. All good trade for me, though.'

'You know, Jim, I think you're very lucky here – nice location, friendly community.'

'Me too, but I don't say it out loud in case it turns my luck.'

Arriving at the restaurant near the middle of Salchester, Jim was relieved to find that Tony, Anna and Boots were only just ahead of them. He quietly told Tony what he'd arranged for the Pritchards, and was really pleased that he had, as Tony had completely forgotten it was for today. This was so out of character for him that Tony started mulling over recent events and conversations to see if he might have missed anything else, but Anna soon brought him back to earth by asking if she could have a glass of sherry to start the meal.

'I don't think so, young lady, but what about you, Pauline?' he asked.

'That'd be lovely, thank you,' she replied, only to feel a blush developing as she realised that he was actually asking her opinion on whether Anna should have one. Thankfully, a burst of laughter from Jim and a 'Well done, Mum!' from Boots, saved her from trying to get out of the hole she'd started digging.

The evening turned out to be yet another of those occasions when sitting down to enjoy a meal together was proving to be a great way of getting to know people. Pauses while food was enjoyed gave time for both questions and answers to be created and considered, and there were very few occasions when voices clashed.

Then, at a point when Tony and Jim were into a tax-related discussion, Pauline took the chance to quietly say to Anna that it was a pity her dad didn't have a lady friend with him.

'Silly man doesn't even look for one, as far as I can tell,' she replied. 'And he doesn't have to look far to find somebody that would suit him down to the ground.'

'You have somebody in mind then?' asked Pauline.

'Yes, and I'm not the only one,' she replied. 'Everybody that knows them thinks the same – it's just that neither of them talks about their private lives, so there's no chance for anything to happen.'

'What about the people around them when they meet?'

'That's the trouble, they only meet at work, and then there's only work that gets talked about.'

'But still...'

'Look Pauline – is it alright to call you Pauline, Mrs Clark?' The nod got her to continue. 'The person concerned is Julie, who works with him and Reg. The three of them really are the Salchester company, as well as the Enterprise, so they're always meeting, but it's always about work!'

'I see what you mean.'

'But,' Anna continued, having seen an opening, 'now that you know that Julie exists, there'd be no harm, and probably a lot of good, if you got the chance to ask him something about her.'

'Thanks, Anna, I'll bear that in mind.'

Some time later, and in all innocence, Pauline asked Tony if he'd decided on a seating arrangement for the weekend trip.

'Sorry, love,' he replied, 'I don't follow – what do you mean?'

'Well, if you're taking Boots as well as Anna, which of them is going to sit up front with you and help navigate?'

'Ah, I see what you mean – what about it, you two? Who's going to make sure I get you to the places you want to see?'

'Aw, Dad, Boots is only here for the weekend so there's not much time for us to chat – do you really need someone in the front with you? We can have the map in the back and tell you what road to take.'

'Not the same, love. I need someone to help remember landmarks as well, to help with the journey back.' He looked thoughtful as he contemplated his next forkful of food, then went on. 'I wonder about Whacker – but I suppose he'd want Tina along as well, and that's the car overloaded.'

'Sorry, Tony, but Tina's on duty as a sort of stand-in when I'm not in – like this evening. Anyway, I don't think Whacker would be up for it. Tina said that he sounded pretty upset about something when she rang him just before we came out.'

'Mm, wonder what that could be – Whacker's usually the sunniest of people.'

'Isn't there someone else you could you take?' asked Pauline.

'You don't want to come along, do you?'

'Not at all, Tony, but surely there's someone you know that'd enjoy the day out?'

'Like who?'

'Oh, I don't know what friends you've got – is there somebody on their own, perhaps?'

'What about Scatty Hattie?' Jim jumped in with a laugh.

'Thanks for that, Jim – I'd drive blind-folded first! Right, you lot, any other bright ideas, or do we draw lots?'

'Have you thought about Julie, Dad?'

'You mean our Julie? Julie at work?'

'Unless you know any others that you're keeping quiet about.'

'But she only knows me through work, and she won't want to risk talking about that all day long. No, I can't see her being at all interested.'

'That's the problem, Dad – you can't see what's around you sometimes! Didn't you once tell me she'd dipped into her savings to help you buy the manor when your shares weren't enough? Surely that shows she's interested in what you do, what happens to you? Why not just give her a ring so she's got time to be ready – we're setting off fairly early, aren't we?'

Without waiting for a reply, and striking while the iron was hot, Anna beckoned over the waiter and asked if her dad could make an urgent call from the restaurant phone. Then, to make absolutely sure, she even went with him and stood in the doorway to the small office while he placed and started the call.

When the pair returned to their table, Anna was full of smiles while Tony looked slightly bemused.

'But that's our Julie,' he kept saying. 'We used to call her the dragon when we started at Mr Hady's. You had to knock at the office door and not dare go in until she called out.'

'I guess she never told you why, did she?'

'What was there to tell?'

'Simply that she just couldn't understand Mr Hady's accounting system, so she noted things in her way – the way she'd been taught in book-keeping classes at school – and when she'd got them sorted she transferred them into his books. She wouldn't let anybody into the office while she'd got notes all over the place, that was all.'

'Well, blow me!'

'Looks like you've got a lot of catching-up to do tomorrow, Tony,' said Pauline. 'But don't forget you'll have a valuable cargo with my lad and your daughter on the back seat – just be careful how you drive!'

Although she had said it fairly seriously, Pauline's comment didn't dampen the mood of the party. When the evening ended, it was on a happy note, with each group wishing a happy, successful weekend to the other.

CHAPTER 27

The morning after the dinner in Salchester, Jim Parker was feeling a little unsure about what to do about breakfast – although Pauline was at the Red Lion as a paying guest, he found that he thought of her more as being a close friend, almost a personal visitor. The question he'd asked himself a hundred times was – should he invite her to have breakfast with him in the family rooms, as he and Tina often did or, if he shared her table in the dining room, would it look almost as if he were checking on his staff? Deciding that Pauline might not be happy in the family quarters, Jim waited until she came down, showed her to her table, and asked if he might join her – she was happy with that, job done!

Unfortunately, they had not gone beyond ordering their meals when Jim was called away to the phone in the office and came back looking both annoyed and upset.

'Sorry, Pauline, but I won't be able to take you into the city today – that was Mike's wife. He's fallen in the bath and cut his head rather badly. She called the ambulance and they're taking him to hospital for stitches and probably an x-ray!'

'Oh, poor Mike – but don't worry about me, Jim, I can still go in on the bus as I'd planned.'

'Would you like me to ask around, perhaps and see if Alison is free to go with you?'

'No, don't fuss, Jim – I'm a big girl and can find my own way around. Though actually I probably won't go much further than last time – I want to spend more time in the cathedral and along the lanes that go out to the salt quay and market. In fact, I'll probably be better on my own without having to wonder if somebody with me is getting bored!'

So that's what happened, and Jim was somewhat pleased about it a little later when he found himself dealing with a rather irate council official accompanied by an engineer from the water company.

'No, sorry, gents,' he replied, when they came in and asked if he had seen, or did he know where they might find, anyone from the Scattergood family. 'Miss Scattergood is often off on the bus into town, but I don't always see her. Do you want to leave a message?'

Obviously the wrong response, as the council chap almost exploded!

'Most certainly not! We've left enough messages and written enough letters – and we know they've received them! This is a health emergency, on top of a pending Compulsory Purchase Order! And we can see some wretched woman sitting in the kitchen, just gazing out of the back window and totally ignoring us! This can't go on! If someone doesn't open the door for us, we'll have no option but to force a way in!'

While this tirade was being delivered, the water company chap was looking more and more embarrassed, and smiled apologetically, before asking Jim, 'Any ideas?'

'I think I know someone who can help, so why not have a seat and try to relax a bit with a tea or coffee on the house while I make a phone call?'

Urged by the engineer, they went over to a table near a window and accepted the drinks brought to them by Tina, who'd overheard most of it.

'If you've seen somebody in there,' she said, 'I think that'll be old Mrs Scattergood – I hear she's very frail and probably couldn't get to the door to let you in, even if she heard you. Anyway, I'm sure my dad will sort something out.'

In the office, Jim was trying to do just that, and started by phoning Loada Cole's home. He was out, but his wife remembered how Eileen had been able to get into the Scattergood home to get a letter, and suggested he rang her, which he did. Having explained the situation, Eileen said she'd come over to the Lion and see what she could do – hoping that Hattie hadn't changed where she hid the spare key.

When Jim reported this back to the men, they were somewhat mollified, but that changed when Eileen arrived and asked to see their authority to enter the Scattergood home.

'But, but....' The man from the council spluttered, while the engineer produced his works identity card and smiled apologetically as he showed it to Eileen.

Even as the second card was produced, identifying the man as John Hudson of the County Council's housing department, Eileen continued to state her terms. 'All I'll do is go into the home to tell them you're there and ask if you can go in – if the occupants are not willing to let you into their home, then that's final, OK?'

'But there's the health problem and the Compulsory —'

'I'm sorry,' she interrupted, 'but that's the resident's rights and I'm representing them, so those are the terms, take it or leave it!'

Seeing they had little option, the men, naturally represented by the council official, agreed to the terms, finished their coffees and set off. Eileen was not as sure of her ground as she'd tried to sound, so she beckoned Jim over and asked if he'd kindly join the group, if only to be a witness to whatever might transpire. He agreed, and they set off to follow the two men towards Parsons Lane but, before they arrived, Eileen quietly asked Jim to try to cover up where she went for the hidden key.

'I wouldn't put it past that Hudson chap to sneak back and let himself in if he sees where the key is left,' she explained. Naturally, Jim said he'd do what he could to distract them.

Arriving at the Scattergood home, Eileen went round to the side and returned a moment later holding a key aloft.

'Right, gentlemen, I'm going in, and you're to wait there – Mr Parker is here as a witness, so I don't want anybody trying to follow me in, OK?'

There were quiet mutterings from John Hudson, but Eileen turned her back on them, unlocked the door and called out, quietly, 'Hello Mrs Scattergood, it's just me again, Nurse Eileen. Some gentlemen from the council just need to pop in and have a look at a couple of things – is that alright?'

The figure gazing out of the kitchen window gave no response, not even any indication that Eileen had been heard. So, assuming the old lady was dozing, Eileen approached the rocking chair and gently touched her on the shoulder.

The men, standing expectantly outside, suddenly heard an almighty piercing scream followed by a soft thud, for all the world as if Eileen had been clubbed and fallen to the ground. The water engineer, being both the youngest and a trained first-aider, was first through the door, to be confronted by the sight of Eileen, bent double and with a hand covering her mouth, gazing horror-stricken at the now headless figure in the chair.

'Good God,' he exclaimed, 'what on earth has happened here?'

By that time, the other two were in the room and Jim went over to console Eileen. She was as white as a sheet, wanting to, but trying not to, look again at the headless body she had exposed.

Unsurprisingly, it was the man from the council who took control of the situation.

'Right, let's have you all outside – there's nothing we can do for the poor woman and this is obviously a crime scene, so we need the police here ASAP.'

There was no argument with that, and they quickly made their way out again. But, on reaching the door and casting a final look back over her shoulder, Eileen brought the exodus to a halt as she pointed out that there was no blood on, or anywhere near, the top of the body. At about the same time the engineer caught sight of the head where it had rolled under the dining table.

'Hang on, a minute,' he said, 'that's no head, and I bet that's no human body. We need a closer look before we make ourselves look stupid.'

So saying, he went back inside, reached under the table and brought out a head-sized cabbage wrapped in a pale pink towel!

'Blow me!' 'What on earth?' 'What the heck?' were just a few of the expressions being aired, indicating the understandable confusion reigning in the small group.

It was Eileen who was first to put forward a reasonable explanation. 'Looks like Hattie did that to put off anybody who thought the place was empty – and to give herself a bit of a sense of company when she was in here on her own. The poor girl's obviously been having a difficult time and didn't know where to turn for help!'

'That's all very well,' interrupted Mr Hudson, 'but where is the person that dummy is supposed to represent? It looks to me as if the registered resident, a Mrs M Scattergood, is absent – perhaps technically missing – and her absence is being covered up for some reason! I still think this is a case for the police.'

'I'm no expert,' said Jim, 'but I'm inclined to agree with you – just in case a serious crime is being covered up.'

There were nods of agreement, so Jim went on: 'If you're happy here, Eileen, I'll nip back to the Lion and try Loada again – if he's out, perhaps his wife can give me a number and name to ask for in town, I'm sure this isn't urgent enough to call 999.'

There was no disagreement, so off he went, rang Loada's number, spoke to his wife Jenny, and from her got the number in Salchester that soon found him explaining the situation to Loada's boss, Sgt Collins.

'We've had no reports of any incidents to do with that name,' the sergeant said, after Jim had explained the situation. 'But – wait a minute – there were some mutterings in the station a little while ago about a young woman called Scattergood bringing a very unpleasant smell with her – sounds like it could be the same family. But, look, I'll get DC Cole to go over and see what he makes of it. In the meantime, it seems like the chap from the council is the only officially responsible person there, so can you ask him to stay there until Cole turns up? And if that nurse knows the family well, she may spot if there's anything looking out of the ordinary.'

With that seeming to be settled and out of his hands, Jim set off back to Parsons Lane, passed on the messages, and was leaving again just as Loada arrived.

'What started all this, Jim?' he asked. 'Sounds like we've opened a real can of worms.'

'No, I don't think so, Loada – looks like young Hattie made herself a dummy to warn people off, but now she's away somewhere just when her bluff's being called. It's that council chap, Hudson, that's making a mountain out of a mole hill. If it was down to me, I'd get that sewer fixed – it really does need doing – then lock up and wait for Hattie to reappear. He can't sort out any problems when there's nobody there to deal with – but that's officials, for you!'

'Hey, give over, Jim! I'm an official, if you'd forgotten!'

On that note, they separated, and Jim was pleased to get back to a bit of normality at the Red Lion – a normality that saw him having to deal straight away with an unexpected problem.

'Had a call from a Mr Pritchard just now, Dad,' Tina reported. 'They're just leaving a garage where their car was taken for repair yesterday, and he wanted to let us know they still want their rooms for tonight and probably tomorrow. I checked the book and it all looks OK, and I told him that, but he said they might also need another night. I told him I'd tell you, etc., and he seemed happy about that – OK?'

The pleasant meal of yesterday evening, and the kerfuffle this morning, had all helped Jim to forget about the Pritchard family – and their trailer.

'Yes, that's fine, love, as long as I don't find my car marooned outside if he has problems with their trailer and they want to leave it in the garage again. I'd better have a word with Tony and check if he's really got storage space for it.'

'You're probably too late for that, Dad – they were supposed to be off early for the run into Wales, weren't they?'

'Never mind, we'll play it by ear. But if you see Ted Bailey, or Whacker of course, they might know. Oh, and Loada might know because of the coach coming back. Why do we have to take on other people's problems, Tina?'

'That's you, Dad, "Mine Host" with a host of problems!!'

Chapter 28

On that same Friday, the lunch period in the Red Lion was almost over, when a small family group came in – an elderly lady helped by a younger man and a young woman, who turned out to be the man's wife.

'I'm terribly sorry about all the problems we've caused,' the man said, 'but do you think my mother could have a glass of water, and could we all have a sandwich or something simple to eat, please, and cups of tea, if it's no trouble?'

'Of course you can,' replied Jim, signalling Tina to see to at least the water. 'But what problems are we talking about? I don't think we've met, have we?'

'No, we haven't, sorry – there's so much been happening, and plans going astray, it's hard to keep track of where we are, who we've spoken to, and so on. Right, my name's Pritchard, this is my wife, and this is my mother, Mrs Scattergood, and we've been messing you about with not turning up for our room bookings.'

'Ah, the elusive Pritchards!' said Jim with a smile that showed no harm had been done. 'And I'm curious to know if you've fixed up a shelter for your trailer with Mr Philips.'

Before anyone could reply, Tina appeared with a tray holding a glass of water and two cups of tea, put it down and turned to Jim. 'Come on, Dad, give the poor folks time to relax before you start quizzing them. You know we can sort something out for their trailer, whatever happens.'

Turning to the Pritchard/Scattergood family, she said 'Do have a relax. The sandwiches are on their way, and you can go into the Residents' Lounge, if you'd prefer.'

'No, I'm sure we'll be fine here, thanks – gives us room to stretch our legs a bit, as well as get back into the real world after hours in the car – many of them in traffic jams, too.'

Accepting that he'd have to wait to get any more useful information from them, Jim switched attention to a couple of his regulars already into their usual afternoon tipples.

Fortunately, they were at the far end of the bar, more or less out of the earshot of the family.

'Did I hear the name Scattergood mentioned just then?' murmured one of them.

'Think so – it was the older woman – the chap said she's his mother! Different name like that sounds like a second marriage somewhere along the line.'

'Yes – wonder if the Hattie girl fits in there anywhere? Jim'll find out and tell us, won't you Jim?' he asked, as Jim approached to get a nearby bottle from the shelf behind the bar.

'If you're talking about the new arrivals, I'll only tell you anything they say out in the open – you know that. Anything in confidence, even simply in private, it stays that way, so – no public speculation, if you don't mind. I don't want them being embarrassed and deciding to leave!'

That really slowed the two of them down – Jim very rarely spoke as firmly as that, but he was relaxed when he returned to serving the new customer. Then he called for Tina to come through from the kitchen where she usually helped as needed.

'Yes, Dad, what needs doing?' she asked.

'Nothing, love, I just wondered if you'd heard anything from Whacker about Tony setting something up for the Pritchards' trailer? If he's not said anything, perhaps you could give him a ring and find out – I don't really like my car out in the open if Tony's got a place ready for them.'

'Haven't spoken to him today. When I rang to see if he's decided about the pictures tomorrow, Alison said he was still really upset and she was leaving him to come out of it on his own.'

'What's he upset about? That's not like him, is it?'

'Oh, with all the Parsons Lane activity I didn't get chance to tell you. Well, it's about that plush version of a board game he's making. It seems the designer had got all excited again about the game itself and had been trying to find a company to take it on and publish it – if publish is the right word.' A nod from Jim. 'It seems that he'd tried this before, years ago, and got nowhere. But this time he felt stronger about it and was getting really uptight with one particular company that he felt was stringing him along and perhaps even trying to diddle him. Anyway, he'd just come off the phone to them when he had a heart attack and dropped dead!'

'Good heavens! Poor Whacker and poor Ted – they must feel they sort of encouraged his interest, I suppose.'

'It's worse than that, Dad. The chap's wife – sorry, widow – she's said that that's just what they did, and she's banned them from doing any more work on it – ever – and is demanding that they hand over all the material to her solicitors, even the work that Whacker had done.'

'Wow, that's strong stuff – are they doing it, do you know?'

'Well, you know Ted – doing his best to settle into the community, build up his business. But, on the other hand, he wants to protect his lad from what they both feel are unjust accusations. This won't get settled easily, by the sound of it, so I reckon we'd best let them come back to normal in their own time.'

'Poor them, and poor woman too. And I know Ted liked the chap as well – he'd helped him sort out some mortgage issues. Let's hope that time heals things. When you do speak to Whacker or the family, give them by best wishes, won't you?'

'Thanks, Dad, but I think the situation leaves us looking after Mr Pritchard's trailer, unless they tell us different.'

After that, the afternoon moved along on at its usual pace – the Pritchards went to their rooms to unpack and freshen up, and the usual groups of locals came and went in the bar as was their wont.

Then, later than usual, Hattie came in, closely followed by the water company engineer. He thanked Jim for his earlier help, then ordered a long cool soft drink to slake his thirst before setting off for the drive back to his depot and then home.

'Not got Mr Hudson still chasing things?' asked Jim.

'That man!!' interrupted Hattie. 'Officialdom personified. He wouldn't accept that I didn't know where my mother was, so she could come and deal with this purchase order.'

'But I assume that's her here,' said Jim, 'as part of the Pritchard party.'

'Yes, that's right,' she said. 'I met them in the village, but I didn't know if she was in the bar, or the lounge, or if she'd already gone up to her room!' And she put on a really innocent, apologetic look that turned into a smile

The three or four regulars witnessing that, realised that this was a side of Hattie that had never been seen or heard before – they also realised that she wasn't surrounded by her usual awful stench.

Then, one of them spoke up – 'Hattie, did I hear you say your mother was here, in the Lion?'

'That's right, Tom, and you can have a word with her when she comes down for a meal this evening, if you like.' As she often did, she finished with a sweet smile, but this time she didn't switch her demeanour, and the smile remained, leaving the others somewhat puzzled.

'If you're not pulling my leg, young miss, I'll hang around till she appears,' he replied.

'No, Tom, I meant it about this evening. Perhaps if you wait for her in the Residents Lounge, say about half past six, she'll come and find you in there. Is that OK?'

'I suppose it's got to be – but I will be there at half past six, young lady, so I hope she will be, too!'

With that settled, more or less satisfactorily, Hattie went to look for her brother to tell him what had been happening at the Parsons Lane cottage.

Tom Grover finished his drink and left the bar to take a walk, trying to marshal his thoughts and decide what to say to the woman who'd occupied his thoughts for most of his life. Half past six found him, as promised, pacing about the Residents Lounge, but still undecided on what to say and what outcome he hoped for.

When the door opened and Mrs Scattergood started to come in, he stopped, looked at her, and said, 'I'm sorry, madam, but this room's been booked for a private meeting.'

'I know, Tom – it's for me to meet you and explain things.' And she came fully into the room, using a walking stick to aid her progress.

'But I was told Hattie Scattergood's mother would come and talk to me – who are you?'

'Oh, my name is Scattergood, all right, and I'm known as Hattie's mum, but I'm not the woman you once knew.'

'Well, you certainly don't look like I imagined after all these years. But who are you, and does Hattie know who you really are?'

'Oh, yes, Hattie and all the family know – so, perhaps if you settle down, I can explain.'

'Well,' said Tom, rather grumpily, 'somebody had better come up with a reasonable explanation – I reckon I'm being taken for a fool, or I need a good explanation.'

Miffed as he was, Tom remembered his manners, offered her a chair, then went to the door and asked a hovering Jim for a tray of tea for them both. Neither of them spoke as they waited, but Tom's mind was racing, and when the tray arrived and he'd served them both, he could wait no longer.

'Right, madam, let's start by you telling me who you are.'

'I'm Margaret Scattergood.'

'But you're not Hattie's mother, are you?'

'No, I'm her aunt, her dad's sister, but she's always called me Mum – even after we told her my true identity.'

'How long has this been going on, and where is her real mum – Margaret Fenton, as was?'

'Perhaps I should tell you the whole story, and you save any questions to the end – how is that?'

'OK, but it had better not be a fairy story!'

'Oh, Tom, I'm so sorry – I know you're very disappointed. Hattie has told me how you keep asking about her mother.'

'OK, stop trying to butter me up and just get on with it!' It seemed that Tom was finding it hard to treat this woman with the kindness and respect that he had shown when the meeting had begun.

'For a start, I should tell you that Hattie's parents did not have a happy marriage. He had a roving eye and, after David, their first child, was born, he would even go off for a weekend with his latest conquest.'

'How could he do that,' Tom just had to interject, 'when he'd got a lovely wife there?'

'I know, Tom, and she once said she was sure she would have had a happier life with you.'

'Blow me, why didn't she say something?'

'How could she? She didn't even see you in the village. When she was out and about with the children, you were at work. In the evenings and at weekends it was the other way round – she was at home with the family, and you were with your mates.'

'Yes, see what you mean.'

'Anyway, when David was six, along came Harriet, and her dad seemed to be a lot more settled – but after about 18 months or so, he was back to his old philandering ways. Then, without warning, he upped and left – no forwarding address, nothing!'

Tom was quietly seething, wishing he could ring the so-and-so's neck.

'Anyway,' the woman went on, 'I felt the least I could do was to come along and help, but I've never been sure if it was a good thing or not. I more or less took over full responsibility for the home as well as the children while she sank deeper and deeper into depression. She would get the bus into town and just wonder around all day, probably hoping to see him – I followed her once and it was a sad sight. Then one day she didn't come home – she'd fallen under a bus – they called it an accident, but was it? We'll never know, of course.'

She paused and wondered if that was a tear she saw in Tom's eye – she certainly felt the familiar lump in her own throat.

'I had no obligations elsewhere and I really had no option but to stay on and look after the children, and they gradually drifted into calling me Mum.'

'But surely the authorities knew you weren't the real mother?'

'Of course, and it's never been hidden, but we were both Margaret Scattergood – her married name and my maiden name. I was "Miss" and she had been "Mrs", but you don't always have to give your marital status. And if you're wondering about the name Pritchard, when he was old enough to understand what had happened, David properly changed his to my mother's maiden name.'

While that answered all Tom's main queries, he was curious about one other thing. 'How have you both managed to live with that smell that young Hattie carries around with her? I hear it's been coming from an underground pipe, or something.'

'That started after I'd left to go and live with David but, of course, Hattie couldn't smell it so she just wasn't aware of it. She wanted to see if she could find work around here, but she's given up on that and is moving up North to be near the rest of us.'

'Well, that's a sad day for me,' said Tom, looking truly as sad as he probably felt. 'As long as Hattie was there, I lived in hope that I'd get chance to see her mum – her real mum – again. What you've told me is not what I wanted to hear, but thank you for clearing things up. How much can I tell people if they ask me – and they're certain to do that!?'

'There's nothing secret, Tom, you can say as much as you like – and I'm so sorry it's hit you so hard. Will you be alright?'

'Oh, yes. But I might think about moving near my brother, in Lincolnshire – make a fresh start, even though it's a bit late in the day.'

'Whatever you do, Tom, we all wish you well – Hattie has told us about how you cared about her mother and, if you wanted to keep in touch with the family, I can give you our address.'

That was the end of a very sad meeting for them both. Margaret Scattergood's report to the family cast a cloud over their evening meal, while Tom went for a long walk to think things over before returning to his farm cottage.

Chapter 29

Returning to the Red Lion after a full day in Salchester, Pauline was tired and rather relieved to find that Jim was fully occupied that evening. After an early meal she went up to her room, and it was next morning before they could meet up, again to have breakfast together. (Mike had returned to duty that morning, sporting a plaster to protect his wound.) Although she was keen to tell Jim all about her day in the city, Pauline was intrigued by a buzz of conversation around a table in the far corner of the room, and asked Jim about it.

'Ah, you missed all the fun there,' he said. 'That's the Scattergood family, minus the daughter Hattie – but let me tell you about it later when they're not so near.'

Lowering her voice, Pauline just had to ask, 'Why, Jim, they don't all smell, do they?'

It was all Jim could do to grab his serviette to stifle a burst of laughter and pretend it had been a slight cough, before managing to assure her quietly that that particular trait did not run through the family genes. 'I'll tell you later, but first, how was your day?'

'It was great – better than I'd expected,' she began. 'I started at the cathedral to make sure that I had time for a proper look at the copes, and who should be there but the woman who gave me the information about the Embroiderers Guild. Unfortunately, she remembered me and asked if I'd been able to follow it up, and of course I hadn't, except to find that there was nowhere local enough for me. Anyway, she'd come in for a sort of induction process for a new member of the group and invited me to go and have a look, so I did. But that was in the afternoon – for the rest of the morning I did more of the tourist things.'

'Enjoy it?' he asked.

'Yes, I did, and in a tea shop I found a copy of the Aspire magazine that Alison takes around, so I asked a guide in the cathedral about its name. He explained it, and I think it's quite cute, so I'm looking forward to telling Alison – hoping she doesn't already know.'

'And?'

'Well, the chap obviously enjoyed telling the story and had a real twinkle in his eye when he said "It's called that because it's what we've got!" So, I just had to say – "But, aspire is what you do, and if you do aspire, then what you've got is aspiration". "Oh, no," he said, "a spire is what we've got! Have a look up at the roof when you go outside!" So I did, and it's true.'

'So,' again prodded Jim.

'Well, it seems that not all cathedrals have spires, particularly just one of them – the best-known is probably Salisbury – so they're quite proud of the one here, and somebody obviously thought the magazine's name might draw attention to it.'

'Hadn't worked with me,' Jim said, 'but then, I'm not often ambling round the city and looking at the rooftops just for the pleasure of it.'

'If it hadn't been for poor old Mike, you could have done, yesterday.'

That seemed to end that particular train of conversation, and they concentrated more on the meal, until Jim at last felt ready to pick up the thread.

'What about going in today, now I'm on holiday again?'

'Thanks, Jim, but I really had enough yesterday – I'd much rather mooch around the area today – if that's not too boring for you?'

'No, it's OK – I'm beginning to realise I just don't seem to take much time off just to lounge around and do nothing. So where do you fancy?'

'Just around the village would be lovely – and I'd love to go along to the ford again; I found it almost mesmerising last time.'

'That's fine by me.' A slight pause, then, 'Look, if you're not in a rush, there's a couple of points I need to pass on to Mike – but the papers should be in in the lounge if you can give me half an hour?'

With that settled, they went their separate ways, each quietly looking forward to some time in the other's company. So the first thing they did, as planned, was to stroll along to the ford, lean on the handrail and gaze at the water, as countless others had before them.

Eventually it was Pauline who broke the spell to comment, 'I just can't imagine how your wife, or anybody for that matter, could just walk away from here.' She paused for a moment, then looked at him and said, 'I hope I know what you're answer will be, Jim, but I have to ask – you're not a wife-beater, are you?'

For the second time that morning Jim was forced to stifle a laugh at her straight-forwardness, almost naiveté.

'No, Pauline, I'm not,' he managed, after a moment to draw breath. 'If you want the simple honest truth, I was a disappointment to her ambitions.'

'But you own a lovely inn in a pleasant peaceful village, you're well respected, and the inn seems prosperous – what more did she need?'

'All along, she'd compared me with her dad. He was a well-respected figure in their community and I liked him, and admired, and respected him – still do – but I wasn't going to turn into a replica of him. You see, he was big in the commercial side of banking, while I just loved the face-to-face of a high street branch. And when that side of the business started to slim down, I wasn't interested in switching over, in spite of all the hints and digs from her, and offers of help from him. So, really, it came down to the fact that she wasn't happy in my world, and I wouldn't have been in theirs.'

'Oh, Jim, I'm so sorry – and sorry I asked. I didn't want to bring up a painful topic, but I was so happy with my husband, and so devastated when he was killed, I just couldn't imagine anyone walking away from all this – and from you,' she ended, very quietly.

Back in Parsons Lane, the Scattergood family were clearing smaller items from the cottage, and loading them into their trailer. They'd not quite finished when a large van turned up, collected the remaining items – mainly larger pieces of furniture – and took it all away. When the cottage was finally empty and swept out, the family had their last looks around, said goodbye to it, closed and locked the door for the last time, and drove away.

Arriving back at the Red Lion, Hattie was the first out of the car, and was met by a rather agitated-looking Mrs Gilbert – Auntie Viv.

'Oh, Harriet, I'm so glad I've caught you – I thought you might have left already – Mr Gasson, my neighbour, couldn't get his car to start and I just didn't know where to look for you in the village and it's such a pretty place and I'm going to miss our little chats over a cup of tea.' And she stopped, with the hint of a tear in her eyes.

By this time, Hattie's brother had taken their car and trailer round to the pub's car park and come back to find his mother, his sister, and his wife, all gathered around and trying to calm this elderly lady. He was quickly included in the introductions, then shepherded them all inside and into the lounge where Mike soon brought them a tray of teas and coffees.

Hattie had felt that she had already said her goodbyes to Auntie Viv when they met the last time at the cathedral teashop – she had passed across her brother's address where she'd be living, together with the date of the move. What she hadn't mentioned was that the move was prompted by the fact that the cottage she lived in had been virtually condemned and was to be pulled down to make way for an estate of new houses – she felt rather ashamed of that fact even though the situation was nothing of the family's making.

'Well, my dear,' Auntie Viv began, once the initial chatter had tailed off, 'although I'll miss you and our little chats, I won't be far behind you, as I'm moving as well – to be nearer my son Andrew, in Shropshire. I'm not sure exactly where just yet, but I shall keep you informed, and perhaps you might like to visit us some time when we're all settled.'

'Wow, Auntie, I'm so pleased you didn't go before me, I'd have really missed you – and of course I'll keep in touch. And when I go out job hunting, I'll be sure to send you a copy of my Sea View!!' Which drew the expected laugh from them all – Hattie had really enjoyed telling the family all about it.

Just then, Mike popped his head inside. 'Sorry to intrude, Mrs Gilbert, but Mr Gasson says he really has to go in a couple of minutes – are you going back with him or staying?'

'Oh, please tell him I'm sorry to keep him waiting, but I'd like him to take me home, please – I'll be there in a minute.' Then, delving into the shopping bag that she'd placed near her feet, she came up with a gift-wrapped package that she offered to Hattie.

'I'd like you to have this, my dear, a little keepsake from me – I just hope you like it.'

'Can I open it now?' asked a very surprised Hattie.

'Of course.'

With everyone looking on, Hattie rather fumbled the unwrapping, but eventually revealed the George Riley vase.

'Oh, Auntie, you can't give me this – surely it's a memento of your husband!'

'Well, to be honest, that's rather the problem with it – he knew some of the families affected by the fire, and it could bring on a bout of real melancholy, something I'd rather not revive. But I feel that you liked it for what it is, so it would make me happy if it would bring you happy memories of our little chats together.'

Isn't it amazing how thoughts of happy times can bring tears to the eye, because that's what happened as they all stood, then went out to the car to wave off Hattie's probably only true friend in the Salchester area.

Meanwhile, in the manor's stable yard, and unaware of all the action around the Red Lion, Whacker was still trying to come to terms with the major disappointment of having to give up work on the board game.

'What can I tell them at college, Dad? They wanted me to take it in and show how I'd used their ideas on the lettering and the illustrations, yet that wretched solicitor says I can't use any of it for anything – that can't be right, can it? It's certainly not fair.'

'Don't worry about it yet. It was an initial reaction – understandable, really – but I'll follow it up tomorrow, see if we can't get some common sense applied to it – without adding to Mrs Harding's distress, of course.'

Alison had come in from the kitchen and heard the end of that discussion, and added, 'Have you told him about Dave Marshall, Ted?'

'What's this then, Dad?'

'Well, I've sort of signed up to do the cabinetmaking for Dave Marshall, the builder who's doing the new little estate on Parsons Lane.'

'So where do I come in?' asked Whacker, still feeling knocked back by his board game project being stopped. 'You won't be sending me up on the roofs, will you?'

'Oh, no – not our area. We'll be doing cupboards, wardrobes, and all indoor stuff, and as much of it as we can we'll do here, so it'll still be much like it is now.'

'Don't forget to tell him about Tom Willett,' interrupted Alison.

'Isn't that the chap you went to see?' asked Whacker.

'Yes, and he'll be coming to see us. Dave is his uncle, often puts pieces of small work his way.'

'So?'

'Well, he'll want to give him some work on this contract, and I've said we can offer him a work space, so that's the next thing for us to do.'

'Oh, come on, Dad, we can't be the good guys all the time, letting him take work from us and then giving him the space to do it in, as well!'

'Hang on a minute, son – I've met both of these chaps and I reckon they're genuine. Anyway, we'll try and have him here when you're not. But when you're both here, he's offered to teach you woodcarving – the sort that he does for the church. It doesn't look as if he's going to be able to do that much longer so, if you've been trained by him and get his seal of approval, that's a line of work that could well come our way. Does that make you feel any easier?'

'Well, yes, but we're all nicely set up now. When we're all here, where does he work – not at my bench, I hope!'

'No. We'll have to sort out a place for him, probably not too far inside if he's still in a wheelchair.'

'Sorry, Dad, but I reckon it looks like this could be problems for all of us – let's hope he only needs to be here when I'm at college.'

'There's an idea,' interrupted Alison. 'How about I take Whacker in on his college days and then collect Mr Willett and bring him here? Then they'll not be here at the same time.'

'Aren't you forgetting Kelly's sandwich runs, love? Look, let's hold our horses until we see what comes of it all – it could be a couple of months before any work comes our way, and a lot can happen in that time.'

One of the good things that did happen very early in that time concerned Whacker's board game project. At the next Chamber of Commerce meeting, Jim Harding's sudden death was naturally the central topic of conversation, with messages of sympathy and support being sent to his family.

During the lunch break, Ted found himself in a small group who'd known about the game board and inevitably asked him what was happening about it. When he told them of Mrs Harding's reaction to both the game and to their involvement, he got quite a sympathetic response. A solicitor in the group asked what sort of agreement they had had with Jim.

'Well,' Ted started, 'I think you know we weren't going to charge him anything for it, so there was really no need for any formal agreement. But it was my boy's first experience of looking at a job from the very beginning, so I used it as a bit of a training exercise, and got him to do all the usual paperwork but without any costings.'

'Did you show any of it to Jim?' he was asked.

'Yes, he asked to see it, but it was just the typical initial notes that would be the basis of a quote – outlining the job, specifying materials, indicating timescales and so on. I think Jim quite enjoyed the whole idea, not simply seeing his project being handled like a regular job, but knowing it would be beneficial to my lad's training.'

'You say that Jim approved of your approach to the task when you showed him the paperwork?'

'Oh, yes, very much so.'

'He didn't sign anything to indicate his approval, did he?'

'As a matter of fact, he did. I didn't ask him to, but he saw the space for the customer's signature, and he insisted on signing it. I remember him saying that it helped to make the whole thing look authentic and, as we weren't going to charge him for it, what did it matter?'

This explanation had held the solicitor's full attention, and he suggested that if he, or any solicitor that Ted employed, could have a look at the papers, they might find a way to deal with Mrs Harding's embargo on the project.

A couple of days later, after Ted had sent the solicitor a copy of the paperwork, he got a phone call to say he was in the clear. Ted was so used to the document that he had overlooked the small print – this had words to the effect that only the finished article and any items supplied by the client were the property of the client, as all preparatory notes, sketches, calculations, models etc., were the property of the contractor.

'Are you going to tell Mrs Harding, or would you like me to do it?' he was asked.

'That's very kind of you, but I think I'll leave it until a situation arises when we want to do more with the model – the poor lady has enough important things on her mind at the moment. When that time comes, I'll probably go back through her solicitor about it.'

The news left Whacker overjoyed, and he was even happier after his dad told him of a phone call he'd had from Tony Philips later that afternoon. Dave Marshall had agreed terms for renting the middle coach-house, including its use as an occasional workplace. This was obviously intended for Tom Willett, but it allowed Dave to have other small jobs carried out there when necessary. Ted had been informed because of his right to veto any uses that might affect his work or his family home.

CHAPTER 30

Over the following year or so, things in Charlford had changed much as they do in any community – parts of the normal cycles of life, like births, marriages, promotions at work, bumper harvests, lovely holidays, crop failures, and so on. Few of these are of great moment apart from the impact they have on the lives of those immediately affected.

However, there had been significant changes in the two sections of the village with which we have concerned ourselves: the Red Lion and Charlford Manor. (Those around the Red Lion were quite local, and affected fewer people, so we'll set them aside for the moment and deal with them later.)

In and around the manor, the developments were greater in number and more complex – not always visible to outsiders, but nevertheless significant to Tony and the other occupants and users of the premises.

Interestingly, it was an event involving Kelly and the city's new indoor bowls club that had triggered the first change. At the successful end of her probationary period, she had found the club's newly-fitted kitchen so useful, and the club's location so convenient to her home, that it felt irksome to drive to Charlford and spend time every morning sharing the sandwich preparation work with Alison. So, feeling secure in her position at the club, and the combined incomes from club and Kelly's Kitchen, she registered the club as her sole operational base.

She then looked for ways to simplify the sandwich business, firstly transferring all the preparation work to the bowls club. While this meant that Alison lost the task of preparing the sandwiches, she was quite happy to continue delivering them. On weekday mornings, she would drive to the club, leave her car in a club parking space, pick up the van that Kelly had already loaded, then set off on the delivery run. This, however, soon proved to be problematic because the daily build-up of traffic in the city often resulted in deliveries arriving late, a frequent occurrence during the visitor seasons. Although Alison varied her route from day to day, this still left some customers unhappy enough to cancel their orders and revert to bringing a lunch in from home.

Surprisingly, but happily, Kelly found that the demand for meals in the club built up quite quickly to a level that could support her, so she decided to sell the sandwich business. She considered offering it to Alison or to Tony Philips, presenting it as a possible expansion to either Ted's or Tony's businesses. But, before she could follow these ideas through, she was approached by a local bakery seeking to expand its existing network of deliveries. After obtaining their assurances that her customers would continue to be well served, Kelly readily accepted their offer – this allowed her to reduce her costs, by finally terminating her lease of the kitchen in Charlford.

The bowls club's location also had made it easier to attract staff, and Kelly was soon able to take on a full-time assistant. As the majority of cooked meals in the club were required at lunchtime, Kelly had regular free time to produce and deliver buffet meals, cakes and such like for other customers – often for one-off celebration events.

The bowls club developed more rapidly than had been expected, so its management committee decided to seek the services of a professional accountant and business adviser. But this action eventually led to disastrous results for Kelly when someone, somewhere – no-one knew if it was in the city council, or the cathedral, or even the club – threw a spanner in the works.

This unidentified person had studied in minute detail the charter, or whatever the document was, that spelled out the limits to be applied to any future use that could be made of the site where the school had burned down – precisely where the indoor bowls club now stood. Though not common knowledge, the document decreed that the site should not be used for profit – probably to ensure that no-one would benefit financially from the deaths of the children. But now, perhaps spitefully, the document that recorded that decision was brought to the attention of the club's new business adviser. It was soon established that the club itself was protected by its non-profit status, but not so Kelly's Kitchen, which was registered, and widely advertised, as being based at the club, and was therefore in breach of the rules.

Poor Kelly was shattered – she had worked so hard and had become really popular with all her customers at the club, just as she had previously with her sandwich business. The club's management committee offered to employ her simply to do the club meals and run its tea bar but, having lost her dream business just as it was getting off the ground, she just couldn't face continuing to work there. She felt that her reputation had been shattered, almost as if the whole debacle had been her fault – which of course it hadn't been – and she suffered a nervous breakdown.

Although club members were far from happy about what had happened, they eventually accepted that the business adviser had done the right thing. He had probably helped avoid a situation that could possibly have had some serious consequences, including perhaps even a costly court case to avoid the closure of the club, if the situation had been allowed to continue.

Back at Charlford Manor, Tony had had no takers for the empty kitchen, and was wondering where and how to try to market it next, when things took yet another turn for the worse. Totally unexpectedly, this came about after the first couple of houses in the new estate in Parson's Lane were completed.

The Bailey family, Alison in particular, had started to feel a little isolated in the stable yard after Kelly had gone. With the benefit of their first-hand knowledge of the quality of the new houses in Parsons Close – as it was now called – they bit the bullet, sold their old home in Bracknell, and bought the first house that was put up for sale.

The move to the new home also triggered another change when Ted suggested, rather tentatively, that their son should consider dropping his nickname. Ted said that 'Whacker' could be thought to indicate excessive use of a hammer – not at all acceptable in quality carpentry. So, Whacker became Steve.

The next change in the stable yard was the less noticeable one at the middle coach-house. The coach had failed to be returned there after the ORE people had given up on the idea of being able to use it. They had decided it was not worth their while after they'd studied the costs and organisation needed simply to get teams of horses to draw it. One of the people they'd approached did have suitable horses but wasn't prepared to let them leave his land. Instead, he offered to store the coach on his estate, and invited the group of owners – Loada's police friends – to come into the estate and drive it occasionally.

This situation allowed the manor coach-house to come into regular use as a store for builder Dave Marshall. His uncle, Tom Willet, occasionally worked in there on small carpentry pieces. Other clean, quiet tradesmen also went in to carry out minor assembly tasks or to sort out details on pieces of plumbing or electrical items. For the benefit of all the other workers in the stable yard, and their clients, Tony maintained the embargo on noisy or smelly work, even though the Bailey family no longer lived there.

The third coach-house had been emptied and redecorated after the stored items it held were finally transferred to the Northfield Hospice shop in the city. The place was now used for occasional small tutorials attended by followers of one 'Morm' Fadmoor.

Morm, whose real name was Jean, was a noted writer on all things to do with the presentation of the home – its decor, its fabrics, even the meals served therein, and so on. She lived and worked by the mantra that any aspect of a meal or a home could be 'made or marred' by the smallest thing. When considering any addition or change in the home, she insisted that one should always ask oneself 'Will it Make or Mar?' – 'M or M?'; hence she started to be referred to as 'Morm'. Understandably, this all began behind her back but, when she heard it, Jean decided to use the name as her nom-de-plume – perhaps it would provide a protective layer of separation from unhappy periods of her previous life.

It wasn't generally known that Fadmoor was not Jean's real name either, nor her ex-husband's, but the name of the village in North Yorkshire where she had begun this unplanned and unexpected career. Some years earlier, on realising that their house there had become rather too big for them once their children had moved out to college, etc., Jean persuaded her husband that they could offer bed and breakfast accommodation to walkers and other visitors to the area. Although not ideally situated to attract many customers, the people who did stay with them were extremely complimentary about the home, its furnishings, its decor, the meals she served, and even Jean's table settings.

Sadly, the location offered limited openings for this small business to grow. So, when her husband's career prospects suffered an unexpected downturn, they were forced to move on. Eventually, the marriage failed and ended in divorce. But, by this time, Jean had written several articles on home presentation that were published in quality magazines whose editors were always asking for more.

Looking for somewhere less isolated to live, Jean had travelled south and was attracted, first to Salchester, then to Charlford, and eventually to the manor house and the small craft community in its stable yard. This final discovery was made shortly after the Bailey family moved out. As Kelly had already given up the kitchen, Jean took on the tenancy of both cottage and kitchen, and settled down to give more time to writing.

The planned new series of Morm Fadmoor articles was inspired by her new setting, and based on the actual work that she carried out in the cottage to create her ideal home. As for the attached kitchen, it provided space to try out menus and other ideas to add to her portfolio. Then, when the end coach-house had become available, it proved to be ideal for her to create her own decor and then hold small classes in general aspects of home presentation.

Not all went well for Morm all the time, but Tony and others around would step in with practical help or advice when necessary. But, when one of the machines in the kitchen simply would not respond to its controls, Tony decided to ask Kelly for help. At first reluctant to return to the site of much happier times, she came in just for half an hour one morning – and was still there at five o'clock! She was totally absorbed and inspired by Morm's work, and started to visit regularly – eventually she took a significant role in bringing new recipes to reality.

Within the manor itself, still essentially Tony and Anna's home, more changes took place before a stable (*unintended pun*) situation emerged.

Firstly, the Wilkinsons returned from their travels, rather disheartened at not having found a place to settle down for a proper retirement. Theoretically, they came back simply to sort through and collect the remainder of their belongings and then move on. Separately and independently, both they and Anna had privately thought that the cottage in the stable yard would suit them down to the ground – if only they could have afforded it. Unfortunately, Morm Fadmoor had beaten them to it, but they gladly accepted Tony's offer of the small suite of rooms they'd occupied before their recent travels – a purely temporary measure, of course!

One of the first changes they noticed was that Tony went out more in the evenings, something he had previously done only when Anna was either also out or had Tina in for company. Naturally, they said nothing, but were pleased, and not really surprised when, on one of his evenings at home, he was joined by Julie from the office – as they always thought of her. It seemed that this closer relationship had developed and grown after their trip taking Miss Anna and her friend Boots to look at colleges in Wales. ('About time too!' was a comment shared, though rarely heard, amongst people who knew them both.)

Just as life was settling into a pattern that was reminiscent of the times before Mr and Mrs W went walkabout, Tony got an urgent call one morning saying that his father had been injured in a fall at home. Pausing only to ask the W's to tell Anna not to worry, and asking them to look after her, he grabbed his coat and car keys and drove off. Arriving at his dad's home in Glenton, he was met by a neighbour saying that the paramedics suspected a broken hip; she then redirected him to a hospital in Oxford.

Happily, although Mr Philips senior's hip was badly bruised, it was neither broken nor dislocated. But he was kept in overnight while doctors looked for any underlying cause of his fall – fortunately none was found. On being satisfied that he was recovering satisfactorily, he was given firm instructions to avoid staircases and stepladders, prescribed some painkillers, and released into his son's care. As he lived in a bungalow, the stairs restriction was no problem, but Tony wasn't happy about him having to straightway look after himself, and insisted on taking him back to the manor.

'That's very kind of you, Tony, but I've got no stairs at home, and you've got that massive staircase!' he protested.

'Look, Dad, it's not just a question of stairs, it's the shopping and cooking you'd have to deal with at home. Just let us look after you for a few days – all right?'

'OK, but what about the stairs – have you got a room I can sleep in downstairs?'

'No, Dad, we've still got the stair lift that was put in when I was injured a couple of years ago, remember?'

'But you took it out, didn't you? I've not seen it for some time now.'

'No, we just took the chair off, but left the rail in – Billy from the yard looked after it. Remember, he'd joined the transport yard just as the chair-lift owners left and it had to be taken out. But he'd installed it originally, and he used to service it, so he had the records to show it was safe and so on. We'd never have been able to put it in for anybody else, of course, but it was fine for me – and will be for you, too. Reg was getting Billy ready to fit the chair again as soon as I said you're on your way – OK?'

So that's what happened, and Mr and Mrs Wilkinson – unasked – once more adopted their favourite roles in life of caring for someone's non-personal, daily needs.

Chapter 31

As previously mentioned, the past year had also seen significant changes in and around the Red Lion.

Just along the road from the inn, in what had been Parson's Lane where the Scattergoods had lived, houses had already been built and the first two bought and occupied. It was now called Parsons Close and was looking rather nice.

The major change at the inn itself was that Pauline Clark had moved in and made her home there after marrying Jim Parker. She had made several weekend visits to start with, but these soon became more frequent until they were followed by an extended stay. The initial visits were always rather formal, with Pauline being booked in as a guest and allocated what was regarded as the inn's best room, until Jim eventually asked her to marry him.

Fortunately for all concerned, particularly the inn's loyal customers, this change only really affected the members of two families; Pauline's son, Boots, and Jim's daughter, Tina. These two teenagers felt the impact a lot less than might have been the case at other times, simply because both of them were in their final years at school and preparing to move on to college, and inevitably to become more independent.

Incidentally, at about this time, Pauline's son started to drop his nickname and insist on using his proper name, John. This change was triggered by an incident at a theatre workshop when one of the older members of the company asked him where Snudge was – a reference to a very old TV sitcom named after its two main characters, Bootsie and Snudge. To John, Snudge sounded more like sludge, so a name change was definitely needed!

In purely practical terms, the Red Lion had enough rooms to accommodate not only Pauline's son, but those contents of the Clarks' Bracknell household that could not immediately be disposed of. But this aspect of his forthcoming marriage had initially worried Jim because it temporarily robbed him of a couple of the rooms on which he relied for some of his income – and it was happening at a busier time of year. Fortunately, Tony still allowed Jim to use the rooms above the manor's stables – provided, of course, that the guests were prepared and agile enough to use them.

Once settled into the domestic side of life as an innkeeper's wife, Pauline needed no encouragement to spend time behind the bar. She already knew a few of the regulars and was grateful for their warm welcomes and their friendly banter as she learned the ropes and the legalities involved in serving alcohol.

During her visits and stays at the inn over the year, she noticed that several of the topics of conversation just didn't go away, the most regular one being about the manor's coach. Fortunately, Loada Cole was more than happy to answer the questions that continued to be raised. Although he'd been the intermediary between Tony Philips and the group of enthusiasts he had given the coach to, Loada actually shared the view of many villagers that the coach really belonged to the manor and should have been returned to be based there. But, as a member of the group of owners, he had privileged access to it in its new home, and rather enjoyed this status – 'basking in reflected glory,' was how one critic described his attitude!

The situation that Loada kept quiet about was that the estate where the coach was kept was neither grand nor landed gentry, but best described as the hobby of a very wealthy businessman. Most of the other members of the police group were known to the estate's owner through their involvement in police protection, and the security advice and service he'd received over the years. But the landowner was also a philanthropist, and Loada knew that he regularly took in children from deprived backgrounds to introduce them to the animals and crops found in the country. He often gave them rides round the estate in the Charlford coach, but Loada definitely kept quiet about that.

Though Jim and Pauline were aware of the coach situation, neither of them would be drawn into any discussions. Jim's priority was to help Pauline settle into the running of the inn, and was pleased with how, in addition to dealing with staying guests, she enjoyed spending time behind the bar, absorbing and contributing to the atmosphere.

Soon after her earliest visits, Jim found there were two things that had puzzled her. The first was the crossword clues that were often bandied about the bar; she was told that these were cryptic clues – a term that she didn't find helpful at all.

'As I understand it,' said Jim, when they finally got round to talking about it, 'a cryptic clue should have two parts – a definition of the answer, mixed up with words that often contain letters to be used to make the answer.'

'Thanks, Jim, that's really clear – glad I asked you – I don't think!' she replied. 'What about an example?'

'Right,' he said, 'I've actually got one – one that the chaps explained to me, OK?'

'Go ahead – but only if it's clearer than mud!'

'The clue was – Tendency to support leaderless stupidity – 10 letters.'

'No idea, Jim, so you'd better just spell it out.'

'Fine. Well, the answer was "propensity", which means "tendency", OK? The "prop" part of the answer comes from "to support" – then the rest of it is from the word density – meaning stupidity; removing its leading letter gives "ensity". You put the two bits together to get the answer – prop-ensity! There, how's that?'

'Thanks, Jim, that sounds more interesting than I'd expected – I think I'll listen properly next time and try my luck. Now, what about the other thing I wondered about – "Sauce in bottle or ramekin"?' She had been intrigued by this being on the inn's menus, but had only ever noticed sauce going to tables in ramekins.

'This goes back to my early days here and I reckon it was really one of the first signs that my wife wasn't quite happy.'

'Oh, don't go on if it's opening old wounds, Jim.'

'No problem – it actually still makes me chuckle.'

'In that case, let's hear it.'

'Well, one day we had a group of chaps in at lunchtime – salesmen or some sort of businessmen from a company in Yorkshire or Lancashire, I think. And they were a bit flushed with success over something or other. Anyway, I can't remember what the meal was, but we served with it a ramekin of brown sauce. Straight away they called me over and said they wanted proper sauce in a proper bottle – not this homemade namby-pamby rubbish!'

'Oh, Jim, how rude!'

'It was all right, love – I could see the funny side of it because, like now, we only used commercial sauces. Anyway, I decided to do things properly and took in an unopened bottle of sauce, carrying it proudly on a tray as if it was a bottle of fine wine. Well, you should have seen my wife's face – she was appalled! When I told her what had happened, her response was, "Oh, James, how very Northern!" – and it didn't help that both the table concerned and nearby customers heard her and burst out laughing!'

'Oh, Jim, how awful and snobby – I can see why she wasn't happy here!'

These two explanations seemed to complete Pauline's induction into the running of a village inn – at least this particular village inn – and life started to settle into a new normal.

Another topic that might have been expected to be raised but wasn't, was that of embroidery – Jim wondered if Pauline's interest in the cathedral copes might simply have been an excuse to make extra visits to the village, and to him? But it was at a chance meeting between Pauline and Alison Bailey in the cathedral teashop where the subject was raised, and her reluctance to discuss it was aired. Pauline was simply wary – 'scared' was only just too strong a word, she explained – of having to display her very basic skill to a group of needle-women she had seen were far more experienced.

'Well, look,' said Alison, 'I'm here to see someone about the Aspire magazine, so let me raise the subject as if I'm the one that's perhaps interested, and see what we can learn.' So they did, and Pauline's fears were allayed. Alison had been advised to try simple embroidery projects, perhaps using kits she could find in craft shops anywhere, so as to gain confidence before enrolling in one of the recommended courses – a plan that Pauline decided to adopt.

The same visit also found success for Alison's own project – she wanted to write simple articles about village churches when they were featured in Aspire. The idea met with tentative agreement, and Broderick Mitcalfe was authorised to publish them, once the piece had gained the approval of the church's vicar and then of the cathedral. As a result, the two women started meeting to compare notes and share their experiences.

Alison's new pastime was proving to be a beneficial distraction from the day-to-day running of the Bailey household. Although Ted occasionally spent time working in the Parsons Close estate, he was rarely able to call in for as long at their new house as he had done when home and work were so close in the manor's stable yard – and, of course, the same went for Whacker (*sorry, 'Steve'*).

As for Steve, after the initial shock and disappointment of not being allowed to progress with the Knight board game, the lad enjoyed having Tom Willett teach him the craft of wood carving when quiet moments in their work schedules coincided. Tom was mainly interested in the size and nature of the carvings generally found in church buildings, but Steve wanted to try more modern subjects. As a compromise, he tried to make playing pieces for the Knight game but, whilst he had some success with quite large versions, he found it was way too difficult, as yet, to work at a scale to suit the board he'd been making.

When this topic came up in a chat with his pal, Boots (*sorry, 'John'*) during the latter's next weekend at home, they both agreed that sticking with church carvings kept Steve away from the temptation to break the initial embargo that had been placed on the Knight game. They then switched to the topic that Steve did want to discuss – what was it like to actually live in a pub? (*Sorry, village inn.*)

John admitted he still found it a bit confusing – which door to use to come in and go out, where to have his meals, and so on. This last item was most awkward when he wanted to take Anna out for a meal – was he being disloyal to the Red Lion if he took her into Salchester for a change? This was a concern that Steve shared when he wanted to take Tina out – was it mean just to take her to his home in Parson's Close – was Tina being mean when she treated him to a meal in her home? What a confusing situation. (*For me as well as for them!*)

One thing that both the lads experienced when in the Red Lion was the questioning by those who remember them from their first backpacking visits. 'Were they pleased to have moved?' 'Did they still make music?' 'Where was their slim friend?'

But even these questions were sidelined one lunchtime, when who should walk into the bar but Hattie Scattergood! And she'd lost none of her sharpness when she broke the deafening silence with 'And which of you fine gentlemen is going to be first to offer a lady and her friend a seat and some refreshment?'

At this point they looked around and realised that Hattie was accompanied by an elderly lady, remembered by some as the one who had come from Salchester to see Hattie the day she left the village. Fortunately, Jim was behind the bar, realised that the lady was a Mrs Gilbert who had phoned to book a table for two for lunch that day, and came round to escort them both to the dining room.

'This is a real surprise, Harriet,' he said. 'How is your family?'

'Oh, they're fine, Mr Parker. I'm just down for a weekend with Auntie Viv, taking in the sights, meeting old friends.'

'You're not planning to return, then?' he asked, hoping to keep the anxiety out of his voice.

'Oh, no. I'm well settled up there, got a nice job, still living with the family, but looking for a little place of my own.'

'Are you just here for a visit as well, Mrs Gilbert? I seem to remember you were off to be near your son, weren't you?'

'What a memory, young man! No, that didn't need to happen – he found a new job just outside Oxford, so we're near enough to each other.' With that, Jim took their orders and left them to be looked after by the waitress.

Hattie's arrival was naturally the topic of conversation back in the bar, particularly when the absence of aroma was noted. Jim was very quick to put a stop to that, knowing how sensitive Hattie had been when she discovered what had happened.

It was into this rather muted discussion that Tony Philips arrived with his father. Jim gave Tony a quick, quiet update on the Hattie situation, then returned to his place behind the bar and served them their drinks.

'Who are these people he was telling you about then, do you know them Tony?' asked his dad. While Tony could explain about Hattie, he had no idea who her companion was, apart from the name that Jim had given and that she lived in Glenton, so he had to ask if his dad might know of the family.

'No, son, don't know any Gilberts.'

And it was left at that until, on coming out of the dining room, Auntie Viv spotted Tony's dad, and called a cheery, 'Hello, didn't expect to see you here.'

It took Mr Philips senior a moment to realise that he was the one being addressed, and then reply, 'I'm sorry, my dear, but do I know you?'

'Perhaps not really "know", but you're sometimes on my bus going into town. Sorry, I shouldn't have butted in.'

'That's alright,' he said, as the face clicked into place. 'I know – you get on near Olive Franks' place, don't you? Do you come out here often?'

'Oh, no, just that my friend used to live here and she wanted to have another look – what about you?'

'Had a tumble at home and my lad insisted I stay in the village with him for a while.'

'Oh, my!' she exclaimed, looking at Tony. 'Then you must be the Tony Philips that Harriet has told me about.'

Before she could continue, possibly to indicate whether the comments had been complementary or otherwise, Hattie almost dragged her away, the little kerfuffle was over, and life in Charlford settled back to normal.

The End

Acknowledgements

Again, my son Ian has been my principal support by editing, checking and proof-reading, and preparing the files and encouraging me through the on-line publishing process.

Cover illustration this time was a joint effort between Ian, Ruth Burrows and me.

Within the book, many people and activities come from my life.
The Aspire magazine story is how my wife and I met Chris Shilling and began delivering *Rhythm and Booze* to pubs around Sleaford.
My good friend Ian Sampson, the North York Moors writer, allowed me to use his planned non-de-plume 'Broderick Mitcalfe', and to base 'Morm Fadmoor' on his dear late wife Jean – though I chose to leave out the 'cussin' and 'spittin' parts of his description!!

Above all, I acknowledge the generous comments and kind support that *Bed and Breakfast in Charlford* received from relatives, friends and unknown brave readers.

However, I don't think I could have continued with the book if it had not been for my son David. He fully shared with me all that needed to be done after Margaret was taken, and then came and nursed me back to life through the following months – all with the blessing of his lovely wife Susi. 'Thank you' is hardly enough.

I hope this offering lives up to your expectations.
W Henry Barnes

About the Author

W Henry Barnes began his writing career many years ago as a Technical Author in the UK defence electronics industry.

Since retiring to Lincolnshire, he has published two novels around the fictional village of Charlford with a third (and final one, he says) in hand.

Away from writing, he is an active member of the Lincolnshire branch of the REME Association, and keeps mind and body in trim playing bowls at a local indoor club.

Printed in Great Britain
by Amazon